I0608068

# THE REFUGEE RUSE

## THE GAIAN CONSORTIUM SERIES, BOOK 7

### CHRISTINE POPE

DARK VALENTINE PRESS

THE REFUGEE RUSE

ISBN: 978-1-946435-17-0

Copyright © 2018 by Christine Pope

Published by Dark Valentine Press

Cover design & print formatting by Indie Author Services

# CHAPTER ONE

KLAXONS BLARED FROM SPEAKERS ON EVERY SIDE of the bridge—which wasn't technically a bridge at all, but the control room of a space station. Either way, Landon Beck had to ignore the urge to pull out his pulse pistol and shoot all of them, just to stop the din. How in the hell was he supposed to concentrate with that racket pounding at him from all sides?

The heads-up displays in the space station's control room showed that attackers were converging from all sides—a fleet of pirates, mercs, soldiers of fortune. Call them whatever you wanted, but it all drilled down to the same reality. They were opportunists, seizing upon the current chaos in the sector, knowing that Station Zeta Tau not only housed several floors of prison cells, but extensive stores of weapons and ammunition, as well as raw materials that could be sold for ready cash on any number of worlds. And now, with the Consortium collapsing on every side, those opportunists knew that the government wouldn't be sending out a defense force to protect its assets in these far-flung corners of the galaxy.

Zeta Tau's commanding officer, Colonel Malachi Owens, shot Landon an irritated glance. "Increase the power to the shields, Captain Beck!"

Of course Landon had already done that, just as soon as long-range scans had detected the invaders. He knew all too well they were sitting ducks here, as anyone with a full complement of functioning brain cells should have known. Yes, the station had its own defense systems, but they were no match for the motley but overwhelming force converging on them now.

Currently, Zeta Tau housed ninety-five crew and support staff, with forty-five prisoners held in the cells on the lower levels of the station. Career criminals mostly, hardened men and women who'd been awaiting transport back to Gaia for sentencing and imprisonment in the maximum-security facility on Titan. Lawbreakers who couldn't be trusted to the weaker security of out-system jails, and thus had been brought here.

Well, all of them were career criminals...except one. And it was she who occupied Landon's thoughts now. Her crimes had been petty ones, her presence here a mere accident of circumstance. She certainly didn't deserve to be blown into space, or, possibly worse, subjected to the tender mercies of the pirates and mercenaries who threatened to overwhelm the Consortium station at any moment.

"Shields are at maximum, colonel," Landon said. "I can go to the power substation and see if I can increase the feed from there."

Owens scowled, but nodded. He'd always reminded Landon of a bird of prey, with his beaky nose and pale eyes, and right then he looked as though he wanted to take on the station's attackers with his bare hands. "Do it."

That was the opening Landon had been waiting for. He inclined his head in acknowledgment of the command and headed out of the control chamber, urgency adding speed to his movements.

Once upon a time, the maneuver he was contemplating would have certainly ended in his court martial. However, with the Consortium collapsing on every side, Landon doubted there was anyone left in a position of authority who would care that he'd fled his post when faced with a no-win situation. All he had to do was make sure that everyone thought he'd perished in the attack on Zeta Tau. Then he'd be able to start over, in whatever brave new world arose from the breakup of a government that had been an empire in everything but name.

He'd finally be free.

The cell block he sought was six levels down from

the control center. Luckily, the elevators were empty, all personnel deployed to protect the station as best they could. Landon hoped the elevator would be equally unoccupied during his return trip. Awkward questions would only slow him down, and he knew he didn't have much time.

When the elevator door opened, he strode out into the detention block, which consisted of several corridors with windowless doors on either side, all fashioned of the same dull gray synth-steel, the only color at all showing in the control panels set into the walls next to each door. As soon as he approached, a pair of gray-uniformed guards swiveled their heads to see who their visitor was. Above the high-necked dark tunics they wore, their faces looked pale and strained. Although at this lower level, the battle outside only revealed itself in telltale shivers of the floor beneath his feet, Landon could tell the guards knew the station was in jeopardy. He didn't see the officer in charge, which was just as well. His mission would be more easily accomplished if he had only a few enlisted men to intimidate.

"Prisoner transfer," he said shortly. That was the only halfway plausible lie he'd been able to come up, and he uttered an inward prayer that it would work.

The two men exchanged a puzzled glance. "Now, Captain Beck?" asked the one on the left.

"Yes, now," Landon replied. "Orders from Colonel Owens."

Those words had the desired effect. Even now, with the fate of the station precarious at best, neither of the men seemed too inclined to countermand an order given by the fearsome Malachi Owens. Both guards straightened, and the one who had spoken gulped and said, "Of course, sir. Cell number?"

Landon had committed the number to memory some days ago. "B-262."

The second guard, the one who had not yet spoken, saluted and then hurried down the narrow corridor between the two facing banks of cells. Another, larger explosion rocked the station, and Landon barely managed to keep his balance. Damn. That was getting too close. So much for the ships Colonel Owens had sent out to mount what defense they could. Clearly, they hadn't been able to hold the mercenary fleet at bay for very long, and once again Landon found himself praying he would have enough time to pull this off.

In a gratifyingly short period, however, the guard returned with the prisoner in tow, her hands locked before her in a set of silvery metal cuffs, long dark hair braided in a messy plait that fell over one shoulder. The shapeless prison garb she wore still didn't quite manage to conceal the curves of her slender figure, although it was doing its best.

She glanced from her current captor to Landon and then back at the guard, but she said nothing. Landon caught the flicker of a quick, speculative gaze before she lowered her head once more to give the floor at her feet a more thorough inspection.

"Thank you, sergeant," said Landon, tone brisk and efficient even though he was feeling anything but at the moment. He let his hand rest near the pulse pistol he wore at his belt and directed his next words to the young woman. "To the elevators."

She remained silent and did as she was told, moving with a shuffling gait to the bank of lifts that faced the guard station. Landon hit the button to call the elevator to their level and uttered a silent prayer that he wouldn't have to wait long for one. Whether anyone or anything was listening to those prayers, he didn't know, but within a few seconds, the door to the center elevator car opened, and he and the prisoner stepped inside. At once he pushed the buttons for the deck where Colonel Owens' shuttle was located.

"Are you going to interrogate me again?" the prisoner asked. Her voice had the rounded accents of someone from Gaia itself, maybe Britain. The lift shuddered as the station took another apparently direct hit somewhere in their vicinity. She showed aplomb unusual for someone her age, which Landon knew was twenty-four standard years. "Hell of a time for it, I have to say."

Landon didn't bother to reply, but instead shot her what he hoped was a quelling glance even as the elevator car ground to a stop. "Out," he instructed.

Was that a shrug she'd just made? Hard to say,

with the way the deck kept lurching beneath his feet. But at least she kept her mouth shut and moved in the direction he had indicated, toward Commander Owens' sleek Gupta-class ship. A harried-looking NCO rushed toward them, eyes full of curiosity, but Landon raised a hand and forestalled the man's questions by saying, "Business of Colonel Owens."

And since Landon was the colonel's adjutant, and presumably in the process of carrying out his commanding officer's edicts, the deck officer really couldn't protest. He nodded. "You're cleared for take-off, sir, but it's chaos out there. Are you sure the ship can handle it?"

"Of course," Landon replied. Inwardly, however, he experienced a tremor of fear. True, the little ship was fast and new, had vastly amplified shields along with the latest subspace drive, but would all those modifications be enough to get him through the firefight raging outside?

A calculated risk, and better than sitting around and waiting for one of the attacking pirates to deliver Zeta Tau's death blow. Without further comment, he headed up the ramp into the shuttle, where the girl he had freed waited for him.

Once he was inside, he headed immediately to the cockpit, his prisoner trailing only a pace or so behind. As he took his position in the pilot's seat, he heard her ask, a plaintive note in her voice, "Are you going to take these off?"

Landon risked a quick glance to his right and saw her raise her hands, still encased in the cuffs the guard had placed on her. "No time now," he replied, and leaned over to snap her safety harness in place.

"Lovely," she muttered.

The ship had been left in standby mode, which meant Landon had only to engage the pulse jets to lift its mass off the deck and then steer the ship through the hangar opening. Sensors told him the deck officer had already dropped the atmospheric shields to allow them to exit. Landon increased the throttle, feeling the powerful sub-light engines kick in as they burst from the hangar bay and into chaos, pulse bolts in shades of green and purple and blue lighting up the blackness of space and causing him to blink before his eyes adjusted to the glare.

A pair of small, modified Epsilon-class ships screamed by overhead, followed by one of the station's remaining Talon bombers. Luckily, they seemed to be so involved with their face-off that they ignored the shuttle as it sped away from Zeta Tau. Landon increased the power to the shields, but not so much that he compromised their speed. A trajectory had already been plotted in, one that would place them in the correct orientation to line up for the subspace jump to the lawless desert world Iradia, which he figured would be a good place to lie low until he could get his bearings. All they needed was a few more precious seconds, just a little more time to get free —

The rear viewports exploded in a wash of blinding white light. Damn. *Damn.* The attackers must have hit the sweet spot on the station's reactor—not an outcome they would have wished for, most likely, since now the valuable loot they'd targeted was no more than space junk. Landon couldn't let himself think about all the people lost in that explosion, fellow crew-members and officers. Not that he'd been terribly close to any of them, but they still didn't deserve to go out that way.

Well, except Malachi Owens. The man was a petty sadist, and certainly didn't merit having any tears shed over him.

But now Landon had other things to worry about, foremost among them the shockwave spreading out from the doomed station. In the co-pilot's seat next to him, the girl he'd rescued let out a shocked gasp, while Landon stifled a curse and urged more power from the straining engines, just enough to get them ahead of the wild burst of energy.

It caught them anyway, and the little ship bucked and heaved like a bear caught in a trap. Sparks flew, and one of the overhead consoles went dark. This time, Landon didn't bother to hold back the curses that rose to his lips, but at the same time he worked frantically to shunt the power he needed from the shields into the backup navigation system. They'd already gone through the worst the shields would

probably have to take, but they were dead if navigation failed them.

A reassuring row of lights flickered into being,
signaling that the navigation systems were back
online. At the same time, a strident beep let Landon
know they had reached the subspace jump point. He
reached forward and pulled the lever back, and the
shuttle shot out of realspace, leaving the shattered
remnants of Zeta Tau behind them.

Landon let himself fall back against the well-
upholstered pilot's seat, then ran a relieved hand
through his hair. That had been way too close. He
figured his heart would resume its normal rhythm
sometime in the next hour or so…as long as nothing
else went wrong.

A discreet throat-clearing noise made him turn his
head. The prisoner stared back at him, her expression
neutral as she held out her hands in front of her.

*Cool thing, isn't she?* he thought, and despite
himself, he almost smiled. Then he unclipped the
insignia from his chest and waved it over the locking
mechanism of the handcuffs. The chip inside read his
rank and personal data, determined he had the
authority to free the prisoner, and released the lock.

The loosened cuffs fell into her lap. She picked
them up and flung them into a corner of the cabin,
then undid the harness from her seat and turned so
she could face Landon directly. A pair of large dark
eyes fastened on him and gave him a direct stare. "So,"

she said, "are you going to tell me what this is all about?"

Good question. Landon only wished he had an equally good answer to give her. His day had started normally enough, but he certainly hadn't thought he'd end up on the run in a stolen ship with a known criminal as his companion. That his intuition had proved him right once again was cold comfort at the moment.

For days he'd experienced a creeping unease, a realization that Zeta Tau was a symbol of a government falling apart from the inside. It had only been a matter of time before someone seized on the opportunity its resources represented. He'd begun planning contingencies, plotting how best to get away. Even then he'd known that Colonel Owens was the type to go down with his ship—or station, to be more precise. However, Landon had no desire to make that kind of sacrifice. He'd enlisted in the Consortium's Gaian Defense Force ten years earlier because it was the fastest way to get his college loans paid off. The deal was that he'd give seven years of his life to the GDF, and then he could make his own way from there on out. He never thought he'd be sent to serve on a prison station in the ass-end of nowhere, the rules governing the payoff of his loans changing every time he tried to pursue the subject, which meant he'd already served three years longer than he'd ever intended. Clearly, the Consortium didn't give a good goddamn whether he rotted out in that backwater of the galaxy, as long as its station was properly staffed. So he sure as hell didn't owe the government his loyalty any longer.

The girl…well, he supposed he could blame her presence here on temporary insanity, or maybe a crusading streak that refused to die. He had only known of her existence because she'd been apprehended on an obscure little world called Zephyr IV, grifting to stay alive. Her crimes were minor: petty theft, illegal gambling…identity theft. Apparently, she'd managed to fool the local authorities into believing she was the owner of a large estate on that fertile planet, had enjoyed a life of some luxury before the real owner appeared and had her arrested. From Zephyr, she was sent to Zeta Tau.

As soon as Landon saw her image on the prisoner manifest, he'd been struck by her beauty, and saddened that someone so lovely would be sent to the hell of the MaxSec on Titan. However, since there didn't seem to be a damn thing he could do about her situation, he'd only spent a few thoughts on her before being consumed by his duties once again. After all, he might have been the colonel's adjutant, but that didn't mean he had any real power to change her situation.

Then had come the attack on the station, and the cold fear that gripped his gut as he soon as he realized what the approaching marauders had planned. They wouldn't give the crew any quarter. Possibly they would free the prisoners, give them the chance to be absorbed into their own criminal fleet. But he doubted the young woman would have been allowed that same opportunity. No, those criminals would have far different plans for her.

The thought had surfaced then, even as he tried to keep the panic at bay: *No, not her.* Landon would never be able to explain to himself where such an idea had sprung from, nor how he found himself acting on the impulse once he realized he was going to take Owens' shuttle and save his own skin. Yes, the delay his foolhardy rescue mission had required might have spelled his doom—and hers—but despite everything, he had somehow managed to get himself and the woman away.

He stared back at her, even as an unfamiliar uncertainty took hold of him. From the dubious expression on her face as she regarded him, it appeared she expected the worst.

"Does it matter what this is all about?" he said at last. "You're alive. Why is immaterial."

"Typical Consortium reply," she responded, and shook her head. "All right, then. I'm not important enough to be worth saving. Any report from one of my interrogation sessions could have told you that. So why?"

It appeared she had learned something from her interrogators about the power of persistence. Still, Landon had no ready answer to give her. The most obvious—*I wasn't going to leave you there to get raped by pirates*—sounded so utterly bald-faced that he couldn't bring himself to utter it.

"Why not?" he asked instead.

Instead of taking offense, she burst out into a peal of unexpected laughter. "You are a case, aren't you? Fine—if you won't tell me why I'm here, maybe you'd be good enough to tell me where we're going."

That seemed safe enough. "To Iradia. It seems the best place to escape notice. No one's going to pay any attention to us there. It was one of the first places to free itself from Consortium control."

"Um, as a Consortium officer, shouldn't you be heading in exactly the opposite direction?" Without waiting for a reply, she shrugged and added, "Not that I mind you running for Iradia. I can work with Iradia."

Well, of all the—"I did not *run*," Landon ground out. "I made a judicious escape once it was determined the pirate attack had a high chance of succeeding."

"You go on telling yourself that."

Really, for a prisoner she certainly had an uncommon amount of sass. Since he wasn't quite sure how he felt about that, Landon plowed on. "Might I remind you that you would be dead if it weren't for me?"

"Well, that's true." A bit of the sparkle went out of her eyes then, and she pulled her legs up against her chest and hugged them to her. Her bare arms looked very thin and pale against the dark gray prison garb, which consisted of a shapeless, sleeveless tunic and a matching pair of baggy pants. In fact, Landon thought he could see goosebumps standing out against her skin. Unlike the synthetic wool uniform he wore, the woman's lightweight prison clothing provided little protection against the cold air of the cabin.

Now that they were in subspace, Landon didn't need to keep quite so close a watch on the cockpit. It was a long way to Iradia, after all. He rose from his seat and made his way back down the corridor to Owens' cabin, which was utilitarian but also somehow graceful, with its recessed lights and curved built-ins. In the wardrobe, he found several high-necked, dark gray GDF uniforms hanging, neatly pressed and ready to go. Taking the jacket from one of them, he draped it over his arm and then returned to the pilot's cabin. The young woman looked up at him with big, mystified eyes as he handed the garment to her. Even in her current bedraggled state, she was almost heartbreakingly lovely.

"It will help keep you warm," he said.

For a moment she was silent, and then she shrugged her way into the heavy jacket. Colonel Owens was thin enough that it wasn't overly large on her, although the sleeves did extend far down over her hands, covering them almost to her fingertips. She pushed the sleeves up as best she could and then said, "Thank you. If you keep on being this decent, I may have to revise my opinion of the Consortium military."

Landon didn't bother to tell her that the Consortium didn't deserve her high opinion. It was obvious that she thought he was the usual rank-and-file officer, and he didn't feel like going into explanations now, especially since he wasn't sure whether he could explain his actions to himself, let alone a stranger. Feeling a bit off-center, he settled for giving a noncommittal lift of his shoulders before he returned to his seat.

"And how are you going to explain me once we get to Iradia?" she inquired. "It seems a bit odd that you'd save me from imprisonment on your station, just so you could hand me over to whatever passes for the authorities there these days."

Well, she had a point. To be honest, he really hadn't thought that far. It did seem somewhat foolish to have jeopardized his own life to rescue her if all he ended up accomplishing was to transfer her to a different prison. "I suppose I could make a stop to take you home," he said after thinking it over, and trying to ignore the discomfiting idea that he was actually the one who wouldn't get a warm welcome on Iradia. "Where are you from?"

"Gaia," she replied. "So that idea won't exactly wash."

No, he certainly couldn't take her to Gaia, heart of the Consortium. How this girl had fallen into her criminal ways when she'd come from a place where she should have had every advantage, Landon didn't know. Then again, even in his short acquaintance with her, it had become fairly apparent that she had a mind of her own.

"Our options are somewhat limited," he said. "I can bring us out of subspace at some point, but I can't deviate too much from our current course. That is, of course, if I decide to let you go at all."

"Oh?" She crossed her arms, pushing once again at the over-long sleeves of her borrowed jacket. "I thought we'd already established that handing me back over to the authorities was a bad idea."

Landon began to wonder if the best thing really wasn't for him to yank the ship out of subspace and drop her off at the nearest half-civilized world. That decision was taken neatly out of his hands, however, when the nav-computer began a frantic beeping. At roughly the same instant, the ship shuddered once, and Landon was almost thrown out of his seat as the vessel ground its way back into realspace. The young woman wasn't quite so lucky; taken off guard, she slid out of the co-pilot's chair and ended up in a messy heap on the ground. Her fall was accompanied by a very unladylike curse.

"What the hell was that?" she demanded as she pulled herself back up into her seat.

Damned if he knew. They had been pulled out of subspace so abruptly that at first he suspected the intervention of a type of ship he'd only heard rumors about, one that apparently could interfere with another vessel's subspace passage, but preliminary scans showed no other ships in the area. He began running a series of diagnostics, all the while hoping it was something simple and fearing it was not.

The computer beeped again, sounding as exhausted as Landon felt. A string of alpha-numeric codes trailed their way across the readout. He stared down at the screen and thought of a few curses or fifty he'd like to say himself.

"That good?" the girl asked, apparently guessing from his continuing silence that their sudden entry into realspace had not been planned.

"The subspace drive is off-line. My best guess is that the blast that caught us as we were pulling away from the station caused some damage, but it's hard to know for sure."

At least their pulse engines seemed to be working. Landon typed in a series of commands, silently willing their navigation system to still be online. If it had been fried as well, then they were as good as dead. They would drift out here in the dark with no means of finding their way to an inhabited world. Fortunately, the nav responded quickly enough, although the information it had to give him was far from welcome.

"Can you fix it?"

"Of course I can't fix it," he snapped. "Do I look like an engine tech to you? I'm not even a real pilot— I just know enough to get us up and down."

The first flash of fear he'd seen so far crossed her features. "So we're stuck?"

"Not completely." He tapped a few buttons, and an image of the system where they'd found themselves stranded appeared on the flat video monitor built into the console. The place was sparse and desolate-looking; only three planets orbited a pale yellow sun. He pointed at the middle planet. "That's Ordon. Not much there, but at least it's been colonized by humans, and the Consortium had a small garrison in the capital city. The pulse engines should get us there in about two hours."

She nodded, a bit of the tension seeming to leave her shoulders. "Do you think we can find someone on Ordon to repair the ship?"

Landon felt none too sanguine about their prospects, but he replied, "I don't see why not. Even a small colony has to have a few starship mechanics around." *I just have to hope they're good enough to handle this ship*, he thought. *It's not quite the same as working on a basic freighter or in-system craft.*

He did not bother to voice his concerns, however, mostly because he thought if he tried to act as though he was in control of the situation, maybe he'd begin to feel that way. Without speaking, he had the nav-computer lay in the most direct course to Ordon. The ship turned gracefully and began moving toward the planet, which from this distance was barely visible. At least the pulse engines hadn't failed them. Yet.

For a moment, the woman said nothing, but merely stared out into the blackness that surrounded them. Then she asked without looking at him, "What's your name, anyway?"

"Landon Beck."

Her eyebrows lifted. "What, no rank? No serial number?"

For whatever reason, she seemed determined to irk him. Perhaps goading him into lashing out in anger was her way of coping with their current situation. Whatever the case, Landon certainly didn't intend for her to get her way. He might have just jettisoned the last ten years of his life by freeing her from her jail cell on Zeta Tau, but that didn't mean he intended to allow her under his skin…at least, not any more than she'd already gotten. "Captain Landon Beck. I really don't think you need my serial number."

Contrary to his theory that she wanted to see him upset, his mild tone only made her chuckle. "No, I guess I don't. So should I call you Landon, or Captain Beck?"

He sighed. "Landon is fine. It's not as though we're exactly here in an official capacity."

"True," she said blithely. "My name is Dhani

Warlow. That's short for Dhanella. I don't know what my parents were thinking."

Landon began to wonder what *she* was thinking. From her tone and the look of amusement that still brightened her face, one would have thought they were trading pleasantries at a dinner party or a bar somewhere. Surely she didn't have the demeanor of someone who had just been rescued from a jail cell in a Consortium space station, or of a young woman who was now stranded in a backwater with one of her former jailers. At any rate, he decided it was probably better not to inform her that he already knew her name, because he'd seen it on the prisoner manifest. That way, he could at least pretend that their acquaintance had only begun a scant hour ago.

While some part of him wanted to continue the conversation, Landon didn't know whether that was entirely wise. He might let slip something he would rather have kept to himself. Tone neutral, he said, "There are some rations and water packs back in the refrigeration unit, if you need something."

For a few seconds she didn't reply, but gave him a quick, sidelong look from beneath her long eyelashes. Then he saw the slender shoulders lift under the heavy uniform jacket. "I am a bit thirsty," she admitted, and eased herself out of the co-pilot's chair. As she exited the cockpit, she added, "Although right now I think I'd rather have a stiff shot of brandy," just before she sailed off down the corridor.

*You're not the only one*, he thought. Unfortunately, Owens had been a teetotaler, and so there were no secret stashes of alcohol on board the ship. With a mental sigh, Landon turned back to the nav-computer readouts.

———————

Possibly Dhani had accurately ascertained his mood, or maybe the reality of her situation had finally begun to hit her. Whatever the case, she was uncharacteristically subdued as the little ship made its way to Ordon, allowing Landon to concentrate on piloting the vessel instead of deflecting her continued verbal volleys. It wasn't until after they had finally made contact with the authorities at Ordon's one and only spaceport and had received instructions to land that she spoke again.

"So what are you going to tell them?" she asked.

"As little as possible," Landon replied. He made a small adjustment to the engine's power levels in order to give the ship increased fuel efficiency during the descent to the planet's surface. "That I'm on Consortium business, and that it's imperative the ship be repaired immediately. There's still a garrison here, so —as far as I can tell, anyway—they haven't tried to break free yet. I doubt they'll ask too many questions."

Dhani didn't appear terribly encouraged by his comment. "And what about me? I doubt anyone's going to believe I'm your second-in-command or something."

Landon had to reluctantly agree with that statement. Even if Dhani went ahead and donned the rest of Owens' uniform, it would be all too apparent it wasn't hers. And the prison garb she currently wore was a dead giveaway that she shouldn't be wandering around free.

"I'll think of something."

An eloquent lift of her left eyebrow told Landon exactly what she thought of his powers of invention. He couldn't even argue with her silent assessment. He was an administrator—and a fairly unenthusiastic one at that—and although he'd had to think fast on his feet more than once in his career, he certainly was not known for being the galaxy-class flinger of bullshit their current situation seemed to require. About all he could do was hope he'd be able to rise to the occasion.

The ship sliced through Ordon's upper atmosphere, its wings trailing streams of water vapor. At once the forward view-screen darkened slightly to accommodate the bright daylight outside. In Otel, the only settlement of significance on the planet's one continent, it appeared to be late morning. From the air, the town looked like a dusty brown splotch on the mottled green of the surrounding landscape, and Landon felt his spirits sink at its unprepossessing appearance. Of all the backwaters to end up in....

But he said nothing as their stolen ship sailed

majestically into docking bay X-22, as directed. From inside the shabby spaceport administrative offices, a small group of equally shabby-looking people emerged—no doubt Ordon's version of a formal welcoming committee. Accompanying them were several dark-uniformed GDF guards, who took up flanking positions to either side of the dignitaries. The entire group waited at the edge of the duracrete oval that formed the docking bay's floor while Landon went through the necessary steps of securing the landing gear and shutting down the pulse engines. In the co-pilot's seat next to him, Dhani watched in silence as he worked, but a dancing light in her dark eyes seemed to signal she was plotting something. Exactly what, he couldn't begin to guess, which only made him that much more anxious about the story he intended to tell those people standing in the docking bay, expectant expressions on their faces.

"Wait in here until I come to get you," he told her, in tones he could only hope would be obeyed. "Let me speak with them first."

"I live for your orders, captain," she said sweetly. The impish gleam never left her dark eyes.

Oh, of all the—he turned from her and stalked down the corridor, pulling at the hem of his uniform jacket as he did so, making sure that everything was fitting just so. If nothing else, he needed to give a good impression, make it seem as though he had every right to be here, every right to be flying this vessel.

He emerged into sunlight that felt blinding after the dim confines of the ship. With the sunlight came a sense of oppressive heat. The humidity levels on this planet were well above what he—or the Consortium's enviro-engineers—considered comfortable.

The best-dressed of the contingent stepped forward. He looked uncomfortable in his high-necked dress suit, beads of perspiration standing out on his pasty skin. "Greetings, sir. We're pleased to see that the Consortium has chosen to reach out to us in these times of trouble. I'm Governor Janning."

Landon nodded. "Captain Beck," he responded. "I require your assistance, as my ship has malfunctioned and I carry urgent dispatches for Gaia, dispatches that can't be trusted to electronic transmission. If we—"

He broke off as he realized that Governor Janning's attention had abruptly shifted to a spot somewhere farther up the shuttle's ramp. Turning the slightest bit to see what had distracted the other man, Landon scowled as his gaze fell on Dhani Warlow.

She hesitated on the ramp as she surveyed the scene before her. Then her chin went up and her shoulders squared, and it was as if he was gazing at a completely different woman. Despite the ill-fitting uniform jacket and the baggy prison trousers, she looked more like a queen than an escaped prisoner—not that the Consortium had any such things as queens.

Dhani descended the ramp and went straight to Governor Janning, who stared at her, apparently mesmerized. "My thanks, governor," she said, and even her voice was altered slightly, the Gaian accent strengthened, its pitch lower somehow. "On behalf of the Consortium government, I would like to thank you." As the governor blinked down into her face, she went on, "I am Larissa Miles, daughter of Clarence Miles."

She hadn't. She *wouldn't*. Landon wanted to clap a hand to his forehead in dismay, but he knew the last thing he should do right now was betray his consternation at her declaration.

Dhani had just claimed to be the only child of Gaia's wealthiest oligarch.

## CHAPTER TWO

THE CHIME SOUNDED, AND DHANI SET DOWN HER hairbrush and went to the door. She had a good idea who waited for her on the other side.

Sure enough, the door whooshed open to reveal Captain Landon Beck, whose entire lean form seemed to vibrate with exasperation. No sooner had he stepped inside her chamber and she'd shut the door behind him than he snapped, "Have you lost your mind?"

"I don't think so," she replied, and returned to her dressing table. For a backwater provincial dump like Ordon, the locals hadn't done too badly in welcoming Clarence Miles's daughter. The room was large and better-appointed than it had any right to be. Dhani wasn't sure if Governor Janning had divested his wife or mistress—or both—of some of her clothing and jewels, but the collection she had been given for her use was fairly impressive. Perhaps some quiet corner of her soul recognized the reckless audacity of what she had done, but no time for that now. She'd given herself a role, and she knew she had better play it to the utmost of her ability. Both their lives depended on it...and after all, it wasn't as though she had never before assumed an identity that wasn't hers.

Captain Beck scowled. Possibly he thought such an expression made him look fearsome, but Dhani only noted that even a frown couldn't really detract from the even, regular features, the frank friendliness of his blue-gray eyes. It really had been kind of a waste for such a handsome specimen to be stuck on Zeta Tau station out in the middle of nowhere. Arms crossed, he asked, "What do you think they're going to do when they discover you have no more connection to Clarence Miles than they do?"

One thing about the room that was, unfortunately, quite sub-par was the air conditioning; Dhani spied a thin sheen of perspiration along Beck's hairline, but she doubted he would admit to any weakness in front of her by reaching up to wipe it away. Her borrowed gown didn't cover nearly as much as his high-necked uniform, and even she felt uncomfortably warm, although the sun had almost set by now.

"And how exactly do you think they're going to discover that particular fact?" she inquired, returning to the dressing table and giving her appearance one last critical look. Her dark hair lay sleek and shiny over her shoulders, and fell past them to halfway down her back, and her eyes looked much bigger than usual, thanks to some artfully smoky shadow. Not bad, considering she'd been locked in a Consortium detention cell less than seven standard hours earlier. Satisfied, she faced Beck and crossed her arms. "Do *you* know what Larissa Miles looks like?"

He shifted his weight the tiniest fraction from one foot to another, but at least he met her eyes as he replied, "No."

Her estimation of this Captain Beck rose a little. How many other Consortium officers would have openly admitted to such a lack of knowledge? Dhani wanted to smile but kept her expression neutral. "And if you, someone with a position as adjutant to the commander of a military base, someone I assume has access to more information than most people in the Consortium, have no idea what Clarence Miles's daughter might look like, what makes you think these provincials would ever suspect I'm not who I say I am?"

"You have a point." The captain raised an eyebrow. "By the way, how is it that *you* know anything about Larissa Miles? For obvious reasons, her father has done his best to keep any information about her hidden from the public."

True, but Dhani had resources the general public lacked. She'd learned early on that no one gave a good crap about plain old Dhani Warlow, so she'd done her best to cultivate contacts with people who could provide her with a short list of important women whom she resembled. On Gaia itself, with retinal scanning and DNA sampling, she wouldn't stand a chance, but out in the hinterlands, those sorts of security measures weren't used as much, due to their cost. Larissa Miles was very similar to Dhani in appearance —in her middle twenties, with dark hair and eyes, slender, not particularly tall. The oligarch's daughter had always been Dhani's ace in the hole, a secret weapon she hadn't quite dared to deploy…until now.

"I…heard things," she said, after a pause she hoped Captain Beck wouldn't notice but probably did. He didn't seem to miss much, this one, and some of the opinions she'd formed of GDF officers while dealing with the soldiers at various local garrisons on the worlds she'd visited were slowly being revised. Then again, she supposed anyone who had achieved his rank had to have a good deal more going on upstairs than your standard NCO.

"Really." His blue-gray eyes seemed particularly piercing right then, but he made no further comment.

"How long do you think we have?" Dhani asked, feeling inexplicably relieved.

He didn't pretend to misunderstand her. "I don't know. A day or two at the most. Even with lines of communication collapsing, word will get out about the destruction of Zeta Tau station. Lists of victims will be sent out. And then our friends here will realize

I should be a dead man…and that you're sure as hell not Larissa Miles."

His honesty surprised her. She hadn't expected him to admit so openly that the Consortium was falling apart even as they spoke. Something so big and so unwieldy couldn't self-destruct all at once, of course, but the first rumblings had started just a standard month ago, when the bootleg transmissions were blasted across the galaxy by a group of freedom fighters, showing the depths of the human-based government's iniquities. Dhani had known about some of those crimes against both humans and aliens—how could she not, when she'd spent the last five years working in the underbelly of Gaian society?—but even she, who thought she'd long since become hardened to man's inhumanity to man…or Zhore…or Stacian…had been shocked.

Mass incarcerations of political prisoners. Attempted genocide. Desecration of the dead. Sterilization of worlds with their own established life, just to provide more colonies for the Consortium. The litany was long, with each crime seemingly worse than the last.

The first revolts began within a week of the bootleg broadcasts going viral, starting with long-colonized worlds such as New Chicago and Nova Angeles, planets that had just been itching for a chance to assert their independence. The revolution spread quickly to Iradia, which had never rested easily under the Consortium's hand, and smaller places such as Lathvin and Shiva Prime. Outposts like Ordon would be the last to fall, mainly because Dhani knew they feared what would happen to them when the government's supply chain was cut off and they had to try to go it alone on a planet just barely able to sustain human life. But even Ordon wasn't so isolated that she and Landon Beck could shelter here indefinitely— as he'd just pointed out.

He still watched her with those careful, clear, blue-gray eyes of his; like a lot of Consortium officers she'd encountered, he had a typical poker face, revealing little of his thoughts or emotions—and oh, would she like a chance to find out what he was thinking—but Dhani had the impression he expected some sort of reply.

"Well, we'll just have to make sure we're long gone by the time they figure it out," she said lightly. "Let's hope they have a decent starship mechanic here, one who works quickly."

"And if they don't?"

"I'll think of something," Dhani said. "I always do." *Almost always,* she amended to herself. She had to admit she'd blown it with that last con. Otherwise, she wouldn't have been languishing in a cell on the Zeta Tau station. It had been her only real mistake— and nearly would have been her last one, if it hadn't been for the man standing before her now.

Captain Beck's mouth quirked. "If you say so."

Apparently, he was also thinking of where he'd found her. She hadn't been able to talk her way out of that one. Still, Dhani thought she should be able to manage things well enough on Ordon. Even her brief exposure to the officials here had convinced her they weren't exactly the sharpest knives in the drawer. "I'll have you know that I can cry very convincingly on cue."

"Why does that not surprise me?" He smiled at her then, and she couldn't help but notice the way the shift in expression changed his features. An extremely handsome man, this Captain Beck, and probably no more than ten years older than she was.

It was always easier when they were handsome....

He continued, "With talents such as yours, however, I find myself wondering why you didn't pursue a career in the entertainment industry, instead of turning to petty grifting."

She gave a bitter laugh. "Don't think I didn't try. Problem is, most of the leading ladies also happened to be the mistresses and girlfriends of high-ranking Consortium officials. About all I could hope for was to be a piece of background set decoration—which wasn't very appealing to me."

And what a humbling experience that had been. Blithely, she'd thought she could make her way into the business through sheer talent...and looks, if one were going to be perfectly honest...but that naïve belief hadn't lasted very long. Oh, she'd gotten a few offers of the sort other women probably would have refused, but even those hadn't panned out. In the end, learning to work her various cons seemed more honorable than sleeping her way to any kind of success in the entertainment industry, especially since she did her damnedest to make sure the victims of those cons were corrupt officials, dirty businessmen, anyone who clearly deserved to lose some of their own ill-gotten loot.

Unfortunately, her luck had run out on Zephyr IV, of all places. She'd pushed it too far there, she was forced to admit to herself. And she'd been sloppy, because the reports that had just begun to circulate told her the Consortium was already starting to crack at its foundations, and those reports had made her nervous. Anyone in the business could have told her that once you lost your nerve, you were done for.

When Captain Beck rescued her, she'd been convinced sex had to be his motivation. Certainly, she could think of no other reason why he would have risked his own life by delaying his escape in order to save her. But he'd had plenty of opportunity on the ship to "take advantage," as such maneuvers used to be referred to back in the day, and yet he had tried nothing. Dhani wasn't even sure whether she would have put up more than a token resistance. After all, a quick tumble in the ship's one luxurious cabin seemed a fair enough exchange for her life. Anyway, she'd already acknowledged to herself that Beck was good-looking, which was more than she could say for some of the people she'd shacked up with in order to have a place to sleep. She could have done much, much worse.

If seduction was his plan, though, he had a strange way of going about it. When she'd opened the door to her suite a few minutes ago, giving him his first sight of her in her borrowed finery, his gaze hadn't even flickered. Not exactly the response of a man who was lusting in his heart, that was for sure.

Her current revelations didn't seem to have affected him, either. Dhani wasn't sure what to do with that sort of disinterest...or rather, if she'd been able to identify him as homosexual, she would have forgotten about that angle and tried something else. However, she got the impression he was hetero, only...ruthlessly self-controlled? Possibly. At least that would give her something to work with.

Captain Beck gave the briefest nod when she finished speaking, then glanced down at the chronometer on his wrist. "We should go down for dinner. The governor is expecting us."

"Of course," she said coolly, matching his indifferent tone. It wasn't as if she *really* wanted him, anyway. It was only that she would have been willing to give herself to him as a way to show her gratitude. That was all.

Still, she couldn't help wondering if he would offer her his arm as they went down to dinner.

Of course, he did not.

Landon sat at the table, watching in bemused astonishment as Dhani charmed the governor, his attaché, the commander of the local garrison, and just about every other male guest at the hurriedly prepared dinner party. Her reception by the few women in attendance was considerably frostier, but he guessed the irrepressible Ms. Warlow was not much bothered by that.

As for himself, he chose to observe rather than participate. If anyone present thought it odd that a ranking officer of the Gaian Defense Force should be so reticent, they certainly didn't show it. Then again, it didn't seem as if his contributions to the conversation were much missed. Besides a few passing comments on the food—which was surprisingly good —to a narrow-faced woman who had identified herself as Trisha Janning, the governor's wife, he had remained silent, wondering what he would do if Dhani stuck her foot in it and required rescuing. So far, however, that hadn't turned out to be the case.

"I've always thought it very important to get out in the galaxy as much as possible," she said, pausing to sip at a glass of pale greenish-yellow local wine. The heavy gold necklace around her throat glinted as she swallowed. "Perspective, you know. And also, there are so many rumors flying about right now. I wanted people to know that the Consortium is as secure as it ever was. My father was concerned about my safety, but I told him I didn't care about that. It was more important to be a sort of envoy, so to speak."

"Admirable, admirable," said Major Trent, the commander of the Consortium garrison. He was a portly man whose dark gray synth-wool uniform jacket fairly bulged at the seams, the high neck ruthlessly compressing his wattled throat. Landon guessed the uniform hadn't been quite so tight before the good major was posted here; if nothing else, the local cuisine was better than some he'd had back home on New Chicago. It seemed the lush environment here was good for something besides increasing the local humidity. "Your father has instilled in you a true sense of duty, I see."

Dhani's full mouth curved in a smile that managed to be both modest and seductive. Landon wasn't quite sure how she accomplished it, but neither Major Trent nor the governor seemed too concerned about the mechanics involved. Both of them continued to stare at her, mesmerized like a couple of *tarns* cornered by an Iradian sand-snake. Across the table from him, Trisha Janning scowled and poured herself another glass of wine.

"I do what I can," Dhani said. "At one time I thought perhaps I should go into the defense fleet, but my father thought it better that I remain a civilian. But that hasn't prevented me from serving the Consortium in any way I can."

*Laying it on a bit thick, aren't you?* Landon thought sourly. He realized he was apparently the only male at the table not caught in Dhani's spell...and he would do everything in his power to keep it that way. Oh, she was a beautiful woman, no doubt of that, but mere beauty wasn't quite enough to fuse his mental circuits, thank you very much. For a brief moment, he wondered what someone like Dhani might have done to the orderly atmosphere at the military academy he attended on Gaia, and repressed a shudder. The Consortium had enough to deal with as it was.

No, she was far from helpless, this wayward young woman he had rescued from the detention levels of Zeta Tau station. Dhani did have an air of fragility—or at least she cultivated one—but it was becoming rapidly apparent to him that she was about as fragile as a hardened steel airlock.

The impulse that had led him to retrieve her from her prison cell was now beginning to seem like madness. But even though he had only known her a short time, Landon couldn't imagine her brilliant life force snuffed out, gone along with so many others. Why *had* he done it, anyway? Surely it would have been much simpler to save himself. But he had reached out to save her despite the risk involved.

It had been her eyes...something in the wide, dark eyes that stared up at him as he processed her electronic file. Although in the booking image her face had been nearly expressionless, her eyes had the wary, frightened look of a horse about to bolt. Those eyes had haunted him, had remained in some hidden corner of his mind until the imminent destruction of the space station forced him to action, even though he understood the risks, knew that if they were caught, she'd be sent on to the maximum-security prison on Titan, while he would face court-martial and a summary execution. And yet...he somehow knew he would do it all over again if he had to.

As he accepted another glass of wine from the governor's wife, Landon caught a quick, sidelong glance from Dhani while her admiring audience chuckled over something she had just said. The corners of her dark eyes were crinkled in amusement, and in her borrowed finery, she bore absolutely no resemblance to the waifish prisoner in oversized inmate garb he had rescued less than half a standard day earlier. She had not asked to be saved, yet here she was.

Now, even as he watched her, he had a sudden, random flash from a hunting expedition he had undertaken a few years earlier while on leave. For some reason, Colonel Owens had invited Landon to Gaia for a hunt, and of course Landon had accepted —he'd known better than to turn down a "request" from a superior officer. Uncomfortable as the situation had been, he'd acquitted himself well enough, although he had no taste for hunting, had never seen the attraction in preying on animals who had no chance against humans armed with pulse rifles.

The worst of it had been the doe. It had been springtime, and Owens didn't seem to care about the difference between a buck and a doe heavy with young. He had shot her, and she had gone crashing into a thick tangle of underbrush. When at last they found her, she was lying on her side, the life draining out of her in a black trail of blood. She had stared up at Landon with dark eyes that held no hope, no belief in mercy. Her shining flanks rose and fell as she panted out her last breaths. And Landon, knowing there was nothing else he could do, had raised his gun and shot her between the eyes, releasing her from her pain, not caring what his superior officer might think of that one gesture of mercy.

It had been that same look in Dhani Warlow's eyes in her booking portrait…a resignation that recognized no chance of a rescue. He couldn't have done anything to save that poor dying deer on Gaia, but Landon knew the young woman's face would have haunted his nightmares if he hadn't tried to save her life.

Very altruistic, although, deep down, he realized it was more than that. She was so very beautiful…and there had been very few women in his life, thanks to his tenure at Zeta Tau station. Short, meaningless affairs during the brief leaves allotted to him had never seemed that appealing. But there was something about Dhani Warlow, something he wasn't quite ready to admit to himself.

Now her life had been returned to her—and damned if he knew what she meant to do with it. She had certainly proved to be quite resilient. The wary look was long gone from her eyes. If he hadn't seen it for himself, he wouldn't have thought her capable of such an expression. Or had it all been another act, Dhani presenting the face she thought her captors would have wanted to see? What she might have hoped to accomplish with such dissembling, Landon couldn't begin to guess. A trip to the MaxSec on Titan was inevitably a one-way ticket. All the meekness in the galaxy wouldn't have convinced the Gaian authorities to free her.

Her voice brought him out of his reverie. "Don't you think so, captain?"

He felt himself startle slightly at being addressed. His thoughts had taken him a long way from where he was. "I beg your pardon?"

Dhani smiled and then gave a wry little shrug. "I fear the captain has more important things on his mind than my tedious theories. Isn't that right, Captain Beck?"

Since he had no idea what she was talking about, Landon replied, in his most neutral tones, "I fear Ms. Miles enjoys a joke at my expense."

"Not at all, captain." Her right eyebrow lifted. "I was just assuring these gentlemen that what we're experiencing now is only a temporary disruption, and that the government—backed by my father and his allies in the Consortium government—will have everything back to normal in no time. Isn't that right?"

She was enjoying this far too much—of that he was certain. But Landon knew of course he couldn't disagree with her in front of the company assembled there, so he said, "The people of the Consortium want nothing more—as do we all, I'm sure."

Governor Janning lifted his glass. "Hear, hear! A toast to the Consortium, and to Clarence Miles and his family!"

*Sycophantic idiot*, Landon thought, but he raised his glass anyway. Why should he expect the governor to do anything less than toady to the woman he thought was the oligarch's daughter? After all, as loath as he was to admit it, he hadn't behaved all that differently while on that terrible hunting expedition on Gaia. True opportunities for advancement didn't come along all that often, especially for someone trapped on a backwater world like Ordon. A few choice words whispered by Larissa Miles into the correct ear could change a man's fortunes overnight.

All around the table glasses were lifted, and Clarence Miles's health was drunk. A complete waste of time, Landon reflected, since Mr. Miles was probably busy trying to safeguard his fortune as best he could, even as the ground began to break up under his feet. With any luck, their ship would be repaired quickly, and he and Dhani would be well on their way long before their benefactors realized Clarence Miles currently wasn't in any position to grant favors.

No sooner had Landon set his glass back down on the table, however, than one of the governor's aides scurried in and whispered urgently into his superior's ear. Governor Janning's eyes widened, and some of the color drained out of his florid cheeks. Then he glanced over at Dhani, and his mouth tightened.

Ever perceptive, she set down her glass and asked him, "Is there something wrong, Governor Janning?"

He started, then attempted to recover his composure by saying, "Well, I've just heard—that is, I believe—" He appeared to gather himself, and finished, "Perhaps you and I should have a word in private."

Her eyes, wide and guileless, focused on the governor. "Is there something wrong with our ship?"

"No—no, nothing like that."

"Is it something I might assist with?" Landon inquired. Whatever news the governor's aide might have brought him, Landon doubted it was anything good. That meant he needed to make sure he was included in any conversations with Dhani that might result. If nothing else, they needed to keep their stories straight. He didn't want to think what would happen if Governor Janning and his little group of toadies here figured out that their entrancing guest was no more related to Clarence Miles than they were.

"Well, erm—" The governor looked at Landon as if really seeing him for the first time. "Yes, well, of course, what I have to say concerns both of you, naturally. If you and Ms. Miles might accompany me to my office?" He rose and addressed the other guests at the table. "If you will excuse us—urgent business—"

Major Trent looked irked at being excluded from the conversation, but he merely said, "Of course." No doubt he wished to avoid making a scene in front of the supposed "Larissa Miles."

Gracefully, Dhani stood, then gave the assembly an apologetic little smile. "Forgive me—it appears Governor Janning has need of me for a little while. Don't let our departure interrupt your meal." She sent an inquiring look in Janning's direction. "If you will lead us to your office, governor?"

"Of course."

The three of them exited the dining chamber and made their way down a long corridor that terminated in a creaky old elevator. Apparently, Ordon didn't rate much in the way of modern technology. As the elevator jerked its way up to the second floor, Landon risked a quick glance down at Dhani, trying to ascertain whether she had guessed at the probable reason for their unscheduled meeting with the governor. He guessed she had; she gave him a surreptitious nod and then looked away, her face placid and only mildly curious.

The governor's office was large and shabby, furnished with a comm console now at least three or four models out of date. Stacks of paper covered the desk of yellowish native wood, and a few half-hearted sconces glowed from the walls.

Not the best place to deliver bad news. It seemed Janning realized this as well; he bustled about nervously, pulling out a seat for Dhani but forgetting to offer one to Landon. Not that he would have accepted it; he felt it better to take his position slightly to the right of Dhani's chair and wait there, hands clasped behind his waist, shoulders back in the old academy stance that still came to him like second nature.

Landon's formal posture seemed to throw the governor even more off-kilter. He retreated behind his desk, shifted a pile of paper from one corner of the old-fashioned blotter to another, fiddled with the stylus of his handheld, and then finally appeared to work up the nerve to look Dhani in the face. "Ms. Miles, I have just received some distressing news."

Instead of replying, she merely tilted her head to one side and waited.

Janning's gaze flickered to Landon for a second, and then he returned his attention to the young woman seated before him. He swallowed. "It seems there was an insurgent attack on Consortium headquarters in Luna City, an attack that destroyed the domes. I don't have to tell you what that means."

White-faced, her lips pressed together, Dhani shook her head, even while Landon tried to process what the governor had just said. How could HQ simply be gone? Oh, of course the Consortium had other bases, other sector headquarters. But it was from the heart of Gaia that all the true governing took place.

"I'm afraid it's even worse," Janning went on, sweat visibly beading on his forehead. "The reports stated that your father was among those lost in the attack. He had been attending an emergency meeting in Luna City."

A heavy silence fell, broken only by a faint sibilant noise Landon realized was the forced air of the over-worked air conditioning units blowing through the vent above the governor's desk. His heart began to pound, but he held himself as still as he could, even as he prayed that Dhani was a good enough actress to pull this off.

Dhani straightened in her chair; even in the dim light, Landon could see the color drain from her cheeks. Her lower lip gave the faintest of telltale quivers, but her voice sounded firm enough when she spoke. "How do you know this for sure?"

"Ms. Miles, the news came directly from the Gaian relay station on Titan. I have no reason to doubt its veracity."

Her hands knotted in her lap. For the first time, Landon realized she wore borrowed gold on her fingers as well. "How was this even possible? How could the insurgents pull off such an attack at Gaia's heart?" she asked, in the same calm, cold voice. But was that a glint of unshed tears he spied tangled in her lashes?

Janning gathered himself as best he could before replying, "I don't have any more details at this time. Very likely no one knows for certain exactly how they were able to prevail against the in-system forces and even get close enough to mount such an assault." He hesitated. "I am very sorry for your loss."

At his words, her shoulders squared, and Dhani lifted her chin. "My loss, and a loss for the rest of the Consortium as well." Then she looked away from the governor and over at Landon. "Captain, it seems my journey was in vain. What now?"

Taking his cue, Landon stepped forward and directed his reply to Governor Janning. "It's more imperative than ever that our ship be fixed with all haste. The only way to ensure Ms. Miles's safety is to keep moving until we can determine how matters stand on Gaia. We can't risk the insurgents learning of her location and tracking her down."

"Of course," Janning said at once. "I will see to it personally."

Dhani stood, hand trembling as she used the back of the chair to steady herself. "Thank you, governor.

Now I think it would be best if I returned to my quarters. Captain?"

And Landon went to her, offering his arm. She took it, leaning on him as if she barely had the strength to walk out of the office, even though she kept her head high. This was the first time they'd actually touched, but Landon couldn't allow himself to take any pleasure in the sensation of her slender hand resting on his forearm, not when he needed to act official and proper. The governor followed them back out to the hallway; there was no need to use the elevator, as the rooms they had been given were on this same floor, although located at the opposite end of the corridor.

They stopped outside the door to Dhani's suite. Janning began, "If there is anything more I can do—"

"Please make my apologies to your guests, governor," Dhani said. "Captain, if you would come with me?"

Knowing he couldn't refuse, Landon inclined his head and then trailed after Dhani as she entered her room. She palmed the door lock, waited a few seconds, and then began to chuckle.

"So," she said, her dark eyes dancing, "do you think he bought it?"

# CHAPTER THREE

_____

*BOUGHT IT?* LANDON THOUGHT. *I THINK HE would have taken out a loan for future shares if he could.* However, he certainly didn't want to give Dhani any more support for her epic prevarications than was strictly necessary. While her lies had saved them so far, actively encouraging them felt a bit closer to the moral edge than he currently wanted to walk.

"The governor appears to believe your story," he allowed. As her dark eyes lit up and a grin began to tug at the corners of her mouth, he added in quelling tones, "For now. But the longer we're trapped here, the more risk we run of your story being revealed for the complete pack of lies it actually is."

To his dismay, her grin gave no sign of retreating. "Does that bother you, captain? Has your own life been such a model of truthfulness and plain dealing that even a few white lies—told purely to keep us safe —are enough to make you uncomfortable?"

How could he possibly answer that question? It wasn't the actual lies that bothered him, but the possible consequences if those lies were ever found out. Yes, her lies—as she had said—were based on simple self-preservation. That didn't change the fact that they now teetered on a precipice, one on a mountain that was starting to crack from the ground up.

"By going along with your charade, I've made myself complicit in it," he replied, after a significant pause.

At last the grin faltered as his words appeared to sink in. Dhani moved away from him and went to the dressing table, where she began to pull the borrowed rings from her fingers. Not looking at him, she said, "I'm sorry."

He wasn't sure he'd heard her correctly. "Excuse me?"

She turned toward him then, a small frown creasing her delicate brows. "I didn't stop to think— that is, I could tell that you didn't have a real story to give the governor and his people about who I was, or why I would be traveling with you. So I came up with the Larissa Miles idea. I suppose I panicked."

"That didn't look like panic to me." On the contrary—her performance out on the shuttle's docking ramp had all the appearances of something she'd been preparing for some time.

"I assure you, it was." She reached up to undo the clasp of her necklace, but seemed to be having some trouble with it. For a second, Landon considered offering to help. But then her hands lifted, and off came the heavy piece of wrought gold. He felt a small pang, then wondered at himself. Was he really disappointed because he'd lost the opportunity to touch the smooth skin at the back of her neck, if even for a second or two?

*Too much wine with dinner,* he thought. *Or possibly temporary insanity.*

Dhani did seem to have that effect on people.

He cleared his throat. "At any rate, what's been done can't be undone. As I said earlier, our best hope is that the ship can be repaired quickly and that we can be on our way before anyone suspects anything."

"'On our way,'" she repeated. This time her eyes did meet his. He thought he saw worry there, along with another emotion he couldn't recognize. "You still haven't said where that will be."

Should he tell her the truth, let her know that his delay in discussing their next step was because he really didn't know *where* to go? Yes, they'd already discussed heading to Iradia, but what if the governor's technicians couldn't repair the ship's damaged subspace drive? They'd be forced to stay here on Ordon, or at least head to a planet within pulse-drive reach. And with Dhani's lies hanging out there like a time bomb, remaining here didn't seem like much of an option. All it would take would be one news story about Larissa Miles taking over the reins of the family business from her late father, complete with an interview with the bereaved daughter—or a report that she had perished in the explosion as well—and their story would collapse like the house of cards it was.

"Where would you like to go?" he asked, hoping she might offer a suggestion that would be better than his original plan.

The question surprised her, he could tell. Her eyes widened, and her mouth parted slightly. Then she shut it again just as quickly, and shook her head. "Any world where I might want you to take me would present a difficulty—they're not known for being sympathetic to the Consortium. I don't think it matters all that much. I might be from Gaia, but it's been a long time since I was able to call any particular planet home."

Despite his determination to not let her affect him, Landon couldn't help but experience a wave of pity at her words. She'd spoken simply enough, but there was a world of loss hidden beneath that one simple statement.

"I suppose we should stick with our original plan of going to Iradia…if the ship can manage it," he said.

Her full mouth pursed. "I'm still surprised you'd suggest heading there—I'd think that was the last place a GDF officer would want to go. I can't imagine they wasted much time throwing off the Consortium's yoke."

"It's also someplace where the Consortium wouldn't have much luck when it came to looking for either one of us. It's a hub for smuggling, both people and cargo. We'd be able to find some kind of transport for you there."

A flash of anger revealed itself on Dhani's face. It took a moment for Landon to recognize the expression for what it was, since so much of what she did and said seemed to be cloaked in careful artifice. Swiftly following on the heels of that anger was a look of disappointment, this one leveled directly at him.

"'Transport'?" she repeated. "To where? I already told you, I don't have anywhere to go. I don't have *anything*—no money, no identification. Nothing. But fine, drop me in that den of thieves and smugglers and crime bosses. I suppose if I can persuade the governor's wife to loan me some of these clothes permanently, I might be able to find someone to shack up with. But no worries. You'll have satisfied your conscience, right?"

"Dhani, I—" Landon found himself reaching out toward her in an instinctive gesture of supplication, and forced his hands to curl themselves into impotent fists at his side. Just as well, since he'd seen her flinch at his abortive movement. Voice hardening, he said, "Look, I wouldn't just 'drop' you there. I'd make sure you had someplace to go. But...but if the galaxy is breaking apart, I want to make sure we're not around when these people find out we're not exactly who we say we are. Because when people figure out there's no government left to keep them in check...it's never pretty."

For a moment she said nothing, but only stared at him out of those wet-ringed dark eyes. Her cheeks were pale beneath the carefully applied cosmetics.

What else could he say? He needed to know what was happening out there. Even though he'd been chained to the GDF for the past ten years, he still had family on New Chicago. The separatists there probably wouldn't have waited for long to act. Problem was, he couldn't know for sure. Transmissions coming to and from Zeta Tau station had been heavily monitored and censored. The last thing the Consortium wanted was for its soldiers to discover that the home worlds they'd left behind were now at war. But that could be exactly what was happening. And not just civil war, but possibly hostilities with the aliens who shared this galaxy with them. Sure, the Zhore weren't warlike at all, and the Eridanis preferred diplomacy above all else, but the Stacians definitely didn't have those sorts of scruples. They might have already gone on the attack, knowing that a weakened Consortium couldn't mount any kind of cohesive defense.

He was spared from further agonizing by the chime at the door. He moved to answer it, since

Dhani remained where she was, cold and still as a statue.

The governor's pasty-faced attaché waited outside. "I'm sorry to disturb you, sir, but Governor Janning said I should come up to see you right away."

Landon stifled an inward groan. "Is something wrong?"

The chubby man's face looked even more pasty, if that were possible. "Our techs have just completed their diagnosis on your ship's subspace drive system. Unfortunately, the crystal harmonizer is shattered. It has to be replaced, but we don't have the spare parts here on Ordon." His gaze shifted to Dhani, to her stricken face, and he swallowed. "This is a bad time, isn't it?"

Actually, Landon thought the attaché's timing was perfect. He'd caught a glimpse of Dhani's real grief and anger, and the interruption had broken off what was turning into a very uncomfortable conversation.

"Ms. Miles is, as you might imagine, rather overwrought at the moment," he said. "As you know, it's imperative that I get her to Gaia as quickly as possible. Are there any other ships here I might requisition for that purpose?"

The attaché straightened. "Yes, sir. That's actually why I'm here. Governor Janning is well aware of the urgency of your situation and offers you his ship as alternative transport. It's not as fast or as well-equipped as yours, but—"

"As long as it gets us there," Landon cut in. At this point, he'd take the most battered cargo freighter in the quadrant if it meant they could be out of this backwater in the near future. Besides, it wasn't a bad deal. Once Governor Janning was able to get his hands on the parts required to fix the little Gupta-class ship, it would be worth far more than the ship they had taken in trade.

Suddenly Dhani was there besides him, damp eyes glowing, her face a perfect picture of tremulous relief. "That is so generous of the governor," she said. "Please tell him that I'll be sure to inform the right people of his generosity."

"Th-thank you," the young man stammered. "Is there anything else you need?"

"As you know, the pirates that attacked us took everything," she replied. With a gesture toward the borrowed dress she wore, she continued, "This gown is lovely, but if a few changes of more practical clothing could be spared, I would be most appreciative."

"Of course, Ms. Miles. I'll see to it at once." He sketched a short bow, then stopped, as if unsure as to whether that was the correct response.

While his awkwardness was somewhat amusing, Landon felt it was time to put the man out of his misery. "Can everything be ready within the next hour? We don't have any more time to lose."

"I-I think so, sir. I'll see to Ms. Miles's request, and after that all should be prepared."

"Excellent," he said. "Then that should be all for now." He touched his palm to the electronic lock and turned to Dhani, who no longer appeared to be the grieving daughter. To his dismay, the impish look was back in her eyes. "Pirates?"

"Well, it's the truth, isn't it?" she responded ingenuously. "I had to give him some sort of story as to why I didn't have any proper clothes." If anything, the devilish glint in her big brown eyes intensified. "Don't look at me like that. At least this way I'll get some clean underwear."

---

"I'm thinking the governor got the better part in this deal," Dhani said after giving the shabby cabin a quick once-over. Like the rest of Ordon, the shuttle appeared to be at least two generations behind most of the galaxy in terms of its technology.

"It's a ship, isn't it?" replied Landon, who looked decidedly testy.

"Yes," she allowed, "barely."

"Then sit down and fasten your safety harness."

He didn't add, *And be quiet*, but he might as well have. She figured she should do as he said—if nothing else, she wanted off Ordon as soon as possible, and if they had to escape in this cramped little shuttle, then so be it.

Without further comment, she seated herself in the co-pilot's chair and wrestled with the unfamiliar harness for a moment as Landon went through the standard preflight checkup. Tension showed in the tight lines of his jaw and his compressed mouth. No surprise—he'd ended up having a bit of a tussle with the governor over whether one of Janning's men should pilot the shuttle to Gaia, and she'd watched with some amusement as the captain trotted out a series of excuses as to why the offered pilot wasn't necessary. Luckily, Landon had come out ahead in that particular disagreement, but it had cost them further delay.

By then it was the middle of the night, Ordon time. Dhani had thought she would be more tired, but for some reason she felt keyed-up and tense, the way she did after too many cups of coffee. Maybe she was merely picking up on some of Landon's urgency; ever since word had come that they would take the governor's shuttle, the GDF officer been pushing to get them off Ordon before any more precious time elapsed. True, they were playing a dangerous game, and all it would take was one transmission containing the wrong information to completely blow their flimsy story right out of the sky.

She hadn't been able to continue her discussion with Landon as to exactly where they might be headed. At this point, it hardly mattered. Where was she supposed to go, anyway? Gaia was sure as hell out of the question. And she'd never spent more than a few standard months on any other planet after she'd fled her home world. The closest she'd ever come to settling down was the time she'd gone to Eridani. Elon had said he loved her, wanted her to stay there with him. She'd probably been crazy to turn him down. Eridanis were notable lovers, and Elon was no exception. He could have given her a life of security, of comfort.

At the time, she hadn't been particularly interested in either comfort or security. She'd found something oddly exciting about racketing around the galaxy, getting by on her wits—and her looks. Vanity? She didn't really think so. More that she knew her beauty was an asset, just another part of the toolbox. It wasn't as though she'd done anything to *be* pretty. That was just how she'd been born.

Dhani frowned, staring ahead through the yellowed plastic of the forward viewport so she wouldn't have to look at Captain Landon. He seemed to be ignoring her anyway, although of course at the moment he was fairly preoccupied. The familiar thrum of warming pulse engines surrounded her. In this case, the vibration sounded a little rough, as if the ship was in desperate need of a good tune-up.

Well, it wouldn't be the first time she'd traveled on a vessel that probably wouldn't pass a proper safety inspection. The governor had sworn up and down that his mechanics kept the ship travel-worthy at all times, but Dhani found that difficult to believe. Maybe he just had a different concept of travel-worthy than she did.

She'd left Gaia on a ship not so different from this one, wheedling her way onto the creaky Vortex-class vessel through a combination of half-true promises and outright lies. The pilot had been a kid not much older than she was, just taking over duties in his father's courier company. Of course he shouldn't have allowed anyone to ride along with him, but he hadn't been up to the task of refusing Dhani Warlow.

Now she couldn't even remember his name.

The darkness outside the viewport began to move. Landon worked silently at the unfamiliar controls, face intent as he maneuvered the ship up out of its landing bay. Dhani found herself watching his movements out of the corner of her eye, despite her intention to not look at him at all.

It would be easier if she could despise him, the way she despised all Consortium officers as good little drones. But somehow she couldn't find it in herself to do so. Hate the Consortium, sure. That was easy. Besides, it was collapsing under the weight of its own lies, its own shadows. Watching Captain Beck's clean profile, focused, sober, she could only thank whatever gods still existed that he had been the one to rescue her, and not some evil GDF goon like his commanding officer.

The ship rose above the clouds and moved forward into the darkness of space. Ordon had no moon, and the star-field around them was of course completely unfamiliar.

Silence for a moment, as she watched Landon tap coordinates into the navigation computer.

"So did you finally decide where we're going?" she asked.

"Iradia," he replied, not looking up. "Like I said, it's the best place to get untraceable transport. I still have access to my accounts—I can give you the cash you need to start over someplace safe." A pause, and then he added, almost under his breath, "If there's any place left that's safe."

The offer of money out of his own pocket startled her. It seemed clear enough that he now looked on her as his responsibility, since otherwise she would have still been sitting in a jail cell when Zeta Tau was destroyed. She almost told him that she wouldn't accept any funds from him, that saving her life was enough. But the practical side of her mind stopped her. Iradia wasn't the kind of place you wanted to be stranded without a single unit to your name.

"Are you sure?" she asked. "It's a long way from here, and this ship—"

"I know how far it is," he replied, "since I just entered the coordinates into the computer." The grim set to his mouth altered subtly, and he added, "The only way to make sure you're absolutely safe is to take you all the way there."

Dhani had the impression he was mocking her ability to take care of herself, and she felt her own lips thin, just the smallest bit. Protesting that she could manage just fine on her own probably wouldn't do much good, however. After all, Captain Beck had rescued her from a Consortium jail cell. It wasn't as if they'd met at a café or a bar.

Instead, she asked, "Can this rust bucket even get us that far?"

His answer was a lift of the shoulders. After making another arcane adjustment to the ship's controls, he said, "I think so. However, it doesn't have the capacity for long-range subspace jumps. We'll have to hopscotch."

Dhani raised her brows.

This time he almost smiled. Almost. "Pilot slang. It means we'll have to make a series of short hops from system to system. We'll come out of subspace briefly, readjust our coordinates, then head off on the next leg of the journey. It will slow us down, of course, but we should still reach Iradia within the next two standard days."

Two days trapped in this bucket of bolts? She didn't like the sound of that, but reflected at least she had enough clean clothes to get her through the ordeal. Unfortunately, the governor's staff, while outfitting them with food and water and other consumables, hadn't bothered with such intangibles as entertainment. The little ship had no vid-players, and not even a handheld that she could at least use for reading and watching whatever shows might be stored on it. Landon didn't appear to have one of his own, most likely because he'd escaped Zeta Tau station with the uniform on his back and not much else.

No vids, no books, no music. Well, that left just one thing.

She turned toward him and asked, "So, what made you want to join the GDF?"

A long pause. Then Captain Beck lifted his head from the console, gave her a surprised glance, and said, "Excuse me?"

"Well, was it a boyhood dream to see the galaxy? The uniforms? The desire to crush helpless populations beneath your booted feet? What?"

The look of incredulity never left his face. "What in the world are you talking about?"

She crossed her arms and sent him one of her most dazzling smiles. It didn't seem to have much effect, except that he blinked once before returning his attention to the pilot's console.

Well, really. Dhani knew how good that smile was. It had weakened the knees of better men than Captain Landon Beck.

Nettled, she said, "It's called conversation. It's what people do. Especially people who're stuck together in rickety old spaceships with nothing else to occupy their time."

"Ah."

"If you were planning on being this antisocial, at the very least you could have asked Governor Janning for a vid unit."

His expression in profile didn't reveal much, although his mouth twitched slightly. In calm tones, he said, "Maybe I just didn't have the chance. After all, you were quite busy asking him for clothing and toiletries and…other things."

"All necessary items, I assure you." She wasn't about to detail the horrible conditions in the detention cells to someone who so obviously didn't understand what it had been like. How could he? Clearly, Captain Landon Beck had never spent any time in jail. After what she'd suffered on Zeta Tau, the shower she'd taken at the governor's palace had been heaven, and the clean clothes that followed almost as sublime. Experiences such as that tended to make you rank changes of clothing and underwear very high on the priority list.

"Of course," Captain Beck murmured. Still not looking at her, he said, "We're about four hours out from our first stop. I'd say that sleep might be a more useful exercise than conversation."

His inflection remained mild as he delivered this suggestion, but Dhani had the feeling he was not in the mood for arguments. Very well; if he had so little need for her company, then she'd remove herself from his presence.

"I am getting a little tired," she said. She didn't add, *Of you*, but the words seemed to hang in the cabin between them.

Without further comment, she unbuckled herself from the safety harness and made her way toward the rear of the ship, where a small sleeping compartment was located. The mattress was lumpy and the blanket not much better, but it felt surprisingly good to lie down and close her eyes. Perhaps she was more tired than she had thought. Damn him—Captain Beck had been right.

It seemed darkness had barely settled on her before she sat up. The ship had given a slight shudder, which must have been what woke her. She blinked against the light filtering in through the open door from the hallway. It hadn't been a sharp shock like the one that had yanked Landon's shuttle from subspace. No, this must have been a standard reemergence into realspace. They'd reached the first of their hopscotch points.

Dhani pushed the blanket aside and stood. She'd only made it halfway down the corridor when the ship bucked again, this time like a stubborn mule. From up ahead, she could hear Landon curse, and she hurried the rest of the way to the cabin.

"What the hell was that?" she demanded.

"Pulse cannon," he replied without looking up from the controls.

"Someone's shooting at us?"

His jaw was set as he nodded. "Yes, someone is shooting at us. And this piece of shit I'm piloting has the weakest shields I've seen in a long time."

Greenish fire splatted against the starboard edge of the front viewport. She let out a yelp and backed away —not that such a minor retreat would do much good if their attackers managed to blow a hole in the bulkhead.

"Where are we?" she asked, willing her voice to remain calm. There wasn't much she could do to take back that startled little yowl she had just made, but at least she could redeem herself by not allowing herself any further displays of terror.

"The Lathvin system," he replied.

The name sounded vaguely familiar, but she couldn't place it at the moment. "Can't we just jump right back out into subspace?"

"The nav-computer is as slow as the rest of the ship. We need more time." Grim-faced, he typed a few more commands into the console.

Time was definitely something they didn't have. "Is there anything I can do?"

Landon shook his head. "I don't think—"

The comm crackled to life, interrupting his words. "Consortium vessel, this is the independent free trader *Westwind*. You are in violation of

Lathvin space. Prepare to stand down and be boarded."

"'Independent free trader'?" Dhani echoed.

"A polite way of saying 'pirate,' I think." Beck turned to the comm and flicked a switch. "*Westwind*, this is shuttle *Ordonian II*. We are a properly licensed vessel on Consortium business. I demand that you allow us to continue on our way."

A low chuckle drifted from the comm speaker. "You are in a position to demand nothing, *Ordonian II*. Stand down, or we'll blow your crate right out of space."

For one long, agonizing moment, Captain Beck said nothing. Dhani could almost hear his thoughts darting here and there, searching for a possible escape route and finding none. Then he straightened and said, "Standing down, *Westwind*."

"Wise of you. Remain in position."

The comm went silent. Out the forward viewport, she saw the slightly bulbous shape of a Nimbus-class ship move into view. The screen darkened as the larger vessel moved overhead and blocked the light of Lathvin's sun.

Commander Beck turned away from the control console and then stood. He didn't look all that frightened. If anything, Dhani would have said his current expression was one of supreme annoyance.

He crossed his arms and said, "You just *had* to mention pirates, didn't you?"

## CHAPTER FOUR

———

THEY LOOKED FAR TOO CLEAN-CUT TO BE PIRATES. And their movements, while not as crisp and efficient as those of men who had graduated from a Consortium training facility, were still not quite sloppy enough for the freebooters they claimed to be. Trying to puzzle out exactly who these men were did a little to dull the sharp edge of fear that ground on Landon now, fear not so much for himself, but what might happen to Dhani at their hands.

He remained silent as the four men completed their survey of the little shuttle. Dhani, surprisingly following his lead for once, stood quiet at his side.

At length, the one who seemed to be in charge paused in front of Landon. "Captain, huh?" he commented, after taking in the rank insignia on Landon's chest.

"Yes." He assumed they'd ask for name and serial

number next, but he didn't see the point in volunteering any more information than he had to.

The man's dark eyes narrowed. "I'd sort of expect a person with your rank to be flying something with a little more class."

"Yes, I suppose you would," Landon said calmly.

The stranger didn't appear to take offense. "Not sure whether it's even worth keeping, but we'll let Vandemar make the decision." He gestured, and the three other men surrounded Dhani and Landon. She sent him a brief questioning look, and he nodded ever so slightly. Resistance at this point would be worse than useless. Better to meet with this unknown Vandemar person and see if they couldn't make some kind of deal.

Exactly what type of deal, Landon couldn't be certain. As he followed the leader of the boarding party through the umbilical connecting the two ships, he reflected that he had very little to bargain with. The ship was worth next to nothing. He had no cash on hand, no valuables to convince the pirates —if that was even what they were—to allow him and Dhani to walk away with their lives. And he didn't want to think about what they might do with Dhani. Slavery was a thriving business in some of the galaxy's more far-flung systems, even though the Consortium claimed it had put an end to the practice. A beautiful young woman could be a tempting prize. To have rescued her from the destruction of

Zeta Tau station, only to have her taken in such a way —

But it hadn't happened yet, and Landon knew he would do everything in his power to keep her safe. This group didn't seem overly threatening; maybe all they wanted was the ship, and he and Dhani would be left on Lathvin IV, the only habitable planet in the system, to make their way to Iradia as best they could. Not the most optimal situation, but certainly better than a host of other dark fates he could contemplate.

The *Westwind* appeared to be in excellent shape, its corridors clean and shining. The few crew-members he spotted wore similar dark, close-fitting clothing. Not uniforms exactly, but attire that still gave that sort of impression. All in all, they looked as unlike "free traders" as possible, and Landon wondered again who these people really were.

They stopped at the end of a hallway. Their guide and captor palmed the lock, then stepped aside. "He's waiting for you."

That comment didn't sound very promising, but they had no alternative except to go in, Landon leading the way, Dhani a step behind him. Somehow she'd managed to keep her mouth shut during the journey here. He could only hope she would continue to do so. Somehow he had the idea that these men wouldn't take the whole "Larissa Miles" act very well...not to mention that passing herself off as a highly connected young woman would most likely lead their captors to thoughts of ransom. That would make their already precarious situation even worse. Kidnappers tended to get disgruntled when faced with the discovery that their captive actually wasn't worth that much after all.

A man who appeared to be a few years younger than Landon himself rose as they entered. Like the rest of the crew-members on the ship, he, too, wore close-fitting black clothes. For a second, his gaze rested on Landon, then flickered downward to Dhani. Their eyes met, and he let out a shocked exclamation as she darted forward with a laugh.

"Jack!" To Landon's dismay, she threw her arms around the stranger, even as he lifted her up and returned the hug. Once she was back on her feet, she planted her hands on her hips and inquired, "'Vandemar'? That's a new one."

He shrugged. "You're a fine one to be talking about assumed names." Then he looked from her back over to Landon. "Interesting choice in travel companions."

Landon didn't much appreciate the overly familiar way the two were interacting, and he liked even less the look of intense disapproval this "Jack" had just shot in his direction. But he'd had years to practice hiding his feelings, and so he returned the other man's glare with an impassive stare that probably did little to improve his mood.

"Jack," Dhani said in warning tones, "I'll have you

know that Captain Beck here is the only reason I'm still alive."

Jack's expression sobered abruptly. "When there was no word from you after Zephyr—"

"Yes, that's when the Connies caught up with me."

Landon hated that epithet. He could feel a frown etching its way into his forehead and did his best to smooth it away. It wasn't that he expected Dhani to have a high opinion of the Consortium—right now, he really didn't, either—but that casual nickname was just so damn *dismissive*.

She went on, "Just my luck that Zeta Tau station was the closest Consortium holding facility to Zephyr. I spent almost a month cooling my heels in one of the station's prison cells."

At this revelation, Jack shook his head. "Jesus. That's not a place I'd expect anyone to actually escape."

"I wouldn't have, if it weren't for Captain Beck here." The note of gratitude in her voice seemed to be genuine enough, as was the quick smile she threw in his direction before turning back toward Jack. "It was a very close call, but we made it. However, our ship was damaged, which is why we're traveling in the rust bucket you found us in. I suppose we should be grateful to Governor Janning for giving us a ship at all, but as a reliable mode of transportation, it leaves a lot to be desired."

Conflicting emotions seemed to be warring on Jack Vandemar's face. While he appeared to be grateful that Dhani was alive, Landon could tell the other man was attempting to puzzle out why a Consortium officer would rescue a known criminal from the very facility that was supposed to keep her locked up. Judging by the other man's expression, Landon guessed that Jack figured it wasn't for any altruistic reason.

*And that's where you would be wrong*, Landon thought. Although his motives for rescuing Dhani were far from simple, they certainly didn't involve the sort of shady motivations Vandemar probably suspected him of.

"Where are you headed?" he asked, in tones more neutral than Landon had expected.

"Iradia," Dhani said promptly.

Her reply made Jack look even more confused. No doubt he was trying to understand why a Consortium officer would make one of the galaxy's most crime-ridden planets his destination.

"I doubt they'd look for me there," she continued. "And it's the perfect place to figure out my next step. I'm sure Mal—"

At once Jack held up a hand. "That's enough, Dhani," he said. "I'm not sure it's wise to discuss this any further in front of your travel companion."

Who the hell was Mal? The leader of the insurgents in this sector? Possibly. Unfortunately, Landon hadn't been privy to the sorts of communiqués which would involve that kind of high-level information. The staff at Zeta Tau station hadn't been involved in hunting down insurgents, only locking them up once they were captured.

Dhani's expression darkened. "I trust Captain Beck with my life. I wouldn't be alive today if it weren't for him."

"If you trust him with your life, fine." Jack shrugged. "But I don't trust him with any of my secrets." He turned toward Landon. "No offense, captain."

"None taken," Landon replied. Although he had little reason to like the man, he knew that if their roles had been reversed, he would have been just as cautious.

Jack pulled a small, slim handheld out of his breast pocket. "Phelan, come and collect the captain and show him to our guest quarters." After tapping the screen to end the call, he gave Landon a grin and said, "Hope you don't mind if I have a few words with Dhani in private."

Automatically, Landon replied, "Not at all," even though he found he did mind, quite a bit. But he also knew that protesting their separation would be useless and would only serve to make him look ridiculous.

For a few seconds, Dhani appeared uncertain. Then she came toward and grasped both his hands in a gesture as welcome as it was surprising. "I won't be very long, captain. I promise."

Before he could reply, she had released him and turned away, just as the door whooshed open and another man entered the room. Landon could still feel the gentle pressure of her fingers against his. More than anything, he wanted to tell her to stay here with him, to not speak with Vandemar in private, but he knew he hadn't earned the right to say such things to her.

"This way, captain," said the newcomer, and Landon forced himself to turn away from Dhani and follow the man out of the chamber and down a series of increasingly narrow hallways. They paused in front of an oval hatchway. "Probably not as spacious as what you're used to, but I expect you'll manage." Then he touched the lock next to the door.

"I always do," Landon replied calmly. At least the room he saw before him seemed clean, if somewhat cramped. A Nimbus-class ship had space for passengers, but its cabins had never been known for their roominess. Still, it was better than bunking in the brig.

He stepped inside and heard the inevitable *whoosh* of the door behind him, signaling he'd been left alone. As soon as he was sure that his escort was gone, Landon tested the door. It wasn't locked, which meant Dhani's word must mean something with these people. While he wondered what she was up to, his current solitude didn't bother him—he'd never been one for idle chitchat. Especially with members of the insurgency.

For he'd guessed soon enough that these men must be insurgents, despite the lack of recognizable uniforms or any kind of rank insignia. What sort of covert operation they might be running out here, he couldn't hazard a guess. If he recalled correctly, Lathvin had no real strategic value. One inhabited planet still in the process of being terraformed, and that was about all that could be said for Lathvin IV. Its location did provide a convenient jump point, but otherwise it had no real significance. However, maybe its location was enough of an explanation as to why the renegades were operating here.

More troubling than the presence of the *Westwind* in this system was Dhani's apparent familiarity with its captain. Their exuberant greetings seemed to signal the presence of some sort of past relationship. Landon found he didn't like that idea very much at all.

Which was simply foolish. He'd have to be naïve indeed to think that a woman with her looks didn't have at least one or two former lovers floating around the galaxy. Besides, he had no claim on her, no interest in her that way. Actually, this chance encounter might all be for the best. Dhani could stay here with her insurgent friends, and Landon could continue unencumbered by any worry for her.

*And if you actually believe all that, I have some swamp land on Iradia I'd like to sell you,* Landon thought, giving himself a mental kick even as he sat down on the narrow cot closer to the cabin's tiny window. He knew—even if she didn't—that this had already progressed far beyond a simple desire to save her life. As he watched, Lathvin IV floated in the darkness of space, a not very prepossessing sphere in mottled shades of gray and red.

No, he did not want Dhani to stay here, logical as such a solution might seem. He didn't much welcome the idea of never seeing her again. True, he had offered to take her to Iradia, but that world was parsecs away. A lot could happen in the time it would take to travel such vast distances.

Exactly what he expected to happen, he couldn't quite say. Truth be told, she'd already probably taken at least a few standard years off his life with her whole Larissa Miles impersonation. He'd be much better off without the drama that seemed to accompany her wherever she went, no matter how beautiful she was, how full of life...how different from anyone he'd ever met before.

The stars winked back at him from outside the viewport. Possibly one of them was Iradia's sun, although he doubted it was strong enough to be seen at this distance. No, he probably just wanted to think it was out there so the journey ahead wouldn't seem so daunting. He'd never been one to racket around the galaxy, moving from world to world. He'd gone from his home on New Chicago straight into the Academy on Gaia itself, and had been put on the support staff track rather than the command track, which would have allowed him a position on one of the GDF's ships. Although he knew about these worlds by their reputations, he'd never experienced them for himself. And now, instead of doing his best to mentally prepare himself for what might lie ahead, he was sitting in this cramped little cabin and obsessing over Dhani Warlow.

Maybe he would have been better off to leave her in her cell. As soon as the thought crossed his mind, however, he knew it to be both wrong and untrue. Whatever trouble she might get him into—and he guessed it could be quite a lot—and no matter what turmoil she might have created in his own mind, he didn't want to imagine her dead along with all the others who had perished in the destruction of Zeta Tau station.

Why should her death matter to him so much more than the deaths of all the others who had lost their lives out there in the blackness of space? They had been loyal servants of the Consortium. One could argue that they had more right to live than someone who was a known criminal. But it hadn't been one of his fellow officers or even a crew-member who had come along with him on his stolen ship. No, he had instinctively gone to save Dhani.

In that space station, with its crowded corridors and various levels of crew quarters and mess halls and docking bays, she had been the only thing of real beauty. Had some hidden part of his soul finally rebelled against the ambition and backbiting he saw around him every day, his compatriots' apparently blind obedience to the will of the oligarchs who ruled the Consortium?

He wasn't quite sure he wanted to admit that. Not even to himself. Because if he did, he would understand that he'd already made his choice…and he wasn't ready to acknowledge that frightening reality.

Restless, Landon stood and attempted to distract himself by making a cursory examination of the cabin. There wasn't much to see: two inadequate-looking cots with even flimsier bedclothes, an empty chest of drawers, a small bathroom with a shower unit that looked as if it might accommodate Landon—if he sucked in his gut and didn't breathe too deeply while he was inside it.

He returned to his post beside the viewport. Not that he expected to see anything much of interest; obviously, the insurgents had chosen the Lathvin system because it was a quiet little backwater. Still, staring out through the slightly yellowed viewport allowed him to turn his direction outward into the emptiness of space instead of focusing on the increasingly hollow contents of his soul.

"Seriously, Dhani, what in the galaxy are you doing with that stiff?"

Jack's derisive tone brought back all the reasons why she had walked away from their liaison a good eighteen standard months ago. An easy enough breakup, she supposed—she'd gotten word of some interesting prospects on Ceres II, and hadn't so much formally dropped him as just left without a backward glance. He wasn't stupid; she didn't have to leave a diagram to explain what was going on.

Back then, the surname he'd given her was Harrison. She had no idea whether it was the one he'd been born with or just another in a long string of pseudonyms. It probably didn't matter all that much.

She crossed her arms and said, "He's not a stiff. He's a good man."

That response elicited a lifted eyebrow. Jack did have nice brows—dark and just slightly arched. Matched the rest of him, she supposed. Polished and handsome and a bit unpredictable. "By what stretch of the imagination could you possibly consider an officer from a death trap like Zeta Tau 'good'?"

"Besides the fact that he saved my life? I don't know…give me a minute to think."

"Dhani, you're a good actress, but I know you too well to fall for the naïve act."

"I am not being naïve." Perhaps she'd played fast

and loose with the truth in the past, but for now she saw no reason to be anything but honest with Jack. At the very least, he wouldn't be expecting such frankness from her. It might put him off-balance.

"It doesn't take a theoretical physicist to guess why he might have thought rescuing you would be a good idea."

She tilted her head to one side and gave him a tight-lipped little smile, the one she tended to use when she wanted to convey barely concealed scorn. "If that's the case, Jack dear, then why hasn't he made a single move on me? We've been alone together enough that I'm sure he could have tried something if he'd been so inclined."

To her satisfaction, Jack looked a little confused. No doubt he'd been expecting her to admit that she'd expressed her gratitude to Captain Beck with something a little more tangible than a simple "thank you." Of course she would never tell Jack that the thought had crossed her mind, and it was the captain who had held himself aloof.

With a lift of his shoulders, Jack said, "Maybe he's just waiting for the perfect opportunity. How the hell would I know? I do know you can't trust a Consortium officer any farther than you can throw one…and usually not that much."

She didn't have a snappy comeback to that comment. Jack's words merely echoed a sentiment she'd expressed on more than one occasion. Somehow, though, Landon Beck was different from the Consortium stooges she'd maligned in the past. He was kind, and honorable. She might even go as far as to say that he was a gentleman, and she hadn't encountered many of those in her life.

"Anyway," Jack went on, "It doesn't much matter now, I suppose. You're safe here with us. By rights I should throw him in the brig, but I get the feeling you wouldn't like that very much."

"You're right—I wouldn't," Dhani snapped. Then the full import of his words began to sink in. "You want me to stay here with you?"

"Well, of course." The eyebrow went up again, and he gave her a hard look. "Why wouldn't you?"

Why, indeed. She glanced away from her former lover and instead pretended to focus on the starry panorama in the large viewport past his left shoulder. After all, it was the natural thing to do. While there would be no point in her remaining on the *Westwind*, Jack could get in contact with other members of the insurgency and make sure she made it safely someplace where she could quietly disappear, wait, and see how this whole scenario played out. No point in having poor Captain Beck drag her all the way to Iradia when she could just stay here for now.

It all made completely logical sense. So why did she feel a pang at the thought of saying farewell to him now? She should be glad that her predicament could be solved so neatly.

"I think I should discuss this with Captain Beck," she said at length.

"What the hell for?" Jack snapped, brow furrowing. "Since when did you ask anyone's permission for anything? I know you weren't too up for discussion when you left to go to Ceres II."

He couldn't be holding that against her, not after all this time. Besides, he'd never shown any hint that their liaison meant anything more to him than it did to her—a way to pass the time, to forget the uncertainty of their lives in isolated moments of heat. Neither one of them had ever uttered the word "love." So why did Jack have to choose this particular time to play the lover scorned?

"We both go where the wind takes us," she replied calmly. No point in allowing herself to get angry with him for indulging in posturing that was now almost two years too late. "We never made any promises to each another."

"And have you made any promises to *him*?"

Really, this was getting a bit tedious. "No, of course not. But there is a little matter of a life debt between us. I don't know about you, but I generally think that requires just a bit of discussion."

Jack made an impatient movement with one hand, as if he'd meant to run his fingers through his hair and then had decided against it. "If that's what you need to satisfy your conscience. I guess I'm just surprised—I wasn't sure you had one."

That was a bit too much. Hadn't it been her conscience that led her to getting involved with the insurgents in the first place? Well, partially, at least. They'd given her the means to lie low when she needed the cover, but she also believed in what they were doing.

She lifted her shoulders, even as he added, "Besides, what do you think your next move should be? The Consortium's falling apart, so any protection your captain might be offering you now isn't going to last for much longer."

"I don't expect him to protect me," Dhani said, her tone sharp. "Right now we both have a common destination. That's all." As her former lover continued to watch her, one eyebrow lifted at a skeptical angle, she went on, "You really think it's ending that fast? But there are hundreds of colonies—"

"Many of which were just waiting for a chance at freedom. No more heavy taxes, no more crappy contracts with the Gaian Development Corporation. Oh, sure, the shine might wear off eventually, probably when they realize it's going to be harder to get the things they need to survive, that being self-sufficient isn't as easy as it looks. But that's going to take a while. And in the meantime, it's going to be dicey out there, even for a woman who's used to thinking on her feet."

Jack's words dismayed her, but Dhani knew she'd never admit as much to him. Anyway, he was just speculating now. He didn't know any more than anyone else how all this was going to turn out. There was a very good chance that he was exaggerating in the hope that if he painted a black enough picture, she would stay here with him. He'd already made it clear enough that he was upset with her over the way they'd parted; no way in the world would she to confess to him that, even though she'd only known Landon Beck for a few days, she still found herself trusting him more in a pinch than she did her erstwhile lover.

"I think I'd like to talk to Captain Beck now," she said finally. She wasn't stupid enough to hope that Jack hadn't noticed the significant pause which preceded her request.

"Fine," he replied, but he obviously didn't make any attempt to keep the annoyance out of his voice. "I'll take you to your cabin myself. Time I got back up to the bridge anyway."

"Then don't let me keep you."

Without bothering to reply, he moved past her and opened the door, then led her down a series of corridors and stopped at a narrow oval entryway. Before he hit the lock, he reached down to his belt and unclipped the slim portable comm he wore there. "Just buzz me when you're done."

Even now he wanted to keep tabs on her. Fine, she'd take the comm as a show of good faith. The borrowed traveling suit she wore didn't have a belt, but she slipped the flat little unit into a side pocket. "Thanks, Jack."

He shrugged and said, "I hope you know what you're doing," then pressed his palm against the door controls.

*So do I,* she thought, but she merely nodded before she turned away from him and entered the cabin.

It was smaller than she had imagined. The two cots placed up against the walls seemed to consume most of the available space.

Landon Beck stood next to the viewport, apparently watching the serene star-drift outside. He shifted his weight as the door closed behind her, but he remained silent.

"Cozy," she ventured. "All the comforts of home."

Then he did turn. "I suppose so."

Something in his manner seemed even more formal than usual. The epithet Jack had used to describe the commander flitted through her mind. Yes, he did come off as awfully stiff and correct, despite his good looks and relative youth. It was almost as though he made himself deliberately formal in an attempt to be sure everyone he met took him seriously.

For a second, she stared back at him, nonplussed, and then a ludicrous thought struck her. Was Landon Beck actually *jealous*?

"I had a nice chat with Captain Vandemar," she

went on. "Well, it started out as a nice chat, anyway. I'm afraid we ended up having a difference of opinion as to what I should do next."

Maybe that was a hint of a thaw she saw there— the slightest relaxation of the taut lines of his mouth, a small retreat of the wariness she glimpsed in his eyes. At least, she hoped it was. "Why is that?"

"He wants me to stay here on the *Westwind*. You'd be free to go, of course, because of what you've done for me."

"Generous of him," said Beck, but he sounded distinctly unimpressed.

"Maybe. But I got to thinking about it, and I much prefer our original plan."

"You what?" Now he appeared startled despite himself. Most likely he hadn't expected her to pass up a chance to stay on a ship commanded by her former lover.

"I'd rather go with you to Iradia," she told him. "If you don't mind, that is."

"'Mind'?" he repeated. Despite what looked like a manful effort to maintain a neutral expression, Dhani got the impression he was completely flummoxed. He cleared his throat and said, "That is—the most logical plan would be for you to remain here."

"True. I suppose that's why I don't want to stay. Besides, Jack is a crashing bore. Now I remember why I was in such a hurry to leave him in the first place."

That comment appeared to render the captain

speechless. He blinked once, then turned away from her to look back out the viewport.

She'd hoped for some sort of reaction, but that wasn't precisely the one she'd expected. Squeezing past one of the cots, she came to stand next to him, although she kept her gaze on his face, not the starscape outside the window.

"I can stay if that's what you want."

Again he said nothing. Then his eyes narrowed, and he swore under his breath.

Really, was she that much of a burden? She opened her mouth to speak, but to her surprise he reached out and turned her so she squarely faced the viewport.

The starscape had altered subtly. Lathvin IV was now only a dark blot against the sky. That wasn't the real difference, however. The sleek, elongated shape of an Orion-class cruiser now floated against the blackness.

"I think," Landon said, "that right now we probably have more important things to worry about...."

# CHAPTER FIVE

A KLAXON BLARED DOWN THE CORRIDOR outside. Almost at once, Landon could feel the vibrations beneath his feet pick up. The star-field shifted, and the cruiser disappeared from view. But it was still out there, unfortunately.

"It appears your Jack is trying to make a run for it," he said.

Dhani scowled. "He's not 'my Jack.'" A note of worry entered her voice as she added, "What are we going to do?"

Good question. Orion-class vessels were fast ships, and Jack Vandemar had reacted almost immediately. Whether his quick action was enough to get the *Westwind* out of range of the Consortium ship's pulse cannon, Landon couldn't say. Presuming, of course, that the unknown ship's orders were to capture the insurgents' vessel and not simply blow it up.

The ship's vibrations increased. Landon didn't think it was a tractor beam that had caused the odd shuddering. Then realization dawned, and he muttered a curse.

"What?" Dhani asked, and seemed to move closer to him, as if driven by some unspoken instinct of protection.

While he might have thrilled to her proximity under other circumstances, right then he had other things to worry about. Or at least, he made himself worry about them, because he didn't want to focus too much on the way his body was reacting to her presence. "Do you feel that?"

She paused, as if to gauge the movement of the vessel beneath her feet. "Yes."

"It's our ship. It's still connected to the *Westwind* by the umbilical."

"I assume that's not good."

"No. No, it's not." Landon had no idea what an umbilical's maximum load velocity might be, but he guessed they were rapidly approaching the straining point. As soon as it was reached, the umbilical would tear away, leaving the *Ordonian II* to drop off and become just another piece of space junk.

If it survived the process without having a hole ripped in its hull, of course.

That seemed to decide things. Waiting here to see if Jack Vandemar really could make a getaway was not an option. Even if the insurgents somehow managed to flee into subspace without getting caught by the Consortium cruiser or blown into a million pieces, the borrowed ship would be gone forever. Then he and Dhani would be at the mercy of the insurgents' captain. While she seemed to think Jack Vandemar was trustworthy, Landon didn't share that assessment.

And if the *Westwind* was captured, then he would have a bit of explaining to do as to why a Consortium officer had been placed in a regular cabin on an insurgent ship instead of in the brig. It was a difficult enough equation without somehow trying to factor Dhani into it.

That seemed to decide things. "We'd better get moving."

To her credit, she didn't even blink. "Time to abandon ship?"

"Past time, I think." He went to the door and touched the lock. Just as the door slid open, one of the insurgents dashed past in the corridor outside. He didn't even pause to look at them. Obviously, Captain Vandemar's passengers were not a priority at the moment.

Landon gestured for Dhani to follow him, then slipped out into the hallway and hurried aft, back to the hatchway where the umbilical was attached. Although he would have preferred a flat-out run—however undignified it might have looked—he kept his pace down to a trot so he wouldn't outdistance her on his much longer legs.

The floor seemed to slip under his feet as the ship rocked from what had to have been a blast from the cruiser's pulse cannons. Landon found himself flung into a wall as Dhani stumbled and fell to her knees. She swore.

No time to stop and assess the damage. Wordlessly, he reached down to her as soon as he recovered his balance. For once, he saw naked fear on her face, but she only grasped his hand and allowed him to pull her upright.

"Guess they're not interested in taking prisoners," she managed.

"Apparently not."

Her slender fingers felt terribly fragile in his, and he felt a wave of protectiveness wash over him that was as strong as it was unexpected. It was because of him that she was here. He had to get her safely away, or what was the point in saving her from Zeta Tau in the first place?

Luckily, the traveling suit and boots she wore had been designed for comfort and practicality rather than style, so she made a better job of matching his hastened pace than he would have thought. Or maybe it was simple panic that lent her speed. Whatever the cause, the rest of their trip down the corridors of the *Westwind* took less time than he had feared.

Even as they reached the umbilical, the ship rocked from another blow. How many more hits like that could the smaller vessel take? Two? Three?

Landon decided he really didn't want to stick around to find out.

Despite the instinct that told him to get out now, he paused before activating the lock that controlled the umbilical. Dhani looked up at him with questioning eyes.

"Take a deep breath before we go," he told her. "The umbilical is attached, but it could come loose at any time. If that happens, we have no more than thirty seconds to get inside the shuttle before the vacuum takes us. Understand?" He didn't bother to add that if the umbilical came loose from the *Ordonian II* and not the *Westwind*, those thirty seconds of grace wouldn't do them a speck of good.

She bit her lip and nodded.

"All right, then." He sucked in as deep a breath as he could manage, then let go of her hand just long enough to hit the switch that would open the iris-like aperture in the umbilical. It began to slide apart, and he hooked her arm in his and pulled her into the narrow, circular tunnel.

It bounced and bobbed worse than a raft in a raging stream. Almost at once, he was thrown from his feet, his hand torn loose from hers.

It was actually a good thing, he realized. Crawling, he had far more stability than he would have if he'd remained standing. Something scrabbled at the heel of one of his boots, and he realized it was Dhani, getting a firm grip so they wouldn't become separated.

The umbilical spanned only about ten meters or so, but it felt more like a parsec. Landon tried not to think of anything except the hatch at the far end that was their destination. He couldn't do much about the wild, bucking motion of the umbilical, or the increasingly panicked nausea that began to rise in his throat. All he could do was continue to crawl.

Finally, his reaching fingers touched metal. With a relieved gasp, he pulled himself upright enough to activate the controls on this end of the umbilical. Just as his hand caught on the smooth surface of the buttons, the tunnel gave a violent jerk, and air began to whistle past his ears, ears that responded with a series of painful pops.

Dhani screamed. Then he felt both her hands fasten around his ankle, hanging on for dear life as the umbilical began to spew its atmosphere out into the void. The encroaching vacuum dragged phantom claws against his body, but he refused to let go of the controls and grimly hit the buttons in the necessary sequence. The door into the shuttle scissored open. He fell through, dragging Dhani with him as best he could. Escaping air rushed past, and he grabbed her by the sleeve and hauled her the rest of the way inside. If enough precious atmosphere was lost, the *Ordonian II*'s antiquated generators would never be able to keep up.

Gasping, he struggled to his knees and slammed his palm against the airlock controls. The door slid shut, even as he caught a glimpse of the umbilical tearing away, undulating in its death throes like a deep-sea jellyfish caught by sunlight.

No time to watch it any further, and no time to offer any aid to Dhani, who still lay on the floor. Coughs racked her slender frame, but if she had enough energy to cough, then she should be all right for now. The best thing he could do for the both of them would be to get the ship out of there as quickly as possible.

The little vessel had remained on standby while he and Dhani were inside the *Westwind*. Although it would take a few minutes to re-engage the subspace drive, at least the coordinates for their next jump had already been calculated. Just a bit of adjustment to account for their drift during the past half-hour, and then they should be home free. He could only hope that the Consortium cruiser was more interested in larger prey and would overlook the *Ordonian II* altogether.

A splash of green fire burst outside. Landon winced. The shot hadn't been directed at them, or the ship would already have been blown into a million pieces. Still, dead was dead, whether it was intentional or whether you merely had the bad luck to be caught in a crossfire.

As he pulled away from the *Westwind* as quickly as the ship's pulse engines would take them, he reflected that things had come to a sorry pass indeed if he was actively running away from the very people who should have come to his aid. But this was not the sort of situation where lengthy explanations were even feasible. Better to get away, regroup, and figure out what to do next, to go someplace where he wasn't likely to be blown into oblivion simply for being in the wrong place at the wrong time.

A groan and a creak of synth-leather signaled that Dhani had regained herself enough to clamber into the co-pilot's seat. "That was close."

Too close. And they weren't out of danger yet. He was trying to keep the bulk of the insurgents' ship between them and the cruiser for as long as possible, but with the way the *Westwind* kept bobbing and weaving, Landon didn't know how long that strategy was going to work.

"You're not signaling them for help," she added.

"No."

"Why not?"

Her question didn't help his concentration any. He glanced down at the nav-computer. Just a minute more....

"Too risky," he replied, without looking at her. "While this ship has Consortium transponder codes, those can easily be faked. And since we were just attached to an insurgent vessel—"

"Better to get away and sort things out later," she finished.

His estimation of her rose another notch. Whatever her quirks, Dhani was capable of quickly assessing a situation.

Then the viewport darkened suddenly, adjusting to a barrage of pulse fire exchanged by the ships outside. For a second, Landon wasn't quite sure of what he was seeing, half-blinded as he'd been by the unexpected blast. Then he blinked, and blinked again.

Those blasts had apparently come from another starship, one that must have just emerged from subspace. The glare from Lathvin's sun prevented him from getting a clear image of the newcomer, but its rounded outlines seemed to indicate that it was another insurgent ship, not a Consortium vessel. Abruptly, the odds in this particular battle had changed.

He would have been of no help to either ship. If the cruiser's captain was skilled enough, he still might emerge the victor. While the Eridani-built vessel matched the Orion-class ship in firepower, the insurgents' vessel had a thinner hull and weaker shields. But with the *Westwind* running interference, it would be a tough fight.

Knowledge of the outcome would forever elude him. The subspace drive chimed its warning, and Landon wrapped his hand around the T-handle and pushed it forward, tearing the *Ordonian II* from normal space and the firefight that had surrounded the little ship.

Familiar star-streaks in unnameable hues boiled

past the viewport. For a few seconds, Landon could only remain immobile in his seat, unwilling to acknowledge the weak-kneed relief that surged through him.

"Damn good flying, captain," Dhani remarked, dark eyes shining with admiration. "Even if you include the near-suffocation."

"My flying had nothing to do with that."

"You know what I mean." To his surprise, she leaned over and gave his forearm a quick squeeze before she settled back into the co-pilot's seat.

It was stupid of him to feel a little burst of joy at her touch. He'd just left fellow Consortium personnel behind while he turned tail and ran. Never mind that there wasn't a moth's chance in a supernova of the *Ordonian II*'s being any good in a firefight. It was the principle of the thing. Still, even though he knew he should be berating himself for his cowardice, he felt absurdly happy.

To cover up his reaction, he assumed a frown, then said, "Now that we're away, maybe you can tell me exactly what Captain Vandemar was doing in the Lathvin system."

He could have sworn the look of puzzlement that crossed her features was genuine. "How would I know?"

"A single Nimbus-class ship, whether or not it's manned by insurgents, is usually not a target of such importance that the Consortium would send one of its cruisers to dispatch it. Nor would the insurgents usually spare one of their Eridus-class vessels to protect a small ship doing picket duty in a relatively unimportant system."

She lifted her shoulders. "That very well may be true. But Jack didn't tell me anything about what they were doing there." A small glint showed in her dark eyes. "He seemed more interested in convincing me to stay."

Landon had a feeling she enjoyed passing on that particular bit of information. While it annoyed him, he'd already guessed as much from her earlier comments back in the small cabin Captain Vandemar had provided for their use. However, he knew better than to give her the satisfaction of knowing that she had irritated him.

"Too bad," he replied. "Information is always useful."

A toss of the long braid she wore over one shoulder. "Well, if that's what you're concerned about, I'm fairly certain we can get free drinks for weeks with our 'escape from the destruction of Zeta Tau station' story."

"As long as you leave out the little detail about my being the commanding officer's adjutant."

The glint returned to her eyes. "Well, there is that."

Now that they were safely away from the Lathvin system and the *Westwind*, Landon realized how utterly, bone-numbingly weary he was. How long had it been since he last slept? Forty-eight standard hours? Sixty? He couldn't even begin to estimate. True, he'd been trained to go for long periods without rest, but his academy days were far behind him. And, he thought with some ruefulness as he looked at Dhani —who seemed little the worse for wear despite nearly being sucked out an airlock—he wasn't twenty-four anymore. Yes, he'd been that same age only ten scant years ago, but....

"We should be at Corona II in a few hours," he said.

"What's there?"

"Nothing, I hope." With that comment, he undid the safety harness and stood, feeling his bones creak as he did so. Right then, he thought he'd be happy to see thirty again. He added, "It should be quiet enough. I'm going to try for a short rest."

Dhani cocked her head to one side and gazed up at him. "You do look tired."

*Thank you so very much*, he thought, but he didn't bother to reply. Instead, he turned away from her and headed to the small sleeping space—he wouldn't give it the honor of calling it a cabin—at the rear of the ship. Much as he'd disliked admitting any weakness to Dhani, he also knew he had just about reached his limit. Better to rest now, while the ship was safely in subspace. At least this way he would be better prepared to face whatever might come next.

*Iradian slavers*, he guessed, as he settled onto the hard little cot. *Silk smugglers. Bathshevan mercenaries.*

And with those cheery thoughts to keep him company, he drifted off into much-needed slumber.

---

Dhani watched the stars bleed past the viewport. She'd never cared much for subspace travel; the queerly distorted stars disturbed her at some deep, almost atavistic level, and she didn't like the feeling of being somehow outside the galaxy, in some other-where that she couldn't quite understand.

People were easier to understand. Well, most of them, anyway.

If she leaned far enough over the edge of the co-pilot's chair and peered down the shuttle's short hall-way, she could catch a glimpse of Captain Beck stretched out on the cot she herself had used only a few hours earlier. Of course, he was much taller; his booted feet hung off the edge of the inadequate little bed. Even in sleep, he was every inch the Consortium officer. He lay on his back, hands clasped on his chest. If it weren't for his closed eyes and a certain slackness to his features, she would have been hard-pressed to tell he was asleep at all.

In the dim light of the overhead fixture in the hallway, his hair gleamed dark gold, just a little shaggier than that of most of the Consortium personnel she'd encountered. Maybe they hadn't had a good barber on Zeta Tau station.

That thought brought a small laugh bubbling to her lips, one she quickly quelled. The poor man needed his sleep. Somehow she doubted he would be happy to have her wake him up because she was laughing about his hair.

Her smile faded as she recalled the firefight they'd just escaped. What the hell *had* Jack been up to, back there in the Lathvin system? Now that she thought about it, she found she was a little miffed that he hadn't shared any information with her. Oh, he'd asked her to stay—probably because he was starting to get a little itchy and didn't have any better prospects around. That would be just like him. Well, she'd had the last laugh there. She could still see the startled expression on his face when she'd told him she preferred to take her chances with Captain Beck.

But she supposed it was one thing for Jack to try to keep her around to scratch his itch, and quite another for him to be sharing state secrets with her. Come to think of it, the few times she'd had direct contact with the insurgents, no one had ever told her much of anything except where she had to be and what she needed to do. It was as if they had thought of her only as a useful pretty face and not much else. Certainly not someone to be trusted with any sensitive information.

Brow furrowing, she wrapped her arms around her knees and hugged them to herself, huddling in the co-pilot's seat as she stared out at the distorted heavens around her. Why hadn't she thought of this earlier?

*Because you let yourself get caught up in their game*, she thought. *It was all so exciting…for a while. They never gave you a chance to stop and think.*

All right, so the leaders of the insurgent cells who'd given her orders had allowed her to think she was a bit more important than she really was. If that was their worst crime, well—even as angry as she felt right now—she knew the Consortium's government was guilty of far, far worse. Ego bruising didn't quite rank up there with genocide or calculated cradle-to-grave oppression.

So why this sense of betrayal?

Because the insurgents were supposed to be the good guys. It was a lot easier when everything appeared to be black and white. She gave an almost involuntary glance down the corridor to the small bed where Landon Beck slept.

Now it seemed as if everything was a million shades of gray.

Too bad that cot was so narrow. Right then, she felt as though all she wanted to do was lie down next to him and feel his arms go around her. That would be enough for now—simply to lay her head against his chest and hear him breathing, to let the warmth of his body take away some of the chill that seemed to be tracing its way through every vein. Insane that she should feel safer with him than ever she had with anyone else.

A strident little alarm began to sound from overhead, and she jumped. Immediately afterward, the ship shuddered its way back into normal space. As soon as the star-field dropped into place around the ship, the alarm shut off. Dhani let out a breath she didn't even remember holding. *The subspace-drive alert*, she thought. *Nothing to worry about.*

The system possessed a small yellow sun and five planets, two of which were in the habitable band. One glowed green as the absinthe she'd once drunk in a high-end restaurant in Paris.

She craned her head to look around, but saw nothing. No other ships, no orbital platforms. Nothing except a serene little system that appeared as if it had never been touched. Not completely true, of course; someone had to have catalogued it and placed its coordinates in the Consortium's databases. Still, after their eventful arrival at Lathvin, it was something of a relief to have ended up in a place so quiet, so isolated.

Captain Beck's voice came down the corridor. "All clear?"

She looked up to see him standing in the entrance to the bridge. His hair stuck out on one side, and she had to bite her lip to prevent herself from smiling. He must have seen something in her expression, however, because he quickly reached up to smooth back the unruly locks.

Too bad. He was sort of adorable when he was rumpled. "Looks that way," she replied.

He settled himself in the captain's chair and began studying the readouts before him. Whatever data he saw, it seemed to put his mind at ease; his expression relaxed a bit, and he pushed himself back in his seat. "No ships in the immediate area, and no transmissions from any of those planets. It looks as if we're in the clear…for now."

"Rested?" she asked.

"Very much so. Thank you for watching the bridge."

Dhani had thought she was teasing him, but he'd taken her question at face value and had answered her directly and courteously. Looking up at him, at the circles under his eyes that his abbreviated slumber hadn't managed to erase, she felt somewhat ashamed.

"Not much to watch," she said. "So far, this crate is doing a pretty good job. I take back everything bad I ever said about Governor Janning."

"Everything?"

"Well, I still think he's a toadying fool, but since he got us off Ordon, and his wife had the great sense to be close to my size, I'll let that go for now."

"Gracious of you." Beck turned slightly away from her and began tapping away at the nav-computer—

entering the coordinates for the next leg of their journey, she presumed.

"So where next?"

"I was thinking of Nelos. There's little enough to trouble us there, and from that system we'll be in a good place to jump to New Albion, and from there finally to Iradia."

As soon as the word "Nelos," left Beck's lips, Dhani felt another one of those laughs tickling at her throat. Really, what were the odds? In all the systems in all the galaxy, the commander seemed to have an uncanny knack for locating the ones littered with evidence of her not-so-pristine past.

Something in her silence must have alerted him, because he turned around and stared down at her, a frown tugging at one corner of his mouth. "Is there something wrong with my plan?"

"Well, not wrong, precisely. It's just that—" She hesitated, then said, "I wouldn't say there's 'nothing' to trouble us on Nelos. Although actually, maybe he could help us."

"'He'?" repeated Captain Beck in dark tones.

"Um—" Maybe she should have just kept her mouth shut. "His name is Eustis Penn. He was a hacker for the insurgents for a while, but he felt he wasn't being challenged enough, so he left."

That was an understatement. Eustis always had a flair for the dramatic—his departure from the insurgent base on one of Vita III's moons had been accompanied by much flinging of data-cards and paperwork in one of the more epic flounces Dhani had ever been privileged to witness. Unfortunately, the insurgency needed Eustis far more than he needed it; his family had money, and he was so gifted that he could charge a premium for his services. She'd kept in sporadic touch with him simply because he could be amusing, and a girl never knew when she might need the help of someone who could hack through a Consortium database the way a laser cutter could chew through solid rock.

At any rate, that was how she knew he had somehow acquired the abandoned compound on Nelos. From there he sat at the center of a web that touched both insurgent and Consortium operatives— and all the shades of gray in between.

That ferociously expressionless look had returned to Beck's features. It was one she'd come to think of as his "officer" face.

"Is there," he asked, in a tone as neutral and yet as damning as the expression he wore, "any system in the galaxy that *doesn't* contain one of your ex-boyfriends?"

# CHAPTER SIX

As the hatch to the *Ordonian II* slid open, Landon reflected that this Eustis Penn had done a pretty damn good job of choosing a sanctuary for himself.

Cool air scented with exotic greenery greeted the two of them as they made their way down the ship's ramp. Overhead, brightly plumed whisper-birds drifted by. The sky was a soft blue just faintly tinged with green, almost the exact shade of turquoise from one of Arizona's fabled mines back on Gaia. From somewhere off to his right, Landon heard the murmur of flowing water.

"That way," Dhani said, pointing almost directly ahead.

Through the forest, he thought he spied an edifice of towering dark stone, looking grim and incongruous against the lush vegetation. Who had built such an imposing structure on this out-of-the-way world, he couldn't begin to guess. Apparently, though, some enterprising individual had decided to make a pile of units by selling the abandoned "castle" to Penn, who, according to Dhani's wry observations, had a flair for the dramatic.

"Really," she'd said, as they began to make their descent toward Nelos, "what use does a hacker have for a fortress, anyway? He'd have done better with a penthouse on New Chicago or even back on Gaia, someplace like New York or Paris. But I suppose that would be too pedestrian for Eustis."

None of these comments exactly reassured Landon, who was none too happy about having to deal with Eustis Penn after the debacle with Jack Vandemar on board the *Westwind*. But a survey of their supplies had told him that their oxygen generators needed a refresh before they could even think of heading on to Iradia.

So Dhani had sent a message over several of the most widely used frequencies, asking to speak with Eustis Penn. He responded almost immediately; Landon guessed that the hacker had his equipment constantly scanning both normal and subspace channels for any chatter in the area. He sounded surprised but friendly enough.

Too friendly, in Landon's opinion. Unfortunately, at the moment no one seemed to be asking him for it.

They'd had little choice, though, not with their

oxygen supplies in their current state. Landon told himself that dealing with Penn was still preferable to pushing their way on to Iradia, and possibly running out of air and fuel long before they reached their goal. Besides, Dhani swore that she and the hacker had parted amicably enough....

So here Landon was, tromping through the forest after the woman who had managed to turn his life upside down in less than three standard days. He couldn't shake the feeling that if he'd just been a bit more clever or more capable, he could have avoided the current situation completely, but exactly how, he had absolutely no idea.

The planet was beautiful, though. Clean, unprocessed air in his lungs, and a cool breeze ruffling at his hair. He'd forgotten how lovely a world could be, trapped as he'd been in an existence encompassed by metal walls and floors and ceilings, where the air and water were perpetually recycled, and day and night had no true meaning.

A wide door of some dark metal covered in an intricate embossed pattern opened as they approached. A voice came from the speaker directly inside.

"Welcome," it said, in Gaian accents as cultured as the ones Dhani had assumed in her guise as Larissa Miles. "Please come to the reception area on the second floor."

Landon arched an eyebrow at Dhani, and she

shrugged. "Eustis always liked to control a situation. Might as well humor him."

A sigh tickled the back of Landon's throat, but he swallowed it and strode forward through a wide, short hallway that ended in an equally broad staircase. The interior of the building appeared to have been constructed out of the same dark, gleaming stone as the exterior, but gracefully curved sconces on the walls lit the way, making the effect more dramatic than brooding.

As they mounted the final step, an arched entryway led them into a spacious chamber agleam with shifting, subtle light. Landon recognized the pieces mounted at regular intervals on the dark stone walls—he himself had owned one of Lugesh's light paintings, although it had been much smaller than the ones he saw now. Unfortunately, the painting was now gone, blasted into atoms along with everything else on Zeta Tau station.

Odd that the thought of the lost painting should bring a little lump to his throat, the way the thought of his lost comrades-in-arms had not.

A tall man with a head of striking dark red hair strode toward them. He wore an impeccably cut tunic and narrow pants, and was as handsome in his way as Jack Vandemar had been. Naturally, Landon disliked him on sight.

That feeling of antipathy only increased as the stranger—who of course had to be Eustis Penn—held his hands out to Dhani. She took them, smiling brightly as a supernova.

"Thank you so much, Eustis," she said. "I'm afraid our poor ship is in need of some tender care."

"Think nothing of it," Penn replied. Then his gaze shifted away from her to Landon, who had remained off to one side. "And your...companion?"

"Captain Landon Beck," he said, and gave a crisp half-bow. "Your service to the Consortium will be noted."

The remark was something of a gamble, as of course Penn and Dhani had met while working for the insurgency. But as far as he could tell, Landon surmised that the hacker was now a free agent...and although the Consortium was now on shaky ground, it still had far deeper pockets than the insurgents did. While possibly Penn had no need of actual wealth, influence and connections were something else altogether.

It might have been a trick of the shifting light in the room, but Landon thought he spied an avaricious gleam come and go in the other man's eyes. All the better. Simple greed he could work with. It was idealists such as Jack Vandemar who tended to cause the most trouble.

"This is an impressive collection of Lugeshes you have here," Landon went on, moving away from Penn to study the painting closest to the stairs. In its current state, it resembled the northern lights he had witnessed on his only trip to Gaia—a rippling gauze veil in subtle shades of aqua and lavender and shell pink. "This piece would appear to be from one of his earlier periods."

"You are a collector?" Eustis Penn asked, surprise evident in his voice.

"Mostly an admirer. I regret that in my current position, I don't have the time to decorate my quarters as I would like."

*That was nicely done*, Landon thought with some satisfaction. *The implication is that I have the means to collect these works, and it's only the constraints of my service that prevent me from doing so. He doesn't need to know that I'm only a farmer's son from New Chicago.*

Penn's face was a study of grudging respect. Behind his shoulder, Landon could see Dhani's eyebrows performing some complicated gymnastics. No doubt she was trying to decide whether Landon was feeding Penn what he thought the hacker would want to hear, or whether he really did know what he was talking about.

"It's always good to meet a fellow devotee," Eustis Penn said, after a distinct pause. "But about your ship—"

"The oxygen generators need a recharge," Landon said immediately. "Through an odd set of circumstances, I required the loan of a vessel, a loan which the governor of Ordon was good enough to give me.

Unfortunately, his ship was not quite up to fleet standards."

"I'll have my people look into it," Penn replied.

Dhani crossed her arms, and her full mouth pulled into something closely resembling a smirk. "Since when do you have 'people'?"

"Since always, my dear. You just didn't know about them."

Again, one finely arched brow raised itself in disbelief, but she somehow managed to hold her tongue.

Penn turned so he faced her. His tone a limpid drawl, he said, "I'm intrigued, though—how in the galaxy did you end up in the company of a high-ranking Consortium officer? Did he make you a better offer?"

Landon stiffened, although he did his best to hide his outrage. The insult hadn't even been disguised. Clearly, Eustis Penn thought of Dhani as the sort of woman who would go with any man who promised her some sort of advancement. What that said about the hacker himself, Landon didn't know. Obviously, he hadn't scrupled at having some sort of an intimate relationship with the young woman himself.

The sight of her pale, stricken features only infuriated Landon further. No, he wouldn't fool himself into thinking that she was some sort of untouched virginal creature—just the little he had glimpsed of her past was enough to refute that idea. But however littered that past might be with former lovers, he knew they must have been that: men Dhani had cared about, if only for a short time. He couldn't believe she had entered into any of those relationships purely for personal gain.

"Hardly," Landon said, injecting a certain amount of steel into his voice, a tactic that had usually proved quite effective with his subordinates. "It was imperative that Ms. Warlow not perish on Zeta Tau station."

As soon as the words left his mouth, Landon cursed himself for his indiscretion. Had it been necessary for him to reveal *exactly* how they had met?

To his surprise, however, Eustis Penn only nodded, as if he'd already been in possession of that information. "Yes, I knew she'd been detained on the space station."

"What?" Dhani demanded. "How?"

The smile Penn flickered in her direction was so condescending that Landon wished he could forcibly wipe it off the other man's mouth. Since they weren't in anything resembling a position of power at the moment, he could only clench his fists at his side and hope that one day whatever force which guided the galaxy would allow him to give the hacker the beating he so obviously deserved.

"I have my ways," Eustis replied. He shrugged, a negligent little movement that somehow showed off the fine drape of the tunic he wore. "You should know that."

From the brief nod she gave her ex-lover, Landon guessed that she probably did. The man was a hacker, after all—one of the best, if Dhani's words were to be taken at face value. He didn't like to think that the Consortium's databases could be so easily breached, but Landon knew better. It was an ongoing war that echoed the one fought in space, a struggle between insurgent hackers and Consortium coders to see who would triumph: the underground operatives who could dissect code faster than a medical mech could perform an autopsy, or the semi-crazed geniuses who populated the encryption branches in the Consortium's intelligence division.

"At any rate," Landon said, thinking he had somehow just lost some ground and not sure exactly how it had happened, "I believe it is safe to say that Ms. Warlow may be treated as a neutral participant for now."

"Bloom off the rose?" asked Penn. He continued to stare down at Dhani without bothering to mask the expression of disdain he wore. "Grifting lost its charm?"

Her chin went up in the movement Landon already knew so well. "A few weeks in a Consortium detention cell tend to do that to a person." The soft lines of her lips hardened perceptibly. "But you didn't even need that much to walk away, did you, Eustis? All that took was a few command personnel who weren't quite quick enough to worship at your feet."

The barb hit home, Landon could tell; Penn's brows drew down, and he crossed his arms. "Idiots," he said.

"Maybe. Or maybe they were just doing their jobs." For a second longer, she matched her former lover glare for glare, and then she looked away, a distant smile playing about her mouth. "But the past is past, isn't it, Eustis? No need to dredge all that up now. Very simply, we need your help. And we hope that you'll give it."

If Landon hadn't been watching the other man so closely, he might have missed the almost imperceptible pause that preceded Penn's reply. "I would never let down a friend in need."

*Well, at least not if you thought you might be able to get something out of it,* Landon reflected in grim amusement.

The sunburst smile returned to Dhani's face. "We really do appreciate it. Don't we, captain?"

The assistance, yes. The person providing it? Not quite so much.

Landon managed to adopt the expression of pleasant politeness he'd invariably been forced to plaster on his features whenever Colonel Owens or another high-ranking officer made a statement he disagreed with but couldn't openly dispute. "Of course. As I said, your generous offer of assistance will not be forgotten."

Again that gleam came and went in Penn's eyes.

Then he smiled and said, "I went to the liberty of having some rooms prepared for you, as I didn't know the extent of the repairs your vessel might require. I assume a suite with adjoining sleeping chambers will be sufficient?"

"Quite sufficient," Landon replied, without bothering to elaborate further. Let Penn think what he wanted. Separate bedrooms made the situation a bit easier to manage. If the sleeping arrangements were the hacker's not-so-subtle attempt at transmitting his opinion of their liaison, so be it.

"I usually take my evening meal at nineteen-thirty local. Of course I would like you to join me. It seems Dhani and I have some catching up to do."

There were few things Landon thought he'd enjoy less than hearing Eustis Penn and Dhani reminisce over their times together, but refusing would only make him sound discourteous and petty. However, that didn't mean he couldn't inject a little archness into his reply. "We would be honored."

The quick, amused glance Dhani threw in his direction seemed to indicate she was wise to his game. But her expression sobered as she turned toward Eustis Penn. "In the meantime, though, I think I'd like to rest a bit. The strain of the journey and everything."

She didn't look particularly strained, but the excuse worked well enough.

"Of course," Penn said at once. "My majordomo mech will show you the way."

A mechanoid Landon hadn't even noticed came forward out of the shadows. Then again, he was fairly certain Penn had chosen such a dark, gleaming finish for the mech precisely because it allowed the machine to blend into the background.

"If you will follow me?" it said, and gestured toward an elevator located toward the rear of the reception chamber.

Landon nodded, and Dhani came at once to his side. Without speaking, they stepped into the lift after the mech. It pushed a button on the control console and they shot upward, the lights on the indicator panel showing that their destination was a good five floors above the reception area.

He was loath to say much of anything in the mech's presence, and Dhani appeared to be in agreement. Such quiet was uncharacteristic of her, but it reassured Landon that she could be discreet when necessary.

Once they arrived at the sixth floor, the mech led them down a long corridor flooded with natural light from a series of enormous windows. Not very defensible, Landon reflected, but even as the criticism crossed his mind, he noticed the faint shimmer of energy shields distorting the landscape outside.

He wondered if Eustis Penn really had the sort of enemies that a fortress like this seemed to indicate, or whether he simply enjoyed putting on an elaborate show. The energy required to generate such a high level of shields day and night wasn't cheap. Then again, Dhani had already made it clear that money wasn't a particular concern for the hacker.

Landon wished he could say the same for himself. If he had access to ready cash, then none of this skulking around in backwater systems and begging assistance from Dhani's admittedly staggering pool of ex-lovers would be necessary. No, they could simply land where they wanted, purchase whatever goods or services they required, and be on their way. The rank insignia on his uniform would be enough to dissuade those involved from asking too many questions about his unorthodox method of transportation and his even more unlikely traveling companion.

A plan began to form in his mind then, even as the mech ushered them into a large, luxurious chamber. Furnishings that wouldn't have been out of place in an oligarch's mansion decorated the main sitting room, and a wide window let in another astonishing vista, this one of a round blue lake fringed by some kind of elegant, drooping local trees. Their meager belongings had already been brought up from the shuttle and deposited in a rather shabby pile behind one sofa.

"Is there anything else?" the mech inquired.

"No, nothing," Landon said. All he really wanted at the moment was a chance to be alone with Dhani.

Such a situation was by its very nature fraught, and yet he still craved her company.

"Of course," said the mech, and promptly disappeared through the doorway.

Dhani had stopped in the center of the chamber and appeared to be giving its contents a careful appraisal. She remarked, "If I'd known Eustis was worth quite this much, I might not have been so quick to give him the boot."

"Truly a bad business move," Landon replied, refusing to be baited. He thought he'd gotten a bit better at reading her expressions. From the lift of her mouth and the wicked sparkle in her eyes, he guessed she hadn't meant her comment to be taken seriously. He added, "Speaking of which—"

"Yes?"

"I've been thinking about how we could resolve our current cashflow crisis."

"I wasn't aware we had one."

"Do you really believe we would have been forced to all these makeshifts if I'd had easy access to my own accounts?"

She appeared to consider. "Well, when you put it that way—"

"Precisely." He made his tone deliberately casual. "I think the best thing to do would be to have Eustis Penn hack into my accounts and take out what we need."

He'd gone completely mad. That had to be the only explanation. Then again, he didn't look particularly crazy. Landon watched her with a frank, somewhat relaxed air, as if he had just suggested that they take a brief stroll around the lake outside their window.

Dhani found her voice. "Come again?"

"Penn is a hacker, correct?"

"Well, yes."

"One of the best?"

Somehow she didn't like the idea of admitting to Eustis' excellence in the field, but since she'd already said as much, she knew lying would get her nowhere. "As far as I know," she allowed.

"Then it should be a simple enough process for him to access my accounts and withdraw the amount I need. Really, I don't see any harm in it—after all, the only person who would report the funds as missing would be me."

He sounded reasonable—almost too reasonable—but Dhani thought there must be a flaw in his argument somewhere. "You don't think your accountant would notice something like that?"

"Accountant? I don't trust anyone else to manage my money."

That settled it. He had to be crazy. No, she didn't have any idea as to what a man of his rank earned, but she knew it must be a decent chunk. How could someone with that kind of income get by without entrusting its management to a professional, especially when it must have been accumulating all the time he was living on Zeta Tau station? It wasn't as though there was much to spend it on in a place like that, and she guessed he'd never been the type for lavish spending while on leave, either.

Some of her disbelief must have shown in her face, because he said, "What do I have to manage? A few accounts, a small investment portfolio. I don't own any real property. Why would I, when I've spent almost my entire adult life away from my home world?"

She supposed she'd never really thought about it. True, there were some in the Consortium's service who managed to maintain households back home, wives…or, more rarely, husbands…and children they didn't see for months at a time. However, the majority of them lived a life apart, their only home the ship or the base where they were currently stationed.

For some reason, Dhani felt a rush of relief as she realized Captain Beck's remarks meant he had no family stashed away somewhere, no wife or significant other. Why that should matter so much, she really didn't want to say. Not now, at least.

With a shrug she was pretty sure didn't fool him for a second, she said, "So you've just let it pile up."

He tilted his head, his expression noncommittal. "Basically. I think you may have an inflated notion of what the service pays. But even a portion of what I have in savings should be enough for our needs."

"Which are?"

He smiled slightly. "A better ship, for one thing. At the rate we're going, we'll be lucky to reach Iradia before the Consortium collapses altogether. I don't like the way things are headed."

It took a moment for his words to sink in. Did he really think the situation was that grim? All right, in between grifting jobs, she'd done some work for the insurgency, but to her it had always seemed in a way like playing at rebellion. The Consortium was so big, so monolithic, that she didn't see how it could really fall, even with all the shockwaves that had rattled it lately. Voice tight with worry, she asked, "You really think that's a possibility?"

Right then he appeared distinctly uneasy…before he managed to blank the expression down behind his usual polite mask. For a few seconds, he said nothing. When he did speak, his tone was measured, even, but she could still detect a certain tightness to his voice, as though he was holding back his true thoughts. "I think it's gone beyond possibility into probability." He stopped there and gave her a piercing look. "I would think you'd be glad of that outcome."

"I—" She hesitated. If someone had broached this subject to her only a few months ago, she probably would have said that of course she'd be happy to see the Consortium ground down into dust, no longer able to exploit and subjugate the very citizens it was supposed to serve. Now, though, she could only wonder what might rise to replace it…if anything. Was chaos preferable to brutal order? For all she knew, whatever government arose from the ruins of the Consortium might be far, far worse. "Of course I'll be glad. I have friends who've worked very hard toward that end. I guess…I guess I just never thought it would actually happen."

His expression softened, and he shifted his weight, almost as if he'd meant to take a step toward her and then thought better of it. "It's a little frightening, isn't it? Like playing in the waves on the shore of an ocean, only to look up and realize a tsunami is coming straight toward you."

Luckily, she'd actually seen an ocean in person, so she understood the metaphor, although she'd never experienced one of those massive waves for herself. And though Captain Beck's words were far from reassuring, perversely, she did feel somewhat comforted. He wasn't trying to make the situation sound better than it was, and she appreciated that, was glad that he wasn't trying to sugarcoat things for her. Of the two of them, he probably had a deeper understanding of what would happen if the Consortium truly did fall apart. In the face of such a catastrophe, he wasn't trying to take refuge in reclaiming his old life. With Zeta Tau station destroyed and no other survivors to contradict his testimony, he could have offered up any story he liked.

Instead, he'd saved her, had risked his own life to ensure hers would continue. It was easy to hate the Consortium, even as she feared what would happen once it was gone, but she knew she didn't hate Landon Beck.

Far, far from it, if she wanted to be completely truthful with herself.

For now, though, she knew she needed to refocus her energy on their current situation. Landon was right—this limping from system to system had to stop. And she had no doubt that Eustis could pull those funds out of Landon's account as easily as a silk smuggler could slip through a GDF blockade. "So what's your plan?"

He seemed to relax slightly at her question. No doubt he'd expected her to continue the argument. "I'll have Penn transfer the funds to a credit voucher. Once our ship is repaired, we'll go to Peralta. It's the closest system where I feel we can purchase a reliable ship without too many questions being asked."

On the surface, his plan seemed simple enough, but experience had taught her that simple didn't always mean easy. "What if Eustis refuses?"

"Do you really think he will?"

She thought of her time with Eustis, his triumphs, his delight in unraveling whatever fiendish code the

Consortium's programmers had been able to create. No doubt he would consider hacking into Landon's accounts to be ridiculously easy, something he could have accomplished while still in school. On the other hand, the perverse nature of the request might appeal to Eustis' capricious nature. She had to hope so, anyway.

"No," she said. "I'm pretty sure he'll do as you ask."

"Good."

There might have been something else she could have said, some question she could have asked to discover why Landon had suddenly decided that urgency was of the essence. He hadn't seemed too concerned about their leisurely pace before now. Had he begun to tire of her, to see her as a burden he wished to rid himself of as soon as possible, so he'd be unencumbered when the shit really did hit the fan?

If that turned out to be the case, there wasn't much she could do about it. Only thank him, and try to survive as best she could. Good thing she already had a lot of practice.

Dhani realized that she'd somehow hoped Landon would stay with her after they reached Iradia, but that was a foolish fancy. He seemed to be a man of honor, and so he wouldn't abandon her until he saw her safely to that untamed desert world, but the idea of any future beyond that had been only a dream. And really, what in the world had she been thinking anyway, that someone like Captain Landon Beck would throw away everything he'd been for a woman like her?

Never mind that, in a way, he already had. She still didn't know how he planned to explain his escape from the station to his superiors. Maybe he didn't know, either. However, from the way he spoke, it seemed clear enough that he had no intention of allowing anything to happen between them. She was his responsibility...and nothing else.

It was the first time she'd really let her half-formed thoughts on the subject take shape, and she wished she hadn't. Tears burned hot at the back of her eyes, and she turned away from him to go to the adjoining chamber, pausing as she went to pick up her single piece of luggage. He didn't follow her, but maintained his position at the center of the chamber, hands clasped behind his back.

Somehow she knew that his decision to stay where he was and not join her could only be a harbinger of things to come.

# CHAPTER SEVEN

*Why the hell didn't you go to her, you idiot?*

Landon wished he knew the answer to that question. Although Dhani was very good at hiding her emotions when she wanted to, she hadn't been able to completely conceal the quick glitter of tears in her eyes, the way her full mouth had thinned before she scooped up her borrowed case and went into the adjoining room. The door had shut behind her, and she hadn't yet reemerged.

The chrono on his wrist—which had automatically adjusted itself to local time—told him it was almost nineteen-thirty, the hour when Eustis Penn had promised...or threatened, depending on how one looked at it...to feed his unexpected guests dinner. If Dhani didn't appear, what then?

Well, Landon supposed he would have to offer

some sort of a pretext for her absence. Weariness, a temporary indisposition…something. No doubt the hacker would be able to see right through those feeble excuses, but with any luck, he wouldn't ask too many questions. And if she didn't appear, that meant Landon would have to ask Eustis personally about hacking his bank account. That should be interesting. Landon wasn't sure what would be worse—the hacker outright refusing him, or asking for some kind of favor in return. What kind of favor could he possibly do for a person like Eustis Penn?

He'd just taken a breath and steeled himself to go downstairs unaccompanied when the door that joined their two rooms opened. Dhani stood there, long dark hair flowing over her shoulders, her slender form shown off by a simple but perfectly draped gown of Iradian silk in a subtle moonlight-gray tone. Something else she'd borrowed from Governor Janning's wife, obviously. What else was she hiding in that suitcase?

Apparently ignoring the way he couldn't quite prevent himself from staring at her, Dhani approached and arched one eyebrow. "Eustis did say nineteen-thirty, didn't he?"

Landon somehow found his voice. "Yes. Yes, he did."

"Well, then. I suppose we'd better go down."

Did he dare offer her his arm? He'd done so back on Ordon, but that was only because she was pretending to be Larissa Miles, and he'd had to go along with the charade. There was no need for false deference here. Besides, he worried that she might get the wrong impression if he attempted to loop her arm through his. Better not.

Even though he wanted nothing more right then than to be a few inches closer to her, possibly close enough to breathe in the sweet scent of her hair, feel the warmth of her body. Thinking such things was madness, considering their current situation. He couldn't allow himself to be distracted—although Landon didn't think much of the hacker's disposition, he couldn't dispute that Eustis Penn was clever. Too clever. It would be difficult enough to keep on his toes around the other man under normal circumstances. Doing so while letting his thoughts continually wander to Dhani Warlow would be nigh impossible.

"Very well," Landon said after taking a deep breath. He went to the door and opened it for her.

The way she hesitated was obvious, which meant she'd intended for him to see how she'd paused. No doubt her way of expressing her disapproval, but best not to acknowledge that he'd noticed. Wearing the neutral expression he'd honed to perfection over the last decade of his life, he waited until she was out in the corridor, then touched the controls to shut the door and seal the chamber.

Dusk had fallen, lending a purplish tint to the light that still filtered through the west-facing windows of the hall. Landon realized then that he didn't actually know where the dining chamber was located, but decided he would descend to the ground floor in the hope that Eustis Penn would be there to greet them.

That proved unnecessary, however, because in the next moment the hacker's mech approached them and said in its metallic voice, "This way, if you please."

Beside him, Dhani lifted an expressive eyebrow. Clearly, she wasn't overly impressed by having a mech as their guide, although the robots were really quite expensive, and beyond the reach of most ordinary citizens of the Consortium.

Then again, Dhani's hacker ex-boyfriend wasn't exactly someone you could call "ordinary."

They followed the mech down the stairs, through the foyer with its massive ten-meter-high roof, and down a long hallway with holographic projections of a night sky on its arched ceiling. Which particular night sky, Landon couldn't say for sure, since none of the constellations looked familiar to him. However, he allowed himself to be suitably impressed by the display, which was both beautiful and, he guessed, costly.

The corridor opened out into a long rectangle of a room, its walls made completely of tempered glass, so it looked as though it had been somehow suspended in the center of an alien forest. Just beyond one wall was an inlet of the pond Landon had glimpsed on their way to the fortress. Its waters glittered with the light of a pale lavender moon that had just risen above a range of low hills to the west.

In the center of the room was a long table that looked as if it had been carved from a single piece of rock. Basalt? Possibly, as it was dark enough. However, the impression of heaviness was leavened by a series of floating lamps that hovered at the center of the table, their bluish glow reflecting in the polished surface.

As soon as they entered, Eustis Penn rose from his seat at the head of the table and came toward them. Whatever he'd intended to say, it was forestalled by Dhani, who remarked, "This is quite the display, Eustis. You must tell me the name of your designer."

The smile the hacker wore tightened slightly. However, his tone was pleasant enough as he replied, "Her name is Lini Trasten. An Eridani." A pause, and he added, "I doubt you could afford her."

This time it was Dhani's expression that appeared a little stiff. Then she chuckled. "Oh, you know how I am, Eustis—I never settle in one place long enough to justify the expense of a designer. No, I was thinking more of Landon here. He has an idea to retire early and invest in some property."

Which of course was a complete lie. True, with the situation out in the greater galaxy the way it was, there was a good chance that he might be forcibly retired in the not-too-distant future, but he very much doubted that if such a thing came to pass, he'd be too worried about the decoration of whichever place he ended up.

Eustis' sharp gray gaze moved toward Landon. "Well, if that's the case, I'll make sure to give you her contact information."

"Thank you," he replied. "I appreciate that."

For a second, the hacker's mouth compressed, as though he was trying to figure out whether there was any truth to anything either Landon or Dhani had just said. Landon guessed that Eustis probably didn't put much stock in most of what Dhani told him, but he was still trying to take the measure of his other visitor, to determine whether he was as much of a con artist as she was.

Actually, Landon wouldn't put it past the other man to have already taken the DNA sample he'd gotten from shaking hands and run it through the Consortium's databases, in which case he would already know that Landon was no more than what he said he was. What the hacker would do with that information, Landon didn't know for sure. All he could do was wait, and try to react as best he could.

"Please, sit," Eustis said, spreading a hand toward the elegant table. "I thought I'd offer some local game —but be assured, everything on this planet has been thoroughly vetted for human consumption."

Dhani's dark eyes danced for a second, and Landon worried she might make an acid comment about Eustis Penn's humanity. To his relief, however, she took her seat without comment, and lifted the cloth napkin from where it rested so she could spread it across her lap.

Landon did the same, although he asked as he sat, "So there is good hunting on this world?"

"Oh, I don't know about hunting," Eustis said airily. "My cook handles all that for me."

"'Cook'?" Dhani echoed. "So it's not just you and the mech here?"

A chuckle. "Hardly. I have a few trusted people on my household staff—the cook, my security detail, a pilot—"

"A pilot?" Landon asked, realizing too late that he probably sounded far too eager. "You have a ship here?"

"Of course I do. While I enjoy the solitude this planet provides, I also enjoy having the means to escape it when necessary. So I keep a pilot on hand. He's also teaching me to fly the thing myself—but not too quickly, because I think he worries that if I get too good, I won't need to keep him around any longer."

"I can see why that might be an issue," Landon responded, his tone serious enough, although his thoughts had already begun to race. What if, instead of getting Penn to hack Landon's accounts and then having to go off-world to purchase a better ship, they could simply buy Penn's ship outright, throwing in the *Ordonian II* so he wouldn't be completely stranded here? The hacker could purchase a replacement at his leisure, but then Landon and Dhani would have the means to go directly to Iradia, or wherever else they desired.

He shot a veiled glance at Eustis from beneath his eyelashes, watching as the hacker signaled the mech to come over and pour the wine, a pale blue vintage, clearly Eridani. Interesting that Penn seemed to trust the robotic assistant more than he did the humans in his employ, since none of them had yet to make an appearance. True, their services might not be needed at the moment, but still....

"I'm hearing some interesting things over the relays," the hacker remarked as the mech poured a precise six ounces into Landon's wine glass.

"Such as?" Dhani inquired, her tone still somewhat arch. It certainly didn't take a galaxy-class hacker —or a captain in the Consortium's Defense Fleet—to tell that she wasn't very happy about what Eustis had said to her earlier.

Actually, Landon wasn't all that happy, either. Penn could think whatever he wanted, but there was no reason to be so openly rude.

"Oh, that the insurgents are lending their aid to the uprising on New Chicago. Since the Consortium is trying to put out fires all over the galaxy, its forces are spread too thin to really try to stop the rebellion. Looks like Gaia is about to lose one of the jewels in its crown." Eustis' gaze slid over toward Landon. "But I suppose you would know all about that, wouldn't you, captain?"

"I'm afraid I've been rather out of contact the past few days," Landon said stiffly.

"Right—those 'unusual circumstances' you mentioned a few hours ago. That wouldn't have anything to do with the destruction of Zeta Tau station, would it?"

Damn. Landon had hoped Penn would let that matter slide, even though he'd been foolish enough to mention it on their first meeting. "It would. My vessel was damaged by the shockwave, and we were forced to take refuge on Ordon and get what help we could there. So you can see why we haven't heard much of what is going on in the greater galaxy."

"Communications equipment damaged, too?"

"He just said the ship was damaged," Dhani said, irritation clear in her voice. She reached for her glass of wine and took a large swallow.

"He said the ship you escaped in was damaged," Eustis pointed out. "But that wasn't the one you arrived in."

"We got caught in some crossfire," Landon explained. "I'll admit our luck hasn't been the best these past few days. And that, as Dhani told you earlier, is why we hoped you might assist us."

"Dhani always was hopeful." Penn sent her a malicious smile. "That is, she always hoped she'd be able to charm you right out of whatever it was she needed at any particular moment. Isn't that right, Dhani?"

Color burned along her high cheekbones, but she merely gave a practiced shrug and said, "Is it a crime to be charming?"

"It should be, when a person is as 'charming' as you. Obviously, someone else thought the same thing, or you wouldn't have been locked up in Zeta Tau." Before she could begin to retort, Eustis shifted in his seat so his gaze was fixed on Landon. "I'm actually more curious as to why the two of you would be alone together in the only ship that survived the station's destruction. It does seem a little...irregular."

Well, Landon couldn't exactly argue with that remark, not when it was the simple truth. However, he wasn't about to explain his motivations to this smirking, holier-than-thou hacker. "She was being transferred," he said shortly.

A chuckle, and Penn reached for his own wine glass so he could take an ostentatious swallow. "Oh, come on, captain—you'll have to do better than that. No one of your rank is going to be tasked with the transfer of a low-level prisoner like Miss Warlow here. Let me guess—you were struck by her beauty, and so were spiriting her away to a hidden love nest someplace where she could thank you properly for rescuing her."

Landon scowled, partly because the hacker had gotten some of it right. He had been struck by Dhani, although his intentions at the time had been purely honorable. True, as time wore on, he was finding his intentions becoming less and less honorable, but there was no way in the world he'd ever admit to that. "I'm afraid I'm not at liberty to discuss classified matters," he said stiffly.

That response made Eustis Penn laugh outright. "'Classified'?" he repeated, and shook his head. "You forget that I read classified material like some people read their morning news-feeds. I saw Dhani's file. Yes, she was going to be transferred to Gaia, but not for another two standard weeks. There was nothing in her record that showed she was facing anything except a routine transfer, usual complement of grunts to guard the shuttle. No mention of her requiring the escort of a captain, especially the adjutant of the station commander. Not exactly the kind of person who could be easily spared."

It was damn hard to play poker with someone who already knew all the cards in your hand. Landon cast about in his mind for some reasonable explanation, something that would put the hacker off the scent, but he couldn't come up with anything that sounded halfway plausible.

To his surprise, Dhani sent Penn an overly sweet smile and said, "You're right, Eustis. Or rather, you're *partially* right. You've just gotten the 'who' wrong, if not the 'what.'" She paused, then went on, "I'm afraid I was the one struck by Captain Beck. I begged him

to be the one to take me to Gaia—one of the guards
had been hinting that he knew exactly what he
planned to do with me once he had me on the shuttle
and away from the station, and I was frightened. I
asked for an interview with the captain, said I had
more information I was willing to hand over. Once we
were alone in the interrogation chamber, I told him
the truth, that I feared for my safety. I knew I had to
be sent to Gaia, but I asked him to take me personally
because I knew he was a man of honor, unlike a lot of
the other men stationed at Zeta Tau. And he agreed.
That's why we were together in that ship when the
station was attacked."

Landon listened to this pack of lies with growing
astonishment. Oh, he knew that Dhani could weave a
believable yarn with the best of them, but he was still
surprised by how convincing she sounded. If he hadn't
known better, he would truly have believed she'd
thought herself in peril—her voice trembled slightly
as she recounted the tale, and her eyes were dark and
tragic.

Even Penn appeared hesitant, as if he was
attempting to decide whether she really was telling the
truth this time, or whether she had produced yet
another lie from her considerable repertoire. His sharp
gray gaze transferred itself to Landon. "Is this true?"

"Of course," he replied without blinking. Maybe
he'd begun to learn a few tricks from his travel
companion. "Naturally, I couldn't allow her to be

placed in any jeopardy. And since I was about to head to Gaia on leave, it seemed the most logical thing to take her myself."

"And your commanding officer okayed this," Eustis said, clearly skeptical.

"Yes. He had no reason to doubt my word. Besides," Landon added, "while you may find this difficult to believe, Colonel Owens wished to avoid any black marks on the station's reputation. If Ms. Warlow had filed a formal complaint, there would have been an investigation."

Which was more or less true. More often than he would have liked to admit, those sorts of investigations went nowhere—the Consortium was very good at covering up evidence of any wrongdoing—but every once in a while, they bore fruit. A careful commanding officer would have done his best to avoid any whiff of scandal.

Eustis Penn appeared to be thinking about the same thing. He was silent for a moment, his gaze tracking toward Dhani for a moment before returning to Landon. "And then the pirates attacked."

"Yes. Very bad timing, of course…but it would have been even worse if we'd left only a standard quarter-hour later. At least we were able to escape."

"We couldn't make it to Gaia, though, because of the damage to the ship," Dhani put in. "And that's the reason behind our sad tale."

"About your ship," Landon ventured. "What model is it?"

"Mistral-class, latest Gupta-drive engine," Eustis said. Then his eyes narrowed. "Let me guess—you'd like to take it off my hands."

Truth be told, Landon had been hoping for something a little less high-powered. He might have saved almost everything he'd earned over the past ten years, simply because he didn't have much else to do with his money, but purchasing even a slightly used Mistral-class ship would wipe out most of what he'd saved. It probably would be better to simply limp the *Ordonian II* to Peralta, then purchase a much more modest vessel there.

Clearly guessing at the reason why Landon didn't answer right away, Eustis remarked, "A bit rich for your blood, captain?"

"I—"

"Not that it matters," the hacker went on. "The *Persephone* isn't for sale."

Landon allowed himself a shrug. He could only hope the gesture looked sufficiently unconcerned. "Actually, I was hoping for assistance in another area —one where you're the expert."

"That being?"

"He needs you to hack his bank accounts and free up some cash," Dhani said, right before she picked up her wine glass and helped herself to another large swallow of the aqua-tinted liquid inside. "Things aren't quite as fluid as he'd like at the moment."

"Ah." Eustis tapped his fingers on the dark stone tabletop, leaving a few obvious smudges. Landon wondered how many times a day the extravagant piece of furniture had to be wiped down. "Why do you need my help? All you have to do is walk into any Consortium-connected bank on almost any world, and use your official identification and biometrics to access anything you require."

Well, under normal circumstances that might be true, but of course Landon didn't dare do any such thing. That sort of transaction would immediately flag his whereabouts. True, the Consortium probably had bigger fish to fry right now than tracking down a single AWOL captain. Even so, it was a risk he couldn't take.

"Because I choose not to," he said, which of course was about the weakest reply he could give.

To his surprise, Eustis Penn grinned. "I get it. You're supposed to be shuttling Dhani to Gaia so they can fit her for a nice little cell on Titan. Only, you can't really bring yourself to do that. With everything in chaos, you figure everyone's probably forgotten about you, so why do the one thing that's guaranteed to attract attention?"

Landon nodded, even as Dhani said, "Yes, Eustis, that's exactly it. If you hack into the accounts and make the money accessible another way, no one's going to know. It's the sort of thing you could do in your sleep."

"I'll think about it."

Of course Penn wouldn't immediately commit to doing such a thing. Landon didn't know the man well —or at all, really—but he'd already taken enough of his measure to realize that he enjoyed toying with people. Maybe he would say yes, maybe he would say no. However, he wouldn't give any kind of answer until he'd made his audience sweat a little.

A wave of dislike went over Landon then, although he didn't react, only reached for his own wine glass as the mech returned to the dining chamber, now pushing a cart laden with food. The mechanoid servant stopped by Eustis Penn's left hand and set down a platter filled with some kind of meat in a wine-dark sauce. The tantalizing aroma reached Landon's nostrils, and his empty stomach rumbled, although not loudly enough that he thought anyone had heard.

From across the table, Dhani's eyes met his. She was idly playing with the bone handle of her knife, but he could still detect the tension in her posture, the set of her mouth. No, she wasn't happy with Eustis at all. The problem was, Landon didn't see what they could do about the situation. They certainly weren't in a position to force him to do anything he didn't want to do. They'd simply have to wait and see what he decided. With any luck, the hacker's capricious nature and desire to thumb his nose at the Consortium would win out over any misgivings he might have about assisting the man who was now escorting his former lover around the galaxy. Landon's relationship with Dhani was anything but intimate, of course, although attempting to explain that to Penn would probably only make matters worse.

"Think away," she said as she watched the mech finish putting out the rest of the food. Despite Landon's less than positive opinion of their host, he had to admit that Eustis Penn did set a fine table. "We don't *have* to have your help. Right, captain?"

"Well, I—"

Eustis smirked at her. "Oh, yes, you're both doing fine on your own. Which begs the question of why you came here in the first place."

The two of them were starting to remind Landon of his bickering younger brother and sister, neither of whom he'd seen in years. But back when they were twelve and ten, respectively, they'd sounded a good deal like Dhani and Eustis.

"We came to ask for help," Landon said, his tone mild. "We knew there were no guarantees involved. And I suppose we'll be able to limp our ship to the next system, should you choose not to provide any assistance. But—"

"I am providing assistance," Penn broke in, sounding a touch more aggrieved than he should.

"My mechanics are working on your ship as we speak."

"True," Landon said. "And we appreciate that. If you don't feel comfortable doing anything else, I understand."

This mild reply seemed to put off Eustis, as though he had expected more of an argument and now didn't know exactly what he should say next. "I didn't say I wouldn't do anything else. I just said I'd think about it."

"Which is usually your code for 'no,'" Dhani remarked.

"Not always."

Landon shot her a warning glance, and she appeared to subside after that, shifting her attention to the mech, who had just placed equal-sized portions of meat, vegetables, and some kind of flat bread on her plate. She picked up her fork, but didn't begin to eat.

Too bad. Right then Landon thought it might be better if she had her mouth full. Clearly, she was spoiling for a fight with the hacker. Wounded pride over the cutting words he'd uttered earlier, or something else, something from their shared past? It didn't take a great leap of the imagination to picture her being on the receiving end of some other nastiness, but Landon hoped for both their sakes that she'd let it go. The last thing they needed was to anger Eustis Penn so much that he was goaded into throwing them out of his fortress before the repairs on the ship were complete.

A brittle silence fell. The mech dished up food for Landon, and then finally for his master. Unfortunately, even though he was hungry, Landon found his appetite had deserted him. Because he knew he needed to eat, he forced a few forkfuls of food into his mouth. It was good.

*Of course it's good,* he told himself. *It's obvious enough that Mr. Penn doesn't settle for anything less than the very best.*

Not the most generous of notions, but right then, Landon didn't much care. He ate some more food, was glad that everyone had apparently decided to call a truce while they were consuming their food. That gave him some time to think, to weigh his options. Once they got to Peralta, they could sell the *Ordonian II,* but it certainly wouldn't bring in enough money to pay for a better ship. In fact, it would probably only get them enough funds to pay for food and lodgings for a few weeks.

Maybe it was worth the risk to do as Penn had said, to go to a financial institution, present his credentials, then take the money and run. Surely Consortium authorities were occupied with more important things than tracking down a runaway officer who wasn't quite as dead as everyone had thought.

The glassware on the table rattled faintly, and

Landon looked up from his plate to see Eustis Penn frowning and Dhani with her head tilted to one side, as though straining to hear something. Then it came again, that rattling of the dishes and glasses, this time accompanied by a low rumble Landon recognized immediately.

An explosion.

*What the—?*

In the next second, Penn had a wafer-thin hand-held out of his pocket and in his palm, was speaking urgently into it. "Oleson, status. *Oleson!*"

Nothing but a hiss of static.

The hacker rose from his seat. "It appears we're under some kind of attack. You didn't bring along any friends you failed to mention, did you?"

Considering the bad luck that had been dogging Landon ever since he rescued Dhani from Zeta Tau station, he couldn't say such a thing wasn't a possibil-ity. However, he only stood as well and replied, "None of our scans indicated any other ships in the vicinity when we came into this system out of subspace."

"That doesn't mean someone couldn't still have been tracking you."

Another explosion, this one louder...which most likely meant closer.

"True, but—"

The glass on the western wall of the dining chamber shattered. Dhani screamed and dropped under the table, the heavy stone shielding her from the shards that flew every which way. A few of them stung Landon's face and hands, but otherwise, the heavy fabric of his uniform protected him fairly well.

Then he didn't have time to worry about the glass, because a squad of men in the dark gray jumpsuits and black battle armor of the GDF's security forces burst into the room and began to move forward in a fashion that could only be described as menacing.

"What the hell do you think you're doing?" demanded Eustis Penn. Dots of blood marred his lean face, but he seemed oblivious to the personal damage he'd suffered, was instead focused on what the intruders had just done to his dining room. "I'm a private citizen with a lawful homestead on this world. You have no right to be here."

"Oh, but we do," a familiar voice said. The shock troops parted to reveal a tall man in a dark uniform. His icy gaze settled on Landon. "We're pursuing a couple of fugitives—one of whom is my former adjutant."

Landon's breath strangled in his throat. It was impossible. The man had to be dead. And yet…there he was.

General Owens, commander of Zeta Tau station.

## CHAPTER EIGHT

As soon as she heard that voice, Dhani's blood turned to ice in her veins. Her every instinct told her to stay under the table, so that was what she did. All right, not her proudest moment, but survival had always trumped pride in her world.

Problem was, from her vantage point down on the floor, she couldn't really see what was going on. She inched closer to the edge of the table, hoping the empty chair occupying that spot would provide enough of a shield. Cautiously lifting her head, she peered out, could just barely see Eustis standing at the head of the table, his arms crossed, every inch of his body thrumming with righteous indignation. Her former lover had always been pretty good at the whole "righteous" thing.

In contrast, Landon was stiff and silent, his face a blank. She'd already come to realize that his lack of expression was only a mask to cover up what was actually going through his mind, so she looked for other tells—like the way the one hand she could see had clenched itself into a fist, the knuckles looking very white against the dark gray of his uniform.

When he spoke, however, his tone only indicated surprise. "Colonel, it's good to see you. When I saw how those pirates destroyed Zeta Tau station, I naturally thought—"

"You thought I was dead? I suppose that would have been convenient. No one to contradict whatever story you planned to tell."

Thank God she couldn't actually see General Owens, could only hear his voice. Although in a way, that was worse. She'd heard enough of that voice already.

"I had no plans to tell anything but the truth."

"Is that so? Then why that wild tale you told Governor Janning on Ordon?"

Oh, hell. Dhani had no idea how he'd accomplished such a feat, but clearly the colonel had managed to track them from system to system. Was it on his orders that the Consortium cruiser had appeared in the Lathvin system? No, that particular explanation didn't sound right. Owens might be a colonel, but he certainly didn't have the kind of rank required to set up that kind of attack. He would have had to send such a request through fleet HQ.

*Like it matters,* she thought. *The only thing that*

*matters is that he's alive…and that he's managed to catch up with us.*

A chill ran through her, raising goose-pimples on her exposed arms. Right then, she wished she'd worn something more covered up. She'd wanted Landon Beck to see her in this dress, to hopefully admire her.

Want her.

Now, though, the thought of Colonel Owens' cold gray gaze taking in the amount of skin the gown exposed made another shiver pass over her flesh. About all she could do was skulk down here and pray that he wouldn't notice how the third party was conspicuously missing from this little tableau.

That particular hope was dashed with his next words, however. "And where is the enterprising Ms. Warlow?" the colonel asked. "I see three place settings here."

"She went back upstairs to her chamber," Captain Beck replied. "She hasn't been feeling well."

Damn it, but Landon Beck was a bad liar. She'd have to give him some lessons—if they somehow managed to survive this.

Apparently, the colonel didn't think any better of Landon's lying skills than she did. "I don't think so," Owens said.

From her place under the table, Dhani couldn't see exactly what he'd done as he was speaking. Given some sort of signal, apparently, because in the next moment, harsh gloved hands grasped her by the arms and hauled her upright. She blinked, finding herself flanked by two of the colonel's commandos. Their synth-leather-clad fingers bit into her biceps, but she forced herself not to react.

Across the table, Landon's dismayed blue eyes met hers, but he also remained still, as though he knew that to try to come to her aid would only make matters far worse.

"Ah, there she is," Owens said, satisfaction showing in the set of his thin lips. He didn't smile; he didn't need to. A certain glint in those icy eyes told her that he'd taken in every detail of her appearance, from the bare arms to the deeply cut neckline and the faint shadow between her breasts that it revealed. "How are you, Ms. Warlow? Or is that Ms. Miles?"

She gritted her teeth and didn't reply. The tooth-gritting was necessary, because otherwise she would have spat out a retort she knew she'd soon regret. It was better to stay silent.

"All right, so you found them," Eustis said, sounding almost bored. "Obviously, *I* didn't know they were fugitives. Dhani is an old friend of mine. It wasn't so strange that she'd want to see me."

"And your 'old friend' somehow neglected to mention that she was a fugitive?"

A shrug. "I didn't ask."

"Unfortunate oversight," Colonel Owens said. He turned his attention to Landon Beck, who was taut as a bowstring, although he'd remained silent as the colonel's commandos manhandled her. All right, maybe being hauled upright by the biceps didn't exactly constitute manhandling. She couldn't blame Landon, who would certainly be outnumbered if he tried to intervene. "You still haven't explained yourself, captain."

"There's nothing to explain," Landon replied.

Owens' brows drew together. "You might as well attempt to get your story in order now, Beck. Soon enough you'll have to repeat it in front of a military court."

At those words, Eustis let out a sound suspiciously close to a snort. Immediately, the general turned toward him, his frown deepening.

"Something amuses you, Mr. Penn?"

A shrug, and then Eustis bent to retrieve his wine glass and take a sip. The dark-visored faces of the commandos holding Dhani swiveled in his direction. One of them cocked his head slightly, and General Owens made a small movement with one hand, as though telling them to stand down.

After allowing himself another ostentatious swallow of the glinting blue-green wine, Eustis said, "I just wanted to know if you've been paying much attention to what's going on out there in the galaxy. From what I've seen, it seems pretty optimistic to think there's going to be a military court on Gaia that gives a good damn whether or not your man there helped a pretty prisoner escape custody. Bigger fish to fry, you know."

Owens' already thin lips thinned even further. Dhani watched him, wondering whether Eustis' intentionally dismissive remarks would be enough to set a spark to the colonel's anger. Her instincts told her probably not; everything the man did was calculated, cold. But still, her erstwhile lover did have a particular talent for getting under people's skin.

"What we're experiencing is a temporary disruption, nothing more," Owens said. "A few malcontents. It's certainly not enough to break down our military, or its courts of justice."

"Hmm." Another swallow of wine, and Eustis added, "I suppose we'll know in another month or two. I doubt it'll take much longer than that. You did hear that both New Chicago and Nova Angeles have broken free of the Consortium?"

Anger glittered in Owens' cold gray eyes. "Again, temporary, minor successes on certain worlds are not enough to destroy a government that has been in existence for more than three hundred years."

"Perhaps you're right." Eustis set down his wine glass. At almost the same moment, the butler mech reappeared with another bottle of wine. "In the meantime, I don't see the point of all these hostilities. A glass of wine, colonel? The '23 is a very good year."

"I don't—" Colonel Owens began...but he didn't get any further than that, because several panels on the mech's gleaming body opened up, revealing hidden micro-size pulse cannons.

Shock momentarily loosened the commandos' grips on her arms. Dhani took advantage of their confusion to tear herself from their grasp and throw herself under the table. Good timing, because almost at the same instant, the mech opened fire, the micro pulse cannons tearing through the body armor they wore.

Apparently Landon had the same idea she did, because she saw him drop and roll as well. His startled eyes met her in the dimness under the table. He jerked his head toward the far end, clearly indicating that they should take advantage of the cover the heavy stone surface provided for as long as they could. After giving a quick nod of agreement, Dhani began to scramble in that direction, cursing the long, dragging skirt of the gown she wore, while at the same time hoping she wasn't completely destroying it. Who knows—if she survived this, she might have an occasion to wear it again.

From overhead came an awful racket, the clatter of booted feet on the stone floor seeming to indicate that additional troops had appeared to replace their fallen comrades, while the piercing sound of rapid pulse fire continued. A gasp, a man's cry of pain.

Had the mech gotten Colonel Owens? Dhani risked a quick glance backward and had to muffle her own cry of shock and despair. Lying on the

floor, his eyes staring sightlessly at her, was Eustis
Penn.

Landon must have seen him, too, because he said
in a harsh whisper, "Keep going. Break left toward the
door as soon as you're clear of the table."

She nodded, trying to ignore the grinding ache of
loss within her breast. No, she didn't love Eustis Penn.
But there had been a time when she thought she did,
and that was why she wished she could weep now.

No time for that, unfortunately. As she reached
the edge of the table, she pushed herself to a standing
position, then bolted for the door. A wild pulse shot
went over her head and she cringed, but she didn't
stop, didn't look back. She could only pray that
Landon was still behind her.

Which she discovered soon enough, since, with
his longer legs, he caught up to her quickly. He
reached out with one hand to take her by the arm,
guide her around a corner of the fortress, running
down a stone-paved path that cut through the forest.

"Where—where are we going?" Dhani panted.

"The ship," Landon said. A pause. Then, "I'm
sorry about Eustis."

All she could do was shake her head. Maybe later
she'd have a chance to analyze the emotions coursing
through her right now. But there wouldn't be a later if
they couldn't get to their ship.

They'd left the *Ordonian II* on one of several
landing pads outside a complex of low-slung buildings

Eustis had said were the repair facilities. As they approached, however, Dhani experienced a sinking feeling somewhere in her stomach. Oh, the ship was still there. But it wasn't going anywhere, not with the engine compartment open to the elements, complicated bits and pieces she couldn't begin to identify scattered on the ground.

"Well, hell," Landon said, his tone expressing pretty much what Dhani was feeling, even though she guessed she would have used a stronger word.

"I thought he said he was going to fix it." She didn't quite dare to utter Eustis' name out loud. Not yet, anyway.

"It looks like someone was," Landon replied. "But they got interrupted."

The source of that interruption became clear in the next moment, as new pulse fire erupted on the other side of the maintenance complex. The captain's jaw tightened; Dhani saw the way his hand went to his belt, as though searching for the sidearm that should hang there. Probably out of courtesy to their host, he'd left it back in their borrowed rooms. At the time, that had seemed like a good idea. Now, though....

Still with his jaw set, Landon went over to the ship, heading toward a large metal tool case that stood next to the engine's disarray. He rooted around in one of the drawers and drew out a heavy, oversized spanner.

"Better than nothing," he said briefly, and began to move toward the source of the pulse blasts.

Dhani wasn't so sure about that. The crude weapon might give him false confidence, which was the last thing they needed about now. However, she didn't argue, but hurried along next to him, glad that he was using the cover of the building to keep them concealed. Maybe if they could somehow utilize the element of surprise—

As they came around the corner of the structure, she spotted a man in gray coveralls crouched on the gangway of a ship much newer and sleeker than the Ordonian II. He was trading potshots with a group of three more GDF commandos, who'd been forced to take cover behind a stack of metal pallets.

The man on the gangway appeared calm, almost relaxed, as though he could keep doing this all day. As she looked on, Dhani thought she recognized him— Milo Vandergrif, an associate of Eustis', and one of the best pilots she'd ever met. He must have been the pilot Eustis had been talking about, although she wondered why the hacker had never bothered to mention the man's name.

*Jealous, probably,* she thought. Back in the day, Milo had flirted with her a bit, not because he was really that interested, but because he knew his pretended attraction would annoy the hell out of Eustis. And the ploy had worked, too.

Milo must have caught a glimpse of them, because

his teeth showed in a sudden, ferocious grin. "Hey, Dhani," he called out, even as he got off another series of pulse bursts at the crouching commandos, who were probably wishing they could be anywhere else. "Long time."

"Long time," she called back. Should she tell him about Eustis? Would having that information make Milo's assault that much fiercer, or would it only distract him? After a second, she decided it was probably better to say something. "They got Eustis."

Milo didn't blink. "Ah." With only the slightest narrowing of his eyes, he let loose on the commandos once more.

"You know this person?" Landon murmured in her ear.

It was really ridiculous that having him so close, feeling his warm breath against her hair, was enough to make a shiver go through her. She should not be distracted by that sort of thing in the middle of a fire-fight, for God's sake. And he smelled good, too, something sort of warm and woodsy.

"Kind of," she replied. "He's a friend of Eustis. I think he was piloting for him, too. At least, I'm pretty sure that ship belongs to Eustis. Milo on his own could never have afforded it."

"So all we have to do is get on that ship and convince this Milo person to fly it out of here."

"I doubt there's much 'convincing' you'll have to do," Dhani said. "The hardest part is going to be getting on board without having those commandos shoot us up in the process."

Landon went silent. One hand reached up to rub his chin, as though he was considering the problem, analyzing it from all angles. Well, that was what he would have been trained to do, right? Having never attended a Gaian military academy, she was a little fuzzy on what those officers were actually taught. It didn't seem as if you needed to know a lot about tactics to ride a desk as adjutant on a prison station, but maybe she was missing something.

"We need to go back out and come around the side of the building opposite us," he said at last. "With the angles they're shooting at, they should have a more difficult time hitting us if we come in from that direction."

"'Difficult'?" she echoed. That didn't sound so great. She would have preferred he use the word "impossible."

"Yes, difficult," Landon said. "But certainly not beyond the capabilities of trained GDF sharpshooters. We'll just have to hope that your friend Milo can keep them occupied."

Dhani opened her mouth to say she wasn't entirely sure she could classify Milo as a friend—he'd always been more of a flirting partner than anything else—but she decided it wasn't worth arguing about. Instead, she nodded, and silently followed Landon as he took her back around the side of the building and then crossed over to the other structure he'd indicated.

As they both peeked around the corner, she could see at once that here there was a much better angle of approach to the ship. From this side, it was clear that there were two entrances—the one near the cockpit, where Milo was currently crouched on the gangway, and then another, probably back toward the passenger compartment. The door there stood open, and another gangway had been extruded from the opening. Several large metal cases sat on the ground near the gangway, as though Milo had been in the process of loading the cargo area when the commandos showed up. It was probably only a matter of time before some of them circled around so they could catch the pilot in their crossfire. Dhani wondered why they hadn't done so already, then realized that, even though the past few minutes had felt like some of the longest of her life, only a very short time had elapsed since she and Landon escaped from Eustis' dining room.

"Keep low, and get ready to hit the ground and crawl if you have to," Landon said.

Dhani couldn't help letting out a sigh as she glanced down at the skirt of her gown, which was already streaked with dirt from crawling around on the floor of the dining room. However, all she said was, "Got it." The last thing she wanted was for

Landon to think she was more worried about a silly dress than saving her own life.

And it wasn't the dress, not really. She couldn't erase the sight of Eustis' dead, staring eyes, nor the curl of Colonel Owens' lip as he stared at her. Although the evening breeze playing on her bare arms was mild enough, she couldn't help but shiver.

If Landon noticed, he didn't say anything. Or rather, his next words had nothing to do with her shiver, or her dismay over the impending ruination of her gown. "We're going."

He took her hand in his and pulled her toward the gangway. She ran at his side, glad that the shoes she'd borrowed from Governor Janning's wife had only moderately high heels. Yes, in the past Dhani had been forced to run in some fairly serious stilettos, but it wasn't the sort of experience she wanted to repeat.

The pulse fire didn't stop, but she could hear a few staticky exchanges between the commandos over their private comm units. The subject of those convos became clear soon enough, because immediately some of the pulse bolts began to be redirected toward them. By that point, she and Landon had reached the gangway. He shoved her ahead of him, and she stumbled into the opening, even as he fell to his knees.

Oh, God. God, no.

The cry of rage and despair caught in her throat, however, because in the next instant, she realized he hadn't dropped to the gangway because he'd been shot, but had instead gone to his knees to present less of a target. He crawled up the corrugated steel surface, jaw tight with effort. A moment later, he was safely inside and pushed himself to his feet.

Other than giving her a nod of acknowledgment, though, he basically ignored her, moving past her into the passenger compartment. His keen blue-gray eyes scanned the interior—which, Dhani noticed, was extremely plush and quite large, with a small conversation area toward the rear, in addition to several rows of more conventional seats. Then Landon nodded, and went over to one of those seats. Resting on it were several high-powered pulse pistols, along with half a dozen battery packs. Clearly, Milo had been prepping for a trip where he'd have to be well-armed.

Landon picked up two of the pistols, then tucked one into his belt. "I think I'd better give your friend some backup. That way, he can concentrate on getting us out of here."

She nodded. "Sounds like a great idea. I can't wait to get off this goddamn planet."

His eyes narrowed slightly at her words, but he didn't comment. Instead, he went forward toward the cockpit and the other exterior door.

Dhani took the one pistol that remained, checked the charge, and followed her companion. Her heart was beating faster than she would have liked, but she made herself stick close to Landon, hoping that the luck which had helped them escape the ruin of Eustis' dining chamber would hold. At least it seemed as though the ship was taking the stray pulse bolts in stride; while the commandos' sidearms were certainly sufficient to take down most living beings, they didn't have quite the firepower necessary to pierce a spaceship's hull.

Landon paused to one side of the open access door, flattening himself against the wall. He seemed to gather himself, then leaned out so he could get off a couple of shots at the attacking commandos.

From her own position, Dhani couldn't see whether his attack had had any effect. However, a second later, Milo called out, "Nice shooting, Tex! Thanks for the backup."

"No problem," Landon replied, and swiveled again, firing a series of rapid pulse bolts. This time, the amount of return fire seemed to be reduced by at least half, which meant that several of those bolts must have hit their mark.

For a second, Dhani felt only relief. Then she realized what the reduction in return fire also meant.

Landon had fired on fellow GDF soldiers. Up until this point, he might have possessed some plausible deniability when it came to defending his actions since fleeing Zeta Tau station, but she didn't see how he could possibly explain shooting down members of his very own service. Yes, maybe he could say it was all Milo, but she guessed that Landon wouldn't do such a thing. He seemed far too honorable for that.

Which meant…he'd been willing to make that sacrifice for her. The rush of gratitude that followed was tinged with shame, however. She honestly didn't know whether she was worth that kind of sacrifice.

Nothing she could do about it now. Her hand tightened on the rubber grip of the pulse pistol she held. She'd make sure she would do whatever she could to help Landon survive this.

Then he swore, and, despite knowing that she should hang back, that getting herself shot would be poor repayment for his service to her, Dhani couldn't help moving forward so she could see what had made him lose control.

The sight that greeted her eyes made her want to curse as well. Milo lay sprawled on the gangway, pulse pistol still clutched in his hand. Thankfully, his eyes were closed, weren't staring at her in a sort of baffled agony the way Eustis' had been, but the smoking hole in the pilot's chest was enough to tell her that he wouldn't be flying them anywhere.

A bolt of green energy flew over her head, impacting against the ship's hull just above the open door. "Get back!" Landon shouted. "Go close the other door. We're leaving."

She knew better than to argue. Transferring the pistol she held to her other hand, she hurried into the passenger compartment, then ran to the door so she could work the controls to retract the gangway and seal the hatch. Luckily, the ship was new and in perfect order, and the gangway was tucked into its receptacle and the door shut and sealed within seconds.

Landon must have done the same thing at the forward door, because when she came back, she saw it was already sealed as well, and he was buckling himself into the pilot's chair. She took the co-pilot's seat and fastened the harness.

"Can you fly this thing?"

"In theory," he said. "It's even more advanced than the ship we took from Zeta Tau, but the controls aren't that much different."

His long, strong fingers flew over the console, flipping switches, touching the heads-up screen. Beneath her, Dhani could feel the ship come to life, the powerful engines coming online. More pulse fire splatted against the forward viewing screens, but small arms fire couldn't do much against their shields. Several more commandos came to the launch pad and commenced firing as well. Accompanying them was Colonel Owens. His mouth moved as he shouted orders, but of course she couldn't hear him from inside the cockpit.

Thank God.

Even so, she found herself burrowing into the luxurious leather seat, trying to make herself smaller. Could the colonel see inside, see her sitting there? She had to pray he couldn't.

Occupied as he was, Landon shot her a quick

speculative glance, right before he flicked the switches to engage the in-system pulse engines. At once the ship shot upward, the commandos scattering in an attempt to avoid getting hit by a super-heated blast from the powerful motors. One last glimpse of Colonel Owens, his saturnine face twisted by a scowl, before they were up and away, the twilight-tinted clouds surrounding them.

Dhani watched as the clouds disappeared, giving way to the blackness of space. Off to one side, the sun glowed bluish-white. She'd been clutching the armrests of her seat, worried that they'd escape the troops on the planet's surface only to run straight into a GDF cruiser once they were in orbit, but the star-speckled heavens around them appeared empty.

For a long moment, neither of them spoke. Landon worked the controls, clearly getting them set up for a subspace jump. At last he said, "I'm sorry."

"It's all right," she replied. Stupid response. Of course it wasn't all right. She didn't know when it would be, either. Maybe at some point they'd come out on the other side of all this, but the game had turned deadly, and she didn't know what to do. She unbuckled the harness. "I need to get some water."

"Of course. We'll be going to subspace in a few minutes, though, so be ready for the jolt."

"I will."

She turned away then, not wanting to see the concern in his eyes. Moving slowly, she went through the passenger compartment, on into the galley. The refrigeration unit there had pouches of purified water. She popped the tab on one, took a long swallow. It didn't do much to heal the gnawing ache inside her, but at least now her throat didn't feel quite so tight and dry.

Pouch of water clutched in one hand, she went back to the passenger compartment and sat down on the compact sofa in the conversation area. Drank some more water. Felt the tug of the ship transferring over to its subspace drive, dropping out of the real universe so they could hurtle to their destination at speeds barely comprehensible to the human mind.

Dhani realized that she hadn't even asked Landon where they were going.

But then, what did it matter?

# CHAPTER NINE

LANDON LINGERED IN THE COCKPIT FOR A FEW minutes, making sure that everything was operating normally. Of course it was; he had a feeling the ship could handle pretty much anything the universe cared to throw at it. As it was, he'd quickly realized that they had no reason to jump from world to world any longer. This state-of-the-art vessel could hurl them to the edge of the civilized galaxy in less than a standard day. Although he hadn't seen the ship that brought Colonel Owens and his commandos to Nelos, Landon guessed it couldn't be anywhere near as fast as this one.

Owens. It worried Landon more than he wanted to admit that the colonel had managed to track him and Dhani down so easily. That had to be the hunter in him, the cold patience that allowed him to spend hours and hours following his chosen prey. His ruthlessness had stood him in good stead in the GDF, but it also meant he would never give up. Maybe they'd given him the slip…maybe not.

And what bothered Landon even more than that was the fear he'd seen in Dhani's dark eyes as the colonel confronted her. It hadn't been the impersonal fear an escaped prisoner might show toward any authority figure, either—there had been real dread in her face, an emotion she hadn't been able to hide.

So what was going on there? As far as he knew, Landon didn't think the colonel had had any interactions with Dhani Warlow. Certainly, there was no record of him interrogating her.

A frown pulling at his brow, he undid the safety harness he wore and got up from his seat. Now that the ship was safely in subspace, he didn't need to remain in the cockpit. If the impossible happened and something did go wrong, an alarm would immediately alert him.

After straightening his uniform jacket, he headed aft to the passenger compartment. Dhani sat huddled in a corner of the couch there, a half-drunk pouch of water on the low table in front of her. Even from where he stood, he could see the slump of her shoulders, the downcast expression on her face. Grief over losing her former lover and his compatriot…or something else?

For a moment, Landon hesitated. He wanted to sit down next to her, possibly reach out to offer her comfort by touching her hand, or her arm…but what if she had no desire for such contact? There was a very good chance she would see such a gesture as an unwanted intrusion.

A compromise, then. He would sit on the couch, but make no effort to reach out to her. If she needed comfort, he would be there for her, but she would have to make that decision.

He settled himself next to her, although not too close. Tone neutral, he said, "We're on our way to Iradia. The nav-computer estimates we should arrive there in approximately fourteen standard hours."

A wan smile touched her lips. "That's fast."

"Yes."

Another silence. She ran her hands over the dirt-smeared skirt of her gown, pulling the silky fabric taut over her knees. Landon realized then that she had nothing to change into, for of course what little luggage they possessed had been left behind on Nelos. Well, they would be able to find something for her once they got to Iradia, assuming they came up with a solution for their cash-flow problems before then.

"I'm sorry about Eustis, and Milo," he said quietly. "That shouldn't have happened. I had no idea Colonel Owens would be able to track us so effectively."

There it was again—that tightening of her lips, even as an echo of fear showed in her eyes. She smoothed the fabric of her dress again, as though she didn't know what else to do with her hands. However, she didn't speak.

Should he leave it alone? Perhaps that was the better strategy. And yet…that flicker of fear made him both worried and angry. She was hiding something. Landon was almost sure of it.

The words came slowly, stumbling as he tried to come up with the best way to pose the question. "Dhani…is there something you want to tell me about Colonel Owens?"

Her fingers knotted together. Then she shifted on the couch, her eyes meeting his squarely. Despite the way she faced him, he still couldn't get a read on her emotions. Her tone almost as neutral as her expression, she said, "Why would you ask me that?"

"I couldn't help but notice the way you reacted when confronted by him."

She was quiet again for a moment. "He…." And then she stopped, as though she, too, couldn't find the right words.

Landon's veins seemed to go icy cold. He hated to even allow the thought to cross his mind, but how he could do anything else, what with the way Dhani was acting now? "He didn't…."

A bitter smile touched her full lips. "He didn't force himself on me, if that's what you're asking."

Hearing the words stated so boldly only seemed to make matters worse. Landon didn't respond for a moment. Then he said, "Well, that's a relief."

"Is it?" Her shoulders lifted, pale and slender under the flimsy straps of her borrowed gown. "I'm pretty sure that was what he was leading up to. He just hadn't gotten there yet."

Hot anger flared in Landon then, replacing the chill that had flooded through his limbs only a moment earlier. "What are you saying?"

"Someone like Owens...I think he got off on the threat of the act just as much as the act itself. He came to my cell a few times. Of course, the guards looked the other way. Then he had me brought to the interrogation chamber. I didn't have any real information to give him, but that wasn't the point. He just wanted to toy with me, let me know exactly what he had planned for me, once he decided the time was right. Nothing had happened yet, though. Not really." Her eyes shut for a moment, her lashes thick and dark against her pale cheeks. "He liked to put his hand here"—she reached up to touch the back of her neck — "and caress me. Or at least, his version of a caress. I could feel the way his fingers tightened on my skin. He wanted me to know that he could snap my neck if he wanted to. Like I said, he took pleasure in the threat. He enjoyed it...you know, the fear."

Dhani recited these horrors in a flat, calm voice, as though speaking of events that had happened to someone else. Landon's hands clenched themselves into fists, but he made himself sit still. Somehow he knew if he tried to reach out to her, she would only draw away. "I didn't know," he murmured.

"Of course you didn't," she said. Her face was calm, blank, probably because she thought that if she let one betraying emotion slip out, she would lose all her control. "No one did. That was the whole point. Now, I don't have such a high impression of myself that I think the colonel is chasing us only because of me. I'm sure he's just as motivated to get the traitor Captain Beck. But if he manages to capture me as well...." A shrug. "That's just icing on the cake, isn't it?"

A certain anger lanced through him at Dhani's use of the word "traitor," but Landon realized he had to own it now. He had helped a criminal escape custody. He had lied. He had shot at fellow GDF personnel. If those weren't the actions of a traitor, he didn't know what else qualified. "I won't let that happen."

"I know you believe that." She pulled in a breath, plucked at the dust-smeared fabric that covered her knees. "I *want* to believe it. I just don't know if I can."

Landon opened his mouth to protest, then stopped himself. How could he argue with her when he couldn't say for certain that she was wrong? They had been lucky so far—if you could call getting a couple of innocent bystanders killed "lucky." He still didn't know how Colonel Owens had managed to catch up with him and Dhani on Nelos. True, all ships had their own distinctive signatures and transponder codes, and so he supposed those could have led their pursuers to them. It was easy enough to believe that Governor Janning or one of his staff had supplied those codes to Owens. Why wouldn't they? It was clear enough that everyone on Ordon was still loyal to the Consortium.

However, Landon very much doubted that the colonel had access to the codes belonging to the ship that he and Dhani had taken from Eustis Penn's compound. Possibly Consortium hackers would be able to get that data at some point, although Penn wouldn't have made it easy for them. And by the time they were able to access the *Persephone's* transponder codes, Landon and Dhani would be long gone. They could sell this ship, get something less conspicuous, a vessel whose codes had been altered. Iradia would be a good place to procure such a ship, even though Landon was forced to admit to himself that Owens might be thinking the same thing, and would be headed there as well.

There wasn't much Landon could do about that. His only comfort lay in the belief that the colonel didn't have access to a ship faster than this one. As long as the transaction was handled quickly, they still might be able to pull this off.

"Hey," Dhani said, laying a hand on his. Landon didn't quite startle, although he couldn't help being surprised that she would reach out to him in such a way…especially after everything she'd revealed about

Colonel Owens. "I don't blame you. I mean, it's just the two of us in a stolen ship, while Owens can come after us with a good deal of firepower. You've done amazing things so far, but you're not a miracle worker."

"No," Landon replied. He didn't want to move, because he feared that any shift in his position might signal Dhani that he wanted her to remove her hand, and that couldn't be further from the truth. Her fingers were warm and soft, the nails still coated with a pale iridescent polish. She must have gotten them done right before she was captured; while he had to admit he didn't know all that much about women's grooming, he did know that such things could now last a month, or more. "I'm definitely not a miracle worker. But this is a fast ship. I don't know if they can catch up with us or not. I was thinking we should sell it when we get to Iradia, buy something more modest. That would give us some spare cash. The real problem will be getting someone to buy it when we don't have any of the paperwork."

For a second, Dhani just stared at him, her expression blank. Then she lifted her hand from his and put it to her mouth, as though trying to hold back laughter. He gazed at her, wondering what in the world could be so funny.

"I'm sorry," she said, and although her voice had a certain breathless quality, at least she wasn't laughing outright. "It's just—you really think anyone on Iradia is going to care about papers? They'll take the ship, no questions asked. Only you might want to have me handle the negotiations."

He supposed he should have thought of that. So much of his life had been spent following rules and regulations, everything on the straight and narrow, that he hadn't stopped to consider how most of the people they'd be dealing with on Iradia couldn't care less about a ship's registration. Especially now, with multiple planets in open rebellion, and Iradia itself already announcing that it had left the Consortium. And he knew he had to take Dhani's point about her being the better negotiator to heart. Wounded masculine pride certainly wouldn't help them here.

"Very well," he said. "I suppose I must bow to your superior experience in that particular area. But if Iradia is so lawless, then what's to prevent someone there from simply stealing this ship and leaving us with nothing?"

"Not much," she admitted. "Our best move is to find someone who's shady but not completely without morals. In the meantime, though, we might as well search the ship. If I know Eustis, he probably left a few goodies behind."

She got up from the couch, and, with some reluctance, Landon followed suit. He'd liked sitting next to her on the couch, enjoyed the feeling of closeness, even though they hadn't done much more than touch one another for reassurance…briefly.

It was a start, however. All he could do was hope they'd be able to build on that beginning.

---

Dhani was all too aware of Landon following her back to the sleeping compartment. He was silent, apparently content to let her perform the search, since she knew Eustis much better than he did, but that silence didn't erase the reality of his tall form less than a foot away from her, or the crazy way she could still feel the pressure of his hand on hers.

It had felt good. His fingers were strong and lean, just like the rest of him. Part of her wished she'd moved in closer to him, had tried to place her head on his shoulder. She could have used the comfort right then. Two people she'd known, their lives snuffed out in seconds. She hoped that at some point she'd be able to come to terms with that terrible reality, could allow herself some measure of grief. For right now, though, she had much bigger problems to face.

She'd been with Eustis about five standard months, long enough to have traveled with him. Not on this ship; she could tell it was a very recent acquisition. However, she had a feeling he'd already made sure it was well-stocked…unless the supplies intended for this particular vessel were still sitting on the landing pad back on Nelos.

The ship had three cabins, and a well-equipped

bathroom. Dhani went into the largest bedroom first, since she knew that was the one Eustis would have taken for his own use. The wardrobe there had a biometric lock on it, but it hadn't been engaged. Possibly because Milo had been in the middle of loading in supplies? She couldn't really think why else, but she supposed it didn't matter now.

In the wardrobe were clean clothes: shirts and trousers and a few high-necked jackets. Eustis and Landon were roughly the same size, so those items should do to replace the clothing he currently wore. It was probably better not to appear on Iradia in the uniform of a GDF officer. Too much to hope that there would be anything suitable for her, although she supposed she could take one of the shirts and belt the trousers as best she could. Nothing could be done about the ridiculous high heels she had on, but once they sold the ship, they should have some extra cash for new shoes and clothes.

Unless....

"Here," she said, pulling one of the shirts and a pair of trousers from the wardrobe, and handing them to Landon. "See if these fit. That uniform is just a little conspicuous."

For a second he looked startled, but then he nodded. "You're right, of course. But what about you?"

"I'll figure something out."

He began to open his mouth, as if he meant to say

something. Instead, he shrugged and went back out into the hallway. A moment later, Dhani heard the door to the bathroom slide shut.

Good. She grabbed another of the shirts and laid it on the bed. Working quickly, she pulled her gown over her head and dropped it to the floor, and then slipped on the shirt and buttoned it up. The thing was so long that it hung halfway to her knees. Maybe she didn't need trousers after all. No, that was a bad idea. Although she didn't want to admit that she wouldn't exactly mind if Landon Beck ogled her legs, she also thought a shirt with only panties on under it wasn't exactly the best attire for sandy, windblown Iradia, no matter how hot it might be.

The trousers were so big, they slipped down to her ankles even after she'd buttoned them. Great. A quick search of the drawers in the room's one dresser provided a single belt. Well, she'd have to hope that the pants she'd given Landon were close enough to his correct size that he wouldn't have to worry about them sliding down. Or maybe he had a belt of his own. His uniform jacket was long enough that it hid exactly what was going on beneath it.

Hmm…probably better not to think about that for too long.

She'd just finished rolling up the pants' legs when Landon reappeared. As she'd hoped, his borrowed clothing fit him much better than the ensemble she'd put together for herself. In fact, the lightweight open-necked shirt and slim trousers did a very good job of showing off what the heavy uniform had hidden—the way the sleeves strained against his biceps, and how the pants seemed to mold themselves to his thighs.

After realizing that she was staring, she cleared her throat. "Looks like those clothes will work just fine."

"I suppose," Landon said, plucking at one sleeve of his shirt with what appeared to be distaste. Was that because he didn't like the idea of wearing Eustis' clothes, or simply because he wasn't used to being quite so much on display?

Dhani thought it would probably be prudent not to make any further comments on his appearance. "I was hoping that Eustis had a safe in here. Can you help me look?"

Appearing relieved that she'd changed the subject, Landon nodded. "Of course."

He went to the wardrobe and checked the top shelf, then pushed the clothing aside to see if the safe might have been hidden at the back. This search proved fruitless almost at once. "Did you look in the dresser?"

"Yes. That's where I found the belt. I didn't see anything like a safe, though."

Rubbing at his chin, he nodded, then went over to the wall next to the dresser, running his hands over the smooth composite. From where she stood, Dhani couldn't see any visible cracks in the surface, but she supposed that was the whole point.

"I'll go check the other bedrooms." It didn't seem likely to her that Eustis would keep his valuables in a room other than the one where he intended to sleep, but then again, he might have hidden the safe elsewhere simply because any intruders would assume he would have that safe close at hand.

"All right."

She went across the corridor and into the first of the secondary cabins. It was small but still luxurious, with a real bed and an elegant stand made of pale blue Eridani *likka*-wood next to it. The table's single drawer proved to be empty, and so was the wardrobe that stood against the wall opposite the bed. Imitating Landon, she ran her hands over the interior of the wardrobe but didn't find anything.

Just to be sure, she went down on her knees—glad that she'd changed out of that damn dress—and peered under the bed. Nothing there, either, only a shining floor made out of the same composite material as the walls.

Fine. As she left the cabin, Landon appeared in the doorway of the main stateroom. "Did you find anything?"

"No," she said, hoping she didn't sound as exasperated as she felt. "Maybe all his valuables got left behind on Nelos."

"Maybe. But there's still the third bedroom, and the bathroom."

True. "I'll take the bathroom, and you can look in the bedroom."

"Of course."

Dhani couldn't help lingering in the corridor for a moment, just so she could watch him walk into the remaining cabin. Damn, those pants looked good on him.

And then she wanted to scold herself for entertaining those kinds of thoughts when the real owner of those trousers was lying dead in his own dining room. She somehow doubted that Colonel Owens would do the decent thing and have the body properly disposed of. Or maybe he would. Eustis had family, a fairly wealthy family with mining interests in Gaia's asteroid belt. Pretty bad optics to be involved in the killing of someone like that and not at least try to do the right thing.

Dhani paused there, wondering why she hadn't yet wept over Eustis. Simply no opportunity, or something else? She wouldn't lie to herself; she'd never truly loved him, had only been caught up by his bright, biting intelligence and good looks. But still, she should be able to mourn him, even if she hadn't loved him. However, all she felt now was a certain sort of abstract sorrow, overlaid by guilt that, if it hadn't been for her involvement, he'd be alive now rather than slumped on the floor of his dining room.

No, it wasn't her fault. She hadn't killed Eustis. That murder lay squarely on Colonel Owens' head, even if it had been one of his commandos who'd fired the fatal shot.

Maybe one day that sick bastard would finally pay for everything he'd done.

In the meantime, she and Landon had to survive. Mouth grim, Dhani went into the bathroom, opened the storage cabinet. Nothing there except a medi-kit, toothpaste, a set of sonic toothbrushes and some mouthwash. Well, at least she wouldn't have to sleep with gritty teeth…assuming, of course, that she'd even be given the opportunity. She couldn't remember the last time she'd really slept, but she didn't think she was going to feel much like sleeping until she and Landon got someplace where they were truly safe.

And she kind of doubted that place would be Iradia.

Fighting back a sigh, she closed the door to the storage cabinet, then crossed her arms and looked around. The shower stall was larger than most you might find on a starship, but she was fairly sure Eustis wouldn't have his safe hidden in there, since you couldn't count on the moisture not shorting out the electronics, given enough time. The sink was simply a metal basin jutting out from the wall, with no storage space underneath it at all. Above the sink hung a small round mirror, probably made of shatterproof glass.

As Dhani stared at it—trying her best to ignore her own reflection, which looked pale and pinched and tired—she realized the mirror wasn't entirely flush to the wall. In fact, it stuck out more than half an inch.

Hmm.

She went to it and began feeling around the edges. Sure enough, when she got to what would have been the three o'clock position on a clock, she detected a depression in the metal. She pressed on it, and the mirror swung outward on a hidden spring. In the wall behind it was an opening about a foot wide, and inside that opening sat a small square safe.

Her relief was short-lived, however, because in the next instant, Dhani realized the safe was locked up and armed, a tiny red light blinking to show that the keypad had been activated.

Damn.

"You found something?" came Landon's voice, and she looked up to see him standing out in the corridor, expression curious.

"Yes. The safe is in here. Unfortunately, it's locked, and I have absolutely no idea what the combination might be."

A frown pulled at his brows. He came closer, and she had to will herself to stay where she was, to not let her heart begin to beat a little faster at his proximity. It was absolutely ridiculous, the way she reacted to him. Oh, she wouldn't deny that he was good-looking, but there was something more to it than that. She'd been around plenty of handsome men in her life, and none of them had made her feel somehow breathless and tingly, as if she was some silly girl back in school who'd never been kissed.

It had been a *very* long time since Dhani's first kiss.

"How well did you know Eustis?" Landon asked.

A neutral enough question, but for some reason it made the blood flare to her cheeks. She really didn't like having to discuss her past with the hacker, not with the man who was currently sending her gauges into the red.

"How well does anybody know anyone?" she returned. "We were together for a few months. We did some traveling."

"In this ship?"

"No, a different one. This ship is newer."

Landon frowned slightly at that reply, although she couldn't tell whether his disapproval stemmed from such displays of reckless consumption, or because he'd hoped she would be familiar enough with the ship that she'd have some idea as to the lock's code. There was a joke. Eustis might have liked her enough to take her to bed, but he sure as hell would never confessed such sensitive information to her.

"Well, let's try the obvious," Landon said. "His birthday?"

"Eustis never did anything obvious," she told him. "His whole reason for being was kind of the opposite of obvious."

"Your birthday?"

Sweet notion, but she shook her head. "He wasn't the sentimental type, either."

"Try it anyway."

"I'm not sure that's a good idea. A lot of safes like this, if you input the wrong combination too many times in a row, it locks down completely, and only the manufacturer can open it."

Another frown. "How many digits in the code?"

Dhani shoved a lock of hair behind one ear. "This model? Eight."

Landon went silent then, one abstracted hand rubbing at his chin. That seemed to be his usual response when he was trying to puzzle through some-thing. His blue eyes were intent on the safe, but she noticed how he didn't reach out to touch it, as though he was worried that even a single careless brush of a finger against its surface might be enough to somehow lock it down.

"Where was Eustis born?"

Why did that matter? But since she could tell that Landon wasn't joking, she said, "On Gaia. Umm... the East Coast sprawl, although he was always careful to say his family had been in Philadelphia for centuries."

"Philadelphia. Good." Landon retrieved his hand-held from his pocket and began running his fingers over the screen. "Try this: thirty-nine, ninety-five, seventy-five, sixteen."

"What is that?"

"The latitude and longitude for Philadelphia, on Gaia."

All right, that was a little more obscure. Although she knew most people could get at that data if they really wanted to, she knew that in general, Eustis didn't go around advertising where he'd been born. He'd spoken of it to her—more to brag about his lineage than anything else, she was fairly certain—but it wasn't exactly common knowledge.

Not quite holding her breath, she typed out the sequence of numbers on the safe's keypad. Nothing at first, and then the little red light flashed angrily, accompanied by a piercing beeping sound.

"Well, that wasn't it," she said. "I don't know how many tries we have left. Probably just two."

Landon ran a hand through his hair. It was thick, and whatever product he might have used to control it seemed to be failing, because a heavy lock fell forward over his forehead despite his best efforts. Right then, Dhani wanted to reach out and push his hair back, feel for herself how soft it was, but she somehow managed to control herself.

"All right…where were *you* born?"

"Me?" she said, startled by the question.

"Yes, you."

She smiled and shook her head. "Look, Landon, I appreciate the thought, but, just for the record, it's not like Eustis and I had a love for the ages or something. I'm not someone who would inspire the code for the safe on his new ship."

"Possibly." Landon shrugged, then went on, "Maybe it's precisely because you were not that important to him that he would use such data to set the code."

Dhani wanted to flinch at the phrase "not that important," but she knew he hadn't said it to be hurtful. He'd only been trying to point out that she might be looking at this the wrong way. "All right," she said, trying not to sigh. "Chicago. That is, Chicago on Gaia, not New Chicago."

His head tilted slightly. "That not what your records say."

"You saw those?"

"Well, I—"

She lifted a hand. Of course he'd seen her records. He'd been adjutant to the freak who ran Zeta Tau, which meant he'd probably been charged with perusing the personal information of everyone detained there. "I had those doctored. Another hacker 'friend,' way back in the day. I thought it sounded better to be from London." At the time, she'd been running from her past, running from the darkness in the Windy City's streets. Yes, there were parts of Chicago that glittered and gleamed and attracted the wealthy from all over Gaia—and the Consortium itself—but she sure as hell wasn't from any of the sleek high-rises that clustered around the shores of Lake Michigan. "But I did end up telling Eustis the truth."

A pause. Dhani waited for the inevitable questions, and wondered whether she'd tell Landon the truth as well, or whether she'd give him yet another in a long series of facile lies. But then he said, "Chicago, it is," and made the entry on his handheld.

When he repeated the numbers to her, she wanted to protest, to tell him this wouldn't work, either, and that if they screwed up yet another time, the safe would lock them out. But then, what difference would that make in the long run? They couldn't get in now anyway.

However, after Dhani entered the final digit, the little light turned green, and the door swung open. One corner of Landon's mouth lifted, and he said, "What was that about not being important enough?"

"Nothing." She reached inside the safe and pulled out several credit vouchers, as well as actual currency, the shining coins preferred by the free traders and settlers who inhabited the outer systems, the ones who didn't quite trust Gaian banks. They'd have to scan the credit vouchers to see how much each one of them carried, but the currency alone would be enough to get her and Landon accommodations on Iradia, and food and more clothing, no matter how loaded those credit vouchers might be. Knowing Eustis, though, they probably represented a decent chunk of change.

Inside the safe was also an old-fashioned metal

key. She removed it as well and held it up, frowning at the unexpected item. "I wonder what this was for."

"I don't have any idea. Something else hidden on the ship?"

"Possibly. There's still the cargo area below us, although this ship doesn't look as if it was built to carry that much."

She handed the key to Landon, forcing herself not to react as his fingers brushed against hers. Which again was crazy. It wasn't as though they hadn't just touched a half hour earlier.

He frowned at the key. "I haven't seen anything up here in the passenger area that would open with something like this. So I suppose we should go down and inspect the cargo area."

"All right." Dhani didn't like that idea very much, but she knew her reluctance stemmed mainly from a childish phobia of dark, enclosed spaces. Anyway, she wouldn't have to go down there by herself. At least, she hoped she wouldn't. "It's okay to just leave the ship on autopilot, so to speak?"

"We'll only be down a level. Any alarms will sound down there as well. Not that I'm expecting anything untoward to happen."

She'd have to take his words at face value. Anyway, she'd traveled countless light-years herself, moving from system to system, and in ships as small as this one. Interstellar accidents were exceedingly rare. She didn't know why she was feeling so jittery. Was it only that the ship they were now traveling in belonged to a dead man? Or was it the thought that Colonel Owens might still be only a few steps behind them?

Pushing that thought aside, she pulled in a breath and said, "All right. Let's take a look."

# CHAPTER TEN

DHANI SEEMED NERVOUS, ALTHOUGH LANDON could tell she was doing her best to hide her unease. What precisely had set her off, he wasn't certain. Was she trying to grapple with the idea that perhaps she'd meant more to Eustis Penn than she'd thought?

Or possibly precisely the reverse....

The interior hatch for the cargo section was located just a few feet away from the bathroom. Landon released the locks, then raised the door. As soon as it was open, lights blinked on in the shadowy chamber beneath. Yes, this was a good ship. Even minor details appeared to have been attended to with care.

"I'll go first," he said. Not that he really expected to find anything dangerous down there, but he hoped that by venturing into unknown territory first, he might help to put Dhani's mind at ease.

She didn't seem inclined to argue, and only said, "All right."

He put his feet on the top rung of the metal ladder and carefully lowered himself. Once he got to the floor of the cargo hold, he took a quick glance around but didn't see anything terribly suspicious—several crates like the ones that had been left behind on Nelos, a fire extinguisher bolted to one wall, a large metal tool chest fastened to another.

"It's fine," he called up the ladder. "You can come down."

A few seconds later, Dhani began to climb down the ladder, going slowly because of the heels she was wearing. Too bad the ship hadn't been carrying a true change of clothing for her, although she'd been fairly clever in making do with some of Eustis Penn's spare clothes. When she got to the bottom of the ladder, she came toward Landon, even as her own gaze swept the interior of the cargo hold.

"I don't see much of anything," she said.

"We haven't checked in those crates yet," he pointed out.

"True, but none of them look as though they'd need a key like the one we found."

He had to concede that point. "Well, let's take a look around."

Dhani still had that dubious expression on her face. Whatever misgivings she might be entertaining, though, she appeared to ignore them as she moved past him and then around a bulkhead. "Just more crates back here," she called out.

It was entirely possible that the key went to a safe or room or something back on Gaia. After all, Dhani had said that Penn came from a very old family. Perhaps the key belonged to one of his family's properties, and he had it for safekeeping.

However, that particular theory died a quick death as Landon moved in the opposite direction from his companion, past the aft bulkhead. Tucked away in a corner was an enormous wooden wardrobe with intricate carvings at both its head and foot. In its doors were keyholes that appeared to be matches to the key he carried.

"Dhani?" he called out.

Quick footsteps, and she was at his side in only a few seconds. Dark eyes sparkling with curiosity, she said, "Do you think the key goes to that wardrobe?"

"There's only one way to find out," he replied. "Do you want to do the honors, or shall I?"

"I'll do it." She went up to the huge cabinet, so incongruously out of place in the bowels of this modern ship, and inserted the key in the lock, turned it. At once both doors swung outward.

Landon wasn't sure what he'd been expecting to see in there—more clothing? fine liquors? artwork? All he knew was that he certainly hadn't thought he would see what now met his eyes.

A row of gleaming pulse rifles, with some kind of

pulse grenade launchers mounted to them. They were much smaller than any he had previously seen, which meant they were probably easier to use and less tiring to carry for long periods of time. Experimental? Most likely. That would explain why there were only an even dozen of them. On the floor of the wardrobe were several metal boxes, probably spare battery packs.

Dhani let out a whistle. "Oh, Eustis, you sneaky bastard."

"I don't understand," Landon said. "If he wanted to smuggle guns, then why all those packing cases? Surely he could have fit more weapons in those."

"Yes," she replied, "but they would have been subject to search. Eustis hid these guns in what has to be a family antique. The Antiquities Decrees would have prevented any forced inspections. No damage to items more than five hundred years old, remember? I'm not saying that an over-zealous customs inspector might not have tried to break inside, but he or she would have been opening themselves up to a very expensive lawsuit on behalf of the Penn family."

"And an inspector would have searched the cases first, and found nothing incriminating." Landon arched an eyebrow at her. "Perhaps we should take a look at one of those, too."

"You read my mind."

She headed back to one of the cases, pressed the button to activate the electronic latch. At once the lid opened, revealing what appeared to be electronics and computer components, all carefully wrapped in anti-static plastic.

"The sort of thing anyone would have expected him to be carrying, since he always passed himself off as a freelance computing specialist. Actually," she added with a shrug, "I guess that's what he really was. He just tended to explore the less legal aspects of the profession."

"Who would he be delivering the guns to?"

That question earned Landon a sideways look, as though, even after everything they'd been through together, she still didn't quite trust him when it came to topics involving the insurgency, or the people allied with them. Then she gave a small shake of her head. "To be honest? I have no idea. I mean, clearly he wasn't taking them to the nearest Consortium garrison, but my best guess is that he was acting as an intermediary, covering up the transport of the weapons by visiting someone he'd known for a long time, having them handle the final delivery. Eustis really didn't like getting his hands dirty. Also, that way he had a better crack at plausible deniability if he did happen to get caught with illegal firearms in his possession."

That all made sense. Landon supposed he shouldn't be terribly surprised that Dhani didn't know anything more than what she'd just told him; by her own admission, and according to the records he'd glimpsed at Zeta Tau station, she hadn't been anywhere near Nelos or Eustis Penn for some time. Anyway, it didn't really matter now. Whoever had been expecting those weapons was going to be sorely disappointed.

"This appears to solve the mystery of the key we found," he said. "Not that I'm feeling terribly excited about having contraband in the hold."

That remark only made Dhani grin. "Oh, come on, Landon—we're headed to Iradia. That's probably the easiest planet in the galaxy to unload contraband. You can leave it to me."

By this point, he supposed he shouldn't be surprised by anything she said, and yet he couldn't help lifting an eyebrow at her. "Leave it to you? You have experience in arms dealing?"

"Well, I don't *personally*...but I've dated people who did."

Of course she had. Landon forced himself not to respond, except to shrug. "We can get that sorted out once we reach Iradia. For now, though, it's probably best if you try to sleep a little. We're now less than twelve hours out."

She planted her hands on her hips and shot him a disbelieving glance. "You really expect me to sleep?"

"Yes, I do. The beds in the staterooms looked comfortable enough."

As soon as those words left his mouth, he wondered if he should have kept silent. He certainly didn't want Dhani to think he was suggesting anything untoward…even if some part of him that he didn't quite want to acknowledge thought it wouldn't be so bad to try out one of those beds with her.

However, she didn't look offended…or amused, either. Instead, she frowned slightly, then said, "I'd rather stay in the cockpit with you. The co-pilot's seat is pretty comfy."

"I don't think that's necessary—"

"I don't care if it's necessary or not," she cut in. "I'd rather not be separated. Just in case."

From the way her jaw set, Landon could tell that she wasn't going to budge on this. Fine. He really didn't think it all that important where she slept, just as long as she managed to get some rest. And, after everything they'd experienced over the past few days, he could see why she wouldn't want to be alone. She needed the reassurance of another human being, even if that human being happened to be an officer of the very government that had imprisoned her.

Was he, though? For all he knew, Colonel Owens had already drawn up the paperwork to begin court martial proceedings. Of course, considering the general chaos that currently reigned in the galaxy, he might have a hard time getting anyone to follow up on such indictments.

Something to worry about later. At the very least, Landon doubted there would be anyone on Iradia who was in a position to pursue such legal proceedings. No, he and Dhani would touch down, resupply, sell the ship, and…

…and then? He really had no idea. He'd only been looking ahead to Iradia, thinking it would be a good place to purchase transport for Dhani, to find someone who wouldn't care about the price on her head as long as the amount paid for her safe passage was higher. Now, though, he didn't want to think about sending her off into the galaxy, to never see her again. He wanted….

Damn it. He supposed it didn't really matter what he wanted.

"Let's get back to the cockpit," he said.

If she noticed any sign of his inner turmoil, she gave no indication of it. After giving him a quick nod, she headed back to the ladder and clambered up, with slightly more grace this time, even though Landon could tell the high heels were giving her trouble. He waited until she had gone all the way up and was back on solid ground, then made the ascent himself.

Without speaking, they headed forward, then took their respective seats in the cockpit. Dhani huddled into the co-pilot's chair, looking very small in her oversized borrowed clothing. She began to shut her eyes, then said, "Promise you'll wake me if anything happens."

"I promise," he replied. "However, I have a feeling that if something does happen, it will be loud enough to wake you all on its own."

She smiled a little at that comment, then shut her eyes and burrowed even further into the seat back.

How beautiful she was, even in that ridiculous shirt, long enough to double for a dress, and even with her hair tousled and falling down from the elaborate up-style she'd worn for their dinner with Eustis Penn. Landon wished he could reach out and touch her cheek, cup her face in his hands and kiss her. He knew better than to try anything like that, however. They'd shared one or two moments of closeness, but certainly nothing to indicate she was ready for that sort of intimacy.

Repressing a sigh, he shifted in his own seat and studied the readouts in front of him. Everything was working as it should, the ship on course with an ETA of 11:22 a.m., Iradia time. He should probably try to sleep as well, but he knew he was still too keyed up, too tense. Anyway, he'd been trained to stay awake for as much as seventy-two standard hours if necessary. Once they had secure lodgings on Iradia…well, perhaps then he'd allow himself to relax.

He pulled out his handheld and the credit voucher, then opened the application that would allow him to read the voucher's current balance. Luckily, such things were untraceable; the app would only tell him how much money the voucher contained, and nothing more. It was only when he tried to tap into it that those on the lookout for such things might be able to track it down. Even then, however, he thought they would be safe enough. A hacker like Eustis Penn would make sure any vouchers he carried were thoroughly scrubbed.

When the display on his handheld flashed the number in question, Landon wanted to rub his eyes and look again, certain that he must have misread it. But no, there were all those digits, telling him that he hadn't been in error.

*10,500,000.*

Yes, he'd guessed that anyone with a home base like Penn's fortress on Nelos must have access to the sorts of funds Landon could only dream about, but he still hadn't thought the hacker would have carried so much money on his person. The downside of having scrubbed vouchers was that, if stolen, those funds could be accessed by anyone. Did Eustis Penn have so much wealth that he could afford to lose more than ten million units at a time?

Apparently so.

With that kind of money on hand, Landon realized they had no need to sell the ship. Well, except that it must still be registered to Penn, but surely Dhani would know something about how to change that. Or at least she would know people who knew something. Or know how to find the sort of people who could erase a ship's transponder codes.

Landon put the handheld and the voucher away, and scrubbed a hand over his face. If asked, he would have said his compensation was more than adequate

—especially since he had very little occasion to spend any of it—and yet the thought of having millions at his disposal was unsettling, to say the least. Never in his life had he had access to that kind of money.

And that ten million was the contents of only one voucher. They'd found three in the safe.

He glanced over at Dhani and saw that she was truly asleep now, eyelashes fluttering slightly as she dreamed, her chest rising and falling with deep, regular breaths. Good. A single night's sleep wouldn't be enough to erase the shock of the two deaths she'd just witnessed, but he hoped she would awake at least slightly refreshed and ready to face whatever awaited them on Iradia.

Too bad he wouldn't be able to say the same for himself. Still, it was probably better for her to be the alert one in that situation, simply because she had far more experience dealing with the underbelly of the galaxy's society than he did. No judgment on her for that; so far she had let slip very little about her past, and yet he couldn't help thinking that something in her early life must have sent her along this path, that fundamentally she was a decent person driven to these lengths by circumstance.

*Or perhaps that's what you want to believe, because thinking such things makes it easier for you to care for her,* he thought. *The last thing you would want to admit is that you've fallen in love with a hardened criminal.*

Then he had to stop himself, because how could he have allowed that thought to cross his mind? Love her? He barely knew her. At the most he would admit that he felt a certain physical attraction to her. It had been a long time since he'd been intimate with a woman, and now, being thrown into close proximity with one who was quite beautiful, it made sense that he would want her. But a very large gap existed between physical desire and love.

Damn. And yet…and yet as he looked over at her again, he couldn't quite prevent the warm sensation that passed over him, an inexplicable tenderness that made him want to take her in his arms and hold her close, and tell her that no matter what happened, he would be there for her.

Not exactly the reaction of a man who simply wished to take a woman to bed.

*She's too young for you,* he told himself. *And you have nothing in common. In the end, it's the sort of relationship that would never work—even if these feelings of yours were reciprocated, which you know they are not.*

That all sounded very sensible, whether or not he truly believed it. Besides, he needed to tear his thoughts away from Dhani Warlow, focus on the planetfall they were due to make in an increasingly short period of time. In a way, it helped that Iradia was so naturally lawless; the people there would already be used to the state of affairs that had now engulfed the galaxy. If he and Dhani arrived and acted as though they owned the place, they would be less likely to encounter any trouble. In a planet filled with predators, it would not do to seem like prey.

Despite thinking that he would stay awake until they reached their destination, Landon found his eyelids drooping, weariness overcoming him. Surely they would be safe enough for a few hours…just enough time for him to reclaim some of his energy.

And then…and then sleep overcame him at last.

Dhani startled awake at the beeping of the nav-computer. Eyes blinking open, she sat upright in the co-pilot's seat and forced herself to focus. No longer were they surrounded by the strange, shifting light of subspace, nor the infinite blackness between systems. Outside the forward view-screen was a sandy orange planet that seemed to grow larger even as she stared at it.

A quick sideways glance told her that Landon was asleep in his own chair, head tilted to one side. He must have really conked out to sleep through the alarm, the one that told them they'd come back into realspace.

"Landon," she said.

His eyelids fluttered for a second, and then his fingers grasped the armrests of his seat as he came awake. The blurriness in his blue eyes disappeared almost at once, and he said, "We're approaching Iradia?"

"If that's it," she replied, pointing to the viewport. In a way, she was surprised by how quickly he had woken up and become focused. Was that a trick they'd taught him at the academy?

He stared through the view-screen and nodded. "Yes." Leaning forward, he touched one of the controls on the comm unit, then frowned. "That's odd. I know that Iradia isn't known for following all the standard protocols, but I thought even they must have some kind of traffic control."

Dhani couldn't really comment on that. She'd racketed around the galaxy a good bit—more than she would have liked, actually—but she'd never been to Iradia. Probably a good thing; at least if she was a stranger here, there was less chance of her running into anyone who might have a grudge.

Or so she hoped.

As she shrugged, Landon went on, "I'll take us down to Aldis Nova. The spaceport there does have a landing beacon at least. And once we get closer, we'll be able to see which landing pads are open."

"And then?"

"Accommodations," he replied, before flicking a quick glance at her. "Clothing and other supplies. Your friend Eustis left us a fortune on his vouchers, so none of that should be a problem. I also think we should hang on to this ship. I find it unlikely that we'll be able to purchase anything better."

For some reason, those words helped to ease a little of the tension currently knotting her neck and shoulders. Until Landon had spoken, she hadn't realized how reluctant she'd been to sell the ship. Maybe it was simply her fear that, once the ship was gone, he would buy her passage on the next vessel leaving the desert world and walk out of her life altogether. However, now he sounded as though he intended for the two of them to stay together. Was he waiting for her to protest, to say that wasn't what they'd planned?

Well, if that was the case, he'd be waiting a long, long time.

"Sounds good," she said cautiously. "We'll need to change the registration, though."

"I know. That's where I was hoping you would come in."

"Me?" Dhani stared at him blankly. His attention appeared to be focused on the complicated bank of controls before them as he guided the ship closer to Iradia, so she couldn't get an accurate read on his expression. "I don't know anything about doctoring a ship's registration."

"Maybe not, but I thought possibly you would know someone...."

"Not on Iradia."

This time he did look up at her. One corner of his mouth lifted in an ironic smile. There was something so endearing about his expression that she wanted nothing more than to lean over and give him a quick kiss. Since she had no idea how he would react to such a gesture, she made herself remain where she was.

"Do you mean to tell me that we've gone halfway across the inhabited galaxy and bumped into 'friends' of yours at every turn, and yet you don't know anyone on Iradia?"

Should she be offended? No. After all, his statement was mostly true, if a slight exaggeration. "I know you seem to think that I've rubbed shoulders with all the galaxy's underground, Landon, but that's not exactly the truth. Anyway, most of my... projects...were predicated on being in respectable venues. It's hard to grift when everyone around you is a grifter, too."

Now the smile would turn to disgust as he realized that she truly was a criminal, wasn't some innocent caught up in the Consortium's net. Better to be honest, though. Why that should seem so important to her now, when a good deal of her adult life had been spent in telling practiced lies, she wasn't sure.

Actually, she knew exactly why. Because this was Landon Beck she was speaking to, and he deserved the truth.

However, although his expression sobered somewhat, she could see nothing of disgust or contempt in it. He appeared almost thoughtful, as if he was turning her words over in his mind, analyzing them carefully. It meant something, to be taken seriously like that. Dhani couldn't remember the last time someone had treated her with such respect.

"I suppose I hadn't thought of it that way," he said. "It makes sense. That does send us back to square one when it comes to Iradia, though."

She stared out at the planet, now a large ochre disk filling almost half the viewport. They should be making planetfall very soon. "To be honest, I'm not sure the ship's registration really matters all that much. If we're coming in on an automated beacon, that means no one's really minding the store, are they? The registration is there to I.D. incoming ships to a planetary government, right?"

"You may be right. I hadn't thought of it that way."

With any luck, her assessment was correct. Their luck had been a shaky thing of late, however. She had a flash of Eustis lying, lifeless, in the floor of his dining room, of Milo sprawled on the ship's gangway. The only luck involved there had been the bad kind. Her past was not the sort to allow much thought of an afterlife or a kindly God, but she hoped those pleasant myths might be true. If she could think of Eustis and Milo as having moved on to a better plane of existence, maybe she wouldn't feel so guilty about dragging them into her mess.

"I guess we'll find out soon enough," she said,

then added, "All the same…it might be a good idea to arm ourselves with a few of those guns we found down in the hold."

Landon stared at her for a moment, then gave a grim nod. As they headed down to gird themselves for whatever might come next, Dhani tried to reassure herself that the guns would only be for show.

And if not…well, at least Landon had proven back on Nelos that he was a good shot. Even so, he was just one man. There was only so much one man could do.

*One man, plus me,* she told herself. *It will be enough.*

It had to be.

## CHAPTER ELEVEN

The heat that greeted them was so intense, opening the hatchway felt like opening the door to a blast furnace. Landon blinked, his eyes watering almost immediately, although he'd appropriated a pair of Eustis Penn's polarized sunglasses from the dresser in the main bedroom. A second pair protected Dhani's eyes, which meant Landon had a hard time reading her expression as she paused at the hatchway opening and gazed out at their new surroundings.

Not that there was much to see. Their ship now rested on a shallow landing pad, its duracrete surface covered by a thin layer of yellow sand. The air seemed to shimmer, dancing with the waves of heat that rose from the ground. All around them were more ships, most of them also lightly dusted with sand. No doubt the sleek outlines of the vessel that had brought him and Dhani here would become blurred as well, if they spent any amount of time on Iradia's surface.

No one had come to greet them—no officious spaceport personnel, not even a local panhandler thinking that someone who had just set down in such a luxurious ship must have ready cash to spare. Before they'd disembarked, he'd reset the biometric scanner at the front hatch so it would open to either his or Dhani's retinal patterns. Luckily, the process was the same for this ship as it had been for the Consortium vessels he'd trained on—and thank God the controls that handled the reset were located inside the ship, rather than outside, where he was sure he would have dropped dead from heat exhaustion during the procedure.

Sweat was already running down his back, pooling in the waistband of his borrowed trousers. He had to hope the moisture wouldn't interfere with the mechanism of the pulse pistol he had tucked there. They had decided that the guns they'd found in the cargo hold were too large and too conspicuous to carry with them, but they still had the pulse pistols they'd used to fight off Colonel Owens' commandos, and Landon had brought one along as a bit of extra insurance.

"This way," he said, leading Dhani down the gangplank and then threading his way through the assembled ships at the spaceport. They'd landed in Aldis Nova, Iradia's largest settlement, since he'd assumed that would be the easiest place to find transport for the young woman who trotted along at his side, teetering slightly on her high heels.

Now, of course, he had no wish to get that transport for her. However, he would do so, if that was what she wanted. He just didn't want to admit to himself how much he hoped she wouldn't want to leave him in order to seek her own fate elsewhere in the galaxy.

First things first. His handheld had indicated that the oldest and most respectable hotel in Aldis Nova was a walk of some five minutes from the spaceport. At the time he'd looked up that bit of information, a five-minute walk hadn't seemed at all daunting. Now, with Iradia's white-hot sun blazing down at them at high noon, Landon was beginning to wish he'd attempted to make some sort of arrangement for local transportation. Did they even have cabs here?

Dhani's forehead glistened with sweat, but she made no complaint as she walked along next to him. At least they didn't have much in the way of baggage, only a single case of expensive-looking leather that they'd found in Eustis Penn's stateroom.

Perhaps too expensive-looking. Once they emerged from the warrens of the spaceport and onto the streets of Aldis Nova proper, Landon and Dhani were surrounded by the town's citizens, all of them wearing loose, blousy clothing in shades of white and beige and tan, far better-suited to the blazing heat than the dark clothes he and his companion had on.

Well, it couldn't be helped. Not too far to the hotel, and then they'd be safely inside and out of the sun. If they were very lucky, the Iradian settlement would have amenities such as electronic shopping, so they might select the things they needed and then have them delivered directly to their room.

The hotel was impossible to miss. Four stories high, it was surrounded by spiky-looking desert vegetation in enormous clay pots nearly the same reddish-beige as the building itself. The imposing structure was topped by a dome with dark blue and gold mosaic tile that glittered in the sun. Perhaps the hotel's architects had wished to evoke a palace from the Arabian Nights, or a villa from Moorish Spain. Either way, it appeared rather incongruous on this world light-years from its original design inspiration, although Landon had to admit that at least it fit the desert theme fairly well.

Inside, he was immediately surrounded by blessed coolness, the hotel's heat pumps clearly working overtime. He took off his sunglasses so he might see better, for it was quite dim in the building's interior. Dhani did so as well, looking around her with some interest.

The Moorish inspiration continued here, with arched doorways and a floor of ceramic tile. Palm plants that must have come all the way from Gaia were set out at regular intervals. At the far end of the lobby was a long desk of carved wood, the heads-up displays of the hotel staff looking very modern and out of place against all those organic materials.

Jaw set, Landon moved forward, Dhani in his wake. Of course they did not have reservations. He had to hope that the balance on the least of their credit vouchers—some three-quarters of a million units—would be enough to convince the hotel staff to provide a room. The other two vouchers, with their millions of units, were still locked up inside the ship. It seemed safer to do that than to carry all their funds with them. Besides, now that he and Dhani had no need to purchase a vessel, three-quarters of a million units would be more than sufficient to provide accommodations, clothing, and any other supplies they could possibly need.

He had been to hotels that utilized mechs as their front desk staff, but here a young woman with fiery red hair greeted him and Dhani as they approached.

"Welcome to the Flower of the Desert," the desk clerk said pleasantly. If she knew she was staffing the front desk of a luxury hotel set down in the middle of the galaxy's most lawless planet, she certainly gave no indication of it. "Do you have a reservation?"

"No," Landon replied, his tone careless, as if he walked into hotels every day without making any plans for his accommodations. "I'm afraid our trip here was rather a last-minute decision. I was hoping you might have something available."

The young woman's professional smile didn't

falter. "We're nearly full, but let me check." Her fingers flew over the heads-up display, which was cleverly angled so that anyone standing in front of the counter couldn't see exactly what she was doing. "I'm afraid all we have is the Governor's Suite on the top floor. It's fifteen hundred units a night."

"That would be fine," Landon said. If they stayed long enough, that rate might start to put a dent in their one voucher, but he hoped he and Dhani wouldn't be here for more than a day or two, just enough to regroup and decide what they wanted to do next.

His response made the desk clerk blink slightly, as though she was startled by his complete lack of reaction to the room's rate. But then she seemed to recover herself. "Excellent, sir. Your credit voucher?"

He withdrew it from his pocket and handed it over, praying that the transaction would go smoothly. Yes, the app on his handheld had verified the balance, but what if Penn had left some kind of trap, something that would be triggered if a certain code wasn't entered, or a particular verification offered—

Beside him, Dhani shifted, although whether she did so because the heels she wore were starting to hurt her feet, or because she, too, fretted that the credit voucher wouldn't go through, Landon couldn't say for sure. About all he could do was stand there calmly and pretend there was nothing out of the ordinary about their situation.

Then the desk clerk flashed him another smile and said as she slid an electronic key card across the counter, "You're all set, sir. Do you need any help with your bags?"

Considering there was only the one, assistance was the last thing Landon needed. "No, thank you."

"The lifts are to the left, in that alcove. Enjoy your stay at the Flower of the Desert."

"I'm sure we will." He stepped away from the counter and headed in the direction the desk clerk had indicated, Dhani right behind him. It was only after they were inside the elevator and ascending to the top floor that he allowed himself to let out a sigh of relief. "That went better than I'd hoped."

She tilted her head up at him. "Why wouldn't it? They had an expensive suite that was empty, and you had the funds to pay for it."

"I'm still surprised she didn't ask for any identification." And what he would have done if she had, he wasn't sure. Besides the clothes on his back, his military-issued identification was the only thing he'd brought with him from the destruction of Zeta Tau station, and that particular I.D. had to have been flagged by now.

Dhani grinned. "On Iradia? Please. This place may put on airs and pretend to be respectable and posh, but you can't tell me that the management here doesn't know which side its bread is buttered on...so to speak. They're not going to ask any questions that might deprive them of a paying guest. I'm sure if you check your voucher's balance, you'll see that they've deducted a hefty security deposit."

He lifted an eyebrow at her. "I thought you said you'd never been to Iradia before."

"I haven't, but I've been in a few places that were…questionable. I know how all this works."

Thank God she did. Landon would never have called himself sheltered, not after more than ten years in the military, but he had to admit there were certain aspects to life on the fringe he'd never before considered. It felt odd to realize that Dhani was far more experienced in those matters than he could ever be, although he supposed he should be relieved that he had such a knowledgeable guide.

But then the lift reached the top floor and opened onto a short hallway with a door at either end. Here were more tile and mosaics and palm trees, although the air felt slightly warmer, as though the hotel's cooling system had a harder time maintaining the desired temperature up here where there was no shelter from Iradia's brutal sun. He didn't care, though. It was still roughly forty degrees cooler than outside.

He went to the door and swiped the card over the lock, and pushed down on the handle. Dhani peeked past his shoulder and let out a low whistle. "Wow, Landon, you did well."

Perhaps he should have protested that he hadn't

done much of anything at all—it was pure luck that the Governor's Suite was the only available room in the hotel—but he decided he'd rather bask in Dhani's approval. As he entered the suite, he could see why she was impressed. The floor here was of patterned marble, the walls a soft blush color. Large windows, framed by filmy curtains, gave a fine view of Aldis Nova. A fountain in one corner made soft splashing sounds, soothing in this desert city.

"It does look like a good place to rest and regroup," he admitted.

She'd paused by one of the couches so she could remove those damn heels. Now, she stood there barefoot, and laughed and shook back her hair. "I'll say. I can't wait to see the room service menu. And the bathroom," she added. "I need a shower."

Landon knew he should never agree that a woman needed a shower. "It will be good to get cleaned up," he said, his tone neutral. "But perhaps we should see about ordering some clothes first, so you will have something new and fresh to change into after your shower."

"Oh, right." Apparently spying the remote for the entertainment console that was mounted to one wall, she went over to the coffee table where the remote rested and picked it up. She aimed it at the unit, then flicked through the stations, which appeared to be the usual mixture of the same films and shows beamed throughout the galaxy, along with a greater-than-average dollop of local advertising. Eventually, she did find a channel for a local clothing supplier, and began making her selections—a rather alarmingly large number of selections, at least in Landon's eyes. But they had the funds, and if doing so amused her, he wouldn't complain.

Instead, he left the sitting room and headed into the bedroom. A large bed was placed up against the wall, its headboard intricately carved wood. Gaian work, from the look of it. He doubted anything as large as an oak tree actually grew on Iradia.

Far more problematic than the source of the bed frame, however, was the fact that there was only the one bed. If he'd been thinking straight, he would have inquired whether there was a room available with two beds, or separate bedchambers. But no, this had been the only room left in the hotel. He and Dhani would have been forced to go elsewhere, and Landon doubted he would have felt safe in a different establishment. Actually, he wasn't sure if he felt altogether safe here, either, but the Flower of the Desert was definitely their best choice for accommodations on this rough planet.

The bathroom was large and well-equipped, with a shower that boasted an entire wall of sprayers—he wondered how they could afford to waste that much water—and a molecular hair dryer, sonic shaver, and other niceties of civilized grooming. It would feel good to get truly cleaned up...and to get some fresh clothing. Eustis Penn's clothing did not fit too badly, all things considered, but Landon didn't much care for going around in clothes that belonged to a dead man. The ship…well, one might argue that using his ship fell into the same category. However, a spaceship wasn't quite as intimate as a pair of trousers. Besides, from what Landon had been able to tell, Penn hadn't even owned that ship for very long. Dhani had said she didn't recognize it, so it had to have been a fairly recent purchase.

Rationalizing aside, it would be good to have clothes that were truly his, and which fit properly. He and Eustis were close in size, but not an exact match; the trousers were a shade short, the shoulders of the shirt just a trifle too tight.

He went back out to the sitting area, where Dhani was still flipping through the offerings from the local merchants. However, he was somewhat surprised to see that she now appeared to be looking at men's clothing.

"What do you think of this jacket?" she asked, the screen paused on an image of a high-collared gray suit in what appeared to be spider-silk. "That color would be great with your eyes."

While he didn't exactly flush, Landon couldn't help but be somewhat discomfited she'd paid enough attention to his eye color that she would be using it as a basis for whether to buy a jacket or not. "It looks rather heavy for Iradia," he said, his tone neutral.

Dhani arched an eyebrow at him. "I wasn't aware we were going to be staying here."

"We're not," he said. "That is, we stopped here because it was a good way point, but now it's been established that we have plenty of available cash, as well as a more than serviceable ship, there isn't much reason for us to remain here for more than a day or two. I suppose it depends on you."

"Me?" She appeared genuinely startled by his statement.

"Well, what do you want to do next? Where were you thinking of going?"

The silence that followed these questions lasted so long, Landon began to wonder whether she intended to answer at all, and what he would do if she remained quiet. Expression troubled, she turned off the sound for the entertainment unit and shifted on the couch so she faced him. "Do we have to talk about that now?"

"If not now, when?"

Another silence. Then she said, "If we're going to get into the heavy topics this soon, I'm going to need a drink."

While a drink didn't sound like a bad idea, he thought it better if they had some food to accompany any alcohol they ordered. It had been many, many hours since either of them had last eaten anything—and the scant few bits they'd consumed at that aborted dinner party on Nelos certainly weren't enough to have sustained them. Landon could ignore hunger if necessary, but now that he was actively thinking about food, he realized how achingly ravenous he actually was.

"And something to eat," he said.

"And eat," she echoed, turning back toward the entertainment unit. Fingers sliding over the remote, she navigated to the channel with all of the hotel's room service offerings. "Anything in particular?"

"You choose."

Dhani hesitated, then shrugged. "All right. But come and sit down at least—I hate it when you hover like that."

Landon wasn't aware that he'd been hovering, but he decided it was probably best not to argue. Without comment, he came around the corner of the over-stuffed sofa and sat down. It was the closest he'd been to Dhani in some time, and he tried his best to keep his expression neutral, to not reveal how much he wanted to reach out and pull her over to him, borrowed clothes, messy hair, and all.

"Probably some fruit," she said, then shot him a sidelong glance. "Or would you rather have a salad?"

"A salad, I think."

"All right. Salad—the one with the poached pear in it, though—and the chicken skewers, and saffron rice, and bread?"

"That all sounds fine."

"And to drink…." She shuffled through the hotel's offerings. "Sparkling white wine?"

"You mean champagne?" That sounded a bit over the top. Yes, they'd made it safely to Iradia, against all odds, but he wasn't sure whether the situation really called for champagne.

"It doesn't say champagne. See for yourself."

As much as he would have preferred to continue looking at Dhani, Landon made himself turn toward the screen so he could read the offerings for himself. Yes, the wine in question was described as dry and light, with a mild sparkle. Not precisely champagne, but something that seemed as though it would be refreshing, and not too heavy. "All right," he said once he was done glancing over the menu. "That sounds as though it should work well enough."

"Perfect." She used the remote to punch in their selections. Once she was done—and the meal had been charged to the credit voucher on file for the room—Dhani shifted on the couch, her attention returning to him. "Can I shower, or would you like to go first?"

"Go ahead," he replied. "By the time you're done, the clothing you ordered should be here—and the food as well, I should think."

At his mention of the wardrobes she'd just replenished, she seemed to droop a little. "I only ordered you two outfits," she confessed. "Maybe you should get yourself some more while I'm in the shower."

"That won't be necessary," Landon said. "If it seems that we will be here for more than a day or two, then I may order some additional clothing, but I'm sure what you've purchased should be enough for now."

From the way she frowned slightly, he guessed she didn't think such a meager assortment would be adequate. However, she didn't protest, but only got up from the couch, saying, "I'll be as quick as I can."

Landon wanted to tell her not to hurry, to enjoy her shower, but he wondered whether that kind of comment might seem a bit too personal. Better to give a noncommittal nod and allow her to disappear into the bathroom.

Which she did. A moment or two later, he heard the water come on. They'd already been informed that anything over twenty liters a day would be assessed a surcharge, but he wasn't going to worry about that. After everything they'd been through over the past few days, they deserved a relaxing shower.

Sitting here where he could hear the water running proved to be more than a little distracting, however. Landon didn't want to think about Dhani in the shower, her baggy, borrowed clothing tossed aside. No, he shouldn't be thinking about that at all.

With an abrupt movement, he pushed himself up from the sofa and went to the window, where the view of Aldis Nova's streets was blurred somewhat by the room-darkening molecular film embedded in the duraglass. Still, he could see people going to and fro, despite the heat of the day. Perhaps those who were natives of this desert world were used to it, and thought nothing of going out and about when the ambient temperature outside was hovering around fifty degrees Celsius.

Eyes narrowed slightly, he watched the movement of the crowds below, doing his best to determine whether he could detect any sort of pattern to their activity. Although he hadn't seen any sign of pursuit since they'd left Nelos, Landon knew better than to allow himself to relax. After all, Colonel Owens had already caught up to them once.

The mere thought of his former commanding officer made a ripple of cold anger move through Landon. He had no reason to disbelieve Dhani's story, because, unfortunately, it had seemed more than plausible to him. On that long-ago hunting trip on Gaia, he'd witnessed Owens' casual cruelty firsthand. It did not require a great leap of imagination to see Owens transferring that cruelty to the lovely young woman who'd ended up in his possession.

Good thing Dhani wasn't nearly as helpless as she looked.

The chime of the door made him startle for a few seconds, hand reaching for the pulse pistol he still had tucked into his trousers, before he realized that of course they were expecting several deliveries, both of the clothing Dhani had ordered and their meal from room service. He hoped the clothes arrived first; matters would be rather awkward otherwise, although he guessed she would put her borrowed outfit back on if necessary.

To his relief, the person waiting at the door had in fact come from the haberdasher's; he was a young man probably around Dhani's age, but so impressively muscled that he looked as though he would have fared better as a bouncer at a local bar than as the delivery person for Aldis Nova's most upscale clothing establishment. Since the clothes had been paid for in advance, all Landon had to do was thank the young man and hand him a tip—while wondering where he'd gotten the badly set broken nose and the scar on one cheek—and then bring the unwieldy bags that contained their new garments over to the couch. He supposed it would have made more sense to go set everything down on the bed, but it was probably better to stay out here, since he had no idea when Dhani might emerge from the bathroom...and how dressed she would be when she did.

In fact, she came out only a few minutes later, her wet hair bound up in a towel. To his relief, she was wearing a silky white robe that did a good enough job of covering her up, although he could still tell that she had on nothing beneath it.

Either not noticing his unease—or ignoring it— she went over to the couch to inspect the bags he'd set down there. "That was fast."

"Yes, and they got a very good tip for it," Landon said. "Shall I bring these into the bedroom?"

"Sure. I'll lay everything out on the bed while you take a shower."

"Perhaps I should retrieve my new undergarments first."

Was it his imagination, or was that a faint flush on her high, rounded cheekbones? "Oh, right."

Better not to react. Landon picked up the bags and brought them over to the bed, then rifled through them until he found the small packet that contained the underwear she'd purchased for him. He wondered why she seemed embarrassed now, when she didn't seem to have any problem buying the things in the first place. Possibly it had seemed far more abstract to her as an item on the screen, rather than something he'd actually be wearing.

He took the underwear with him into the bathroom, which was still somewhat steamy from Dhani's shower, although drying out fast enough. After that, it was quick work to step into the roomy shower stall, lined in some sort of polished stone, and do his best to wash away the stress and the grime of the past few days. He wouldn't allow himself to luxuriate in the sensation of the warm water hitting his back, however; he worked efficiently, scrubbing himself down, working shampoo through his hair, and then rinsing off and climbing out of the shower enclosure in less than five standard minutes. If they ended up going over their water allowance, he doubted it would be on his account.

A few minutes with the razor to get the stubble off his cheeks and chin, a few more with the molecular hair dryer. Of course, he didn't have the pomade he usually employed to keep his hair military-neat, but he hoped some of the gel the hotel supplied would prevent it from getting too unruly.

When he emerged from the bathroom—carefully covered in the second of the two robes the hotel had provided—he saw that their clothes had already been put away, although Dhani had left one outfit laid out on the bed for him, a loose-fitting shirt with an open collar and a pair of trousers in a neutral shade of tan. The garments were simple enough, as if she'd known he wouldn't accept anything too ornamental, but even so, he felt strangely conspicuous as he got into them and then pulled on the black boots he'd worn with his uniform. She hadn't purchased new footwear for him, possibly because she hadn't been able to guess at his shoe size the way she had with the clothes she'd bought.

Feeling somewhat refreshed, he went out into the main living area of their suite. Dhani sat at the desk there, using it as a dressing table. Her hair was still damp, but lay neatly combed out over her shoulders.

Her bare shoulders. The outfit she wore was simple enough, a pale gray sleeveless tunic with embroidery around the neckline and a pair of softly billowy trousers in a darker shade of gray, but even from where he stood, he could see how the tunic followed the curves of her body, was somehow more tantalizing than the far more revealing gown she'd worn to their abbreviated dinner on Nelos.

She glanced away from the mirror that hung over the desk and shot him a dazzling smile. Apparently, some cosmetics had been included with their care package from the clothing store, for her full lips wore a gloss just a shade or two deeper than their natural rosy hue, and her big dark eyes looked even bigger, thanks to the careful shadows she'd applied there.

Once again, he was struck by how stunning she was. No wonder she'd left a trail of discarded lovers across the galaxy.

That wasn't precisely fair, though. From what he'd been able to tell, some of them had abandoned her… or the break-ups had been a mutual decision. At the same time, Landon couldn't help but wonder what deficiency in those men's character or thought processes had led them to think that they would be better off without her.

He cleared his throat. "Feeling better after your shower?"

"Oh, yes. You?"

"Definitely."

He was saved from having to say anything further by the sound of the door chime. Their food, he guessed, and right on time.

Sure enough, a mech waited out in the corridor with a cart laden with a variety of covered dishes, as well as their bottle of sparkling wine in a silver sleeve of specially conducting metal to keep it chilled to the perfect temperature. Because a mech had brought their food, there was no need for a tip, although Landon thanked the mechanoid before wheeling the cart into the suite and making sure that the door had shut securely behind him.

In addition to the living room with the couches and the bedroom itself, there was a small dining room off to one side, an octagonal-shaped chamber with nearly panoramic views of Aldis Nova, now with the brutal sun just about to slip below the horizon. He wheeled the cart in there, while Dhani set down her cosmetic brush and followed him.

As he removed the covers from the serving dishes and put them down on the tabletop, she took in a deep breath, eyes closing in apparent pleasure. "Real food smells so wonderful."

"Yes, I suppose it does," he replied, barely suppressing a smile.

She sat down and waited until he was done and had taken his own seat. As he reached for the bottle of wine and eased out the cork, she propped her chin on her hands and looked out the windows. Gradually, the nano-film was lightening as the sun went down, allowing them a better view of the city. Already a few lights were beginning to turn on, although Landon had a feeling that they never provided all that much illumination. Aldis Nova was a town that liked many of its deeds done in the dark.

He set the cork aside and filled Dhani's glass, and then his own. She lifted hers and paused. "What should we toast to?"

"I thought you said this wasn't champagne."

"You don't have to have champagne to toast," she replied, reasonably enough.

"True." He stopped to consider her first question. "Why don't we toast to a clean getaway?"

"That sounds like a wonderful idea."

They clinked glasses and both took a sip. As she'd promised, the wine was light and crisp, with just the faintest effervescence, not quite as bubbly as a true sparkling wine. It tasted far better than Landon had expected—or had he simply been in dire need of the sort of muscle relaxant such an alcohol might provide?

Either way, he was glad that she'd suggested that they order the wine. For a moment or two, they were both silent as he dished out their food, doing his best to make sure they got equal portions. Dhani took a bite of salad and once again closed her eyes, clearly savoring the taste.

It had probably been a very long while since she'd had anything fresh. They would have fed her enough in her prison cell to keep her alive, but none of it would have been particularly healthy or anything close to tasty. True, they'd had their meal on Ordon, where the food had been surprisingly good, but that dinner had been interrupted by the news of Clarence Miles's death. And Landon doubted she could even count the few bites of food she'd had at Eustis Penn's home before Colonel Owens' commandos arrived on the scene.

But after they'd both had salad, and drunk a few more sips of wine, she said, "All right, we can talk now."

"About?"

"You know what."

Yes, Landon supposed they needed to discuss what was coming next. He wanted her to stay with him, and yet...what, truly, did they have to bind them together? A shared enemy, he thought, but in that case, it might be far wiser for them to separate, to give Owens two targets instead of one.

However, Landon didn't like that idea very much.

After a long pause, he said, "I suppose what we do next depends on you."

Her fingers slid up and down the stem of her wine glass. "Why me? You're the one in control here."

He hadn't been expecting that response. "Why on earth would you say that?"

"Because you're the one who knows how to pilot that ship. Without you, I'm stranded here."

When she put it that way.... "I would never strand you on Iradia...or anywhere else," he said gently.

To his relief, Dhani smiled just before she sipped from her wine glass. "I know you wouldn't," she replied. "That's not the point. But I can't fly our ship, and so a lot of this is up to you."

Landon couldn't say he appreciated being put in this position. He would much rather that she'd stated clearly what she wanted to do next, so he could weigh the pros and cons of the suggestion and decide whether it was feasible or not. Once again, he found himself forced to hesitate, to stop and think carefully about what he needed to say.

She seemed to understand that he was having a hard time providing her with a response. "If you could go anywhere...where is it you'd like to go?"

Not home to New Chicago, that was for certain. His relationship with his father had always been strained; Landon didn't want to think what Hamilton Beck would think of Dhani Warlow. But someplace where he could be close to the land, could see a world's seasons, breathe fresh air, feel the rain fall on his face. He'd spent too many years in Zeta Tau's artificial environment and wanted nothing like that ever again.

"I can't say the name of the world, because I don't know it," he said. "A colony somewhere, self-sufficient, far away from all this mess." He gestured toward the window, even though the streets outside seemed peaceful enough. But most likely Dhani would know he meant the conflict in the galaxy as a whole. "Someplace with air we can breathe on its own, where people work the land."

"We'll find it," she told him. "I'll admit I don't know of any place like that off-hand, but farming colonies aren't exactly where I did my best work."

That didn't surprise Landon at all. She looked like someone made to wear fine gowns, to eat gourmet food and drink expensive wine. Of course, he knew that wasn't the reality of her existence, not at all, but he could see why she'd been able to blend into that kind of society, even if she hadn't been born to it. Would she settle for being a farmer's wife on some far-flung colony world?

Then he had to wonder where in the world that thought had come from. Wife? He'd only known her for a few days, and even that short acquaintance had been enough to tell him that Dhani Warlow didn't seem much like the type to settle down and live a quiet life.

"You would go to a place like that?"

The smile she sent him was like the sun rising—a gentle, friendly sun, not like the white-hot monster that blazed down on Iradia. "Landon," she said, "haven't you figured out yet that I would go anywhere with you?"

# CHAPTER TWELVE

Dhani really hadn't intended for those words to leave her mouth, and, judging by the flare of shock in Landon's blue-gray eyes, he hadn't been expecting her to say anything remotely along those lines. Now, though, she realized they had been the simple truth. Despite the madness of the past few days, she'd never felt as safe as she did with Landon Beck. He'd stuck by her side through all of this, had never once given up on her, even though he had every right to.

Never in her life had she been with anyone anything like him.

An awkward silence fell. Landon reached for the bottle and poured both of them some more wine. At last he said, "You mean that?"

"Yes," she said simply.

Once again, he was quiet. He drank a swallow of

wine and Dhani did the same, mostly because she could tell he needed this time to gather his thoughts. When he spoke, his tone was thoughtful. "I'm not sure I'm worthy of you."

She couldn't help it. A laugh escaped her lips, even as Landon looked at her with some astonishment. "*You* don't think you're worthy of *me?*" she asked, then went on quickly, before he could reply, "I'm pretty sure that statement should have been phrased the other way around. You're an honorable man, Landon, and I'm just a criminal."

"I don't think—" he began, but she shook her head, knowing she needed to speak her piece before he said anything else.

"No, I really am. I mean, I'm not a murderer or anything like that. I've never hurt anyone physically, or even caused much real damage. I've mostly taken money from rich people who wouldn't even notice that it was missing unless someone pointed it out to them."

She pulled in a breath, forcing herself to meet Landon's gaze. To her relief, he was watching her closely, but not with anything close to condemnation in his expression. She'd been worried about how he would react when she told him the bald truth. Of course, he must have seen her record when she was locked up at Zeta Tau, but he could have tried to convince himself that she was merely a victim of circumstance, not someone who'd voluntarily broken the law on so many occasions, she couldn't keep track anymore. Suddenly, it seemed vitally important that he know the truth about her before they went any further. And once he knew the whole sordid story, it would be completely within his rights to leave her here on Iradia to fend for herself. She deserved such a fate, after everything she'd done.

"I don't think that matters so very much," he said at length, and Dhani allowed herself to let out a breath of relief. Not quite a sigh, but close. "Victimless crimes, right?"

"Well, I'm sure the people I stole from considered themselves victims, but considering they were living off generations of ill-gotten gains...." She stopped herself there and lifted an eyebrow at him. "Since when are you a moral relativist?"

He offered her a smile, one of such sweetness that she felt herself melt a little inside. "I suppose when I realized that I was in love with a woman with a questionable past."

Landon...loved her? The notion was so bewildering, and yet so entirely welcome, that Dhani could only sit there and stare at him, not sure she'd heard him correctly. Yes, she could tell he was attracted to her—long ago she'd learned to read those little tells, and exploit them if necessary—but it was a long way to go from attraction to love.

Because she sat there in stupefied silence for so long, he clearly thought his words must have been unwelcome. "I'm sorry," he murmured, gaze shifting away from hers. "I shouldn't have said that."

At last Dhani found her voice. The last thing she wanted was for him to think that she hadn't wanted to hear him say something so unexpected, so unbe-lievable.

So lovely.

"No," she said, her voice firm. "I'm glad you said it. I—I just didn't think there was any way you could feel something like that for me. All I've done is drag you from one dangerous situation to another—nearly gotten you killed, made you lose your career."

He waited until this litany of transgressions was over. Then, very deliberately, he set his napkin aside and stood. Dhani could only watch him, wondering what he was going to do next. Was he angry with her? Did he intend to walk out of the dining room?

As it turned out, nothing could have been further from his intentions. He came closer, reached down, and took her hands in his so he could raise her from the chair where she sat. And then he was kissing her, quite competently, too.

No, those kisses were far beyond competent. They were also impassioned, as though he had been holding back his true feelings for much longer than she'd thought and could no longer try to hide his need for her. Strong fingers cupping her face, trailing through her partly damp hair. He tasted of the tartness of wine and the sweetness of the dressing on the salads they'd just eaten, and she opened her mouth to his even as she pressed against him, now feeling his arms wrap around her, his body molding to hers.

For a second, he paused and looked down at her, his eyes somehow hungry and gentle at the same time. "Was it...all right that I did that?"

"More than all right," she told him. "I can't tell you how long I've been wanting you to kiss me. And—"

"And?"

She had never faltered in front of a man before, but she realized this was different, that all the times before she'd only played at love. It wasn't that she hadn't cared for those men, but this was different— this was a need that seemed to be consuming her from within, making her entire body tremble slightly. How would Landon react if she stated those needs so baldly? And yet, as much as she enjoyed his kisses, she wanted more.

"Take me to bed," she whispered.

A small pause, and then his arms were around her once more, only this time lifting her from the tiled floor so he might carry her out of the dining area and on into the bedroom. Thank God she'd had the presence of mind put their purchases away while he was in the shower, or there would have been bags and bags of clothes in their way. As it was, Landon only reached with one arm to drag the covers back, and then they were falling onto the bed, his weight on top of her, his mouth hungry against hers once more.

She reached up and clasped her hands against the back of his head, feeling the soft heaviness of his tawny hair against her fingertips. Not so long ago, she'd wondered what it would be like to run her fingers through his hair, and it was even better than she'd thought, probably because he hadn't bothered with putting much of anything in it after he'd showered.

Those were only passing thoughts, however, because his hands were moving over her body, caressing her, and she knew she needed to get these damn clothes off and now, before she forcibly tore them away from herself. She began to fumble with the long hem of the tunic she wore, and Landon obligingly grasped it and pulled it over her head, then slipped his fingers under the elastic waistband of her loose-fitting trousers and drew them down.

That was better. Now she just needed to help him with his own clothes, and within a moment, they, too had been tossed onto the floor. He still wore his underpants, just as she still had on a bra and panties, but still, they'd never been this exposed to one another before.

For a second, he paused, staring down at her. "Good God, you're beautiful."

What was she supposed to say to that? Men had been calling her beautiful since she was fourteen years old, but, as with everything else that involved Landon Beck, this was different. *He* was different.

She said simply, "I love you." And while she might have said those words before, she knew she'd never really meant them. Not like this.

He kissed her, his hands moving to undo the clasp at the front of the bra. As soon as her breasts were freed from the confining garment, he shifted so he could take a nipple in his mouth, suckling.

The spasm of pleasure that moved through her was so intense, she cried out. Yes, her breasts had always been sensitive, but....

No time to think about it, because now he was sliding down her panties, his fingers slipping inside her. And God, she was wet, ready for him already, even though he'd barely touched her. She moved with him, rocking her hips slightly so his fingers would sink deeper. Ah, yes, *there.*

He continued to stroke her, each movement bringing her closer and closer to the edge. In the past, she hadn't always climaxed with her lovers, because either she was having sex to oblige them, or their technique just wasn't that good. No chance of that with Landon—the orgasm hit her only a few minutes in, shocking her with its strength. She clung to him, shuddering, and thought, *If it's like this when he's just fingering me....*

Another shudder went through her, but then she realized she needed to take care of him since he'd just done such a spectacular job with her. Dhani grasped the black briefs he wore and pulled them down, felt a slight start of surprise at the size of him. She wasn't even sure why she should be so surprised, except that someone who always seemed so upright and well-mannered didn't seem like the sort of person to be sporting such an impressive specimen.

Well, she needed to make sure she showed him her appreciation.

Her hand closed around him, and she began to stroke his shaft up and down, slowly, tantalizing him every once in a while by slowly drifting her fingers lightly over the tip. He gasped, and she sent him a lascivious smile before she bent and took him in her mouth, savoring the clean taste of his freshly showered skin, the velvety-soft texture of that skin against her lips. Now he was moaning, one hand reaching down to push her hair back and out of the way, but gently, not in a manner that made her think he was doing so in order to hold her in place.

Good, because she was only doing this to heighten his arousal, get him close to the edge but in no danger of going over it. After a few moments, when she could tell he was about to reach the point, judging by the way his breathing was speeding up and he grew even harder against her lips, she eased herself away, then straddled him. For a second or two, she perched there, feeling his shaft brush against her. The sensation was delicious, but not as delicious as what came next.

She sank down on him, leaning over slightly so her hair slipped over her shoulders and brushed against his cheek. His eyes were wide, staring into hers, still filled with need, but also a certain fierce tenderness, as if he was constantly amazed by her, by what she did to him. She twined her fingers with his, hanging on as they moved together, his cock deeper inside her, faster, filling her, a heat building in her core.

Landon came first, a deep groan wrenched from the depths of his lungs. Dhani hung onto him, riding him, feeling him spill inside her, and there was something about the sensation, about the realization that the man who stared up at her with eyes like the skies of lost Gaia loved her, *her*, Dhani Warlow, with all her faults and foibles and terminal bad luck, that made the climax surge from deep within her, and she cried out, hanging on as the orgasm shuddered through her limbs, blood echoing from every vein, pounding.

At last she couldn't remain upright any longer, and slid off him so she could collapse at his side. Immediately, his arms were around her, holding her close, his lips laying the tenderest of kisses against her temple. For a long moment, neither of them said anything. It was enough to know that they were here together, that somehow they had managed to flee across the galaxy and find warmth and safety in one another's arms.

When Landon finally spoke, his voice was full of

wonder. "You are the most amazing woman I have ever met."

Under ordinary circumstances, Dhani might have replied to such a statement with a quip, sure that the person speaking had to be teasing her. Now, though, she knew that Landon was only telling her his most heartfelt truth, and that it would be cruel to speak to him in such a way. Besides, she knew exactly how he felt, because right then she was convinced that he was the most amazing man in the galaxy.

She snuggled against him and said, "And you are wonderful, Landon Beck. In every way. I think I'm glad I was being held at Zeta Tau station."

Her words seemed to surprise him; he shifted so he could look down at her, see her expression. "You're joking."

"No, I'm not. Because how else would I have ever met you, in a galaxy as big as this one?" Now she thought it was safe to send him an impish little smile. "After all, it doesn't sound as though we kept the same company."

He didn't smile in return, instead looked thoughtful. "I suppose you're right. Still, I would rather you never had to suffer what you did."

Some of the afterglow from their lovemaking faded a little at his comment. Dhani had always been good at compartmentalizing, and so she'd shoved Colonel Owens and his hideous power games off into a remote corner of her mind and carefully locked it so she wouldn't have to think about what he'd done to her. She would have preferred that Landon not bring the matter up at all, but she knew he hadn't spoken as he had to hurt her, but only to express a wish that she could have avoided such ugliness altogether.

"It's all right," she said, hoping he wouldn't press too much on the subject. "It's over with, and we're away from him."

"True." Landon bent and kissed her on the cheek, the brush of his lips against her skin so gentle, so tender, that she wanted to cuddle into him and have him hold her for roughly a hundred years. "And you were—you were protected? I should have asked first, but in the heat of the moment—"

She smiled at him then, a genuine smile. How typical of him to be concerned about such a thing! "It's all right, captain...I've had my shots." Of course she had. She might have used a few wiles to ensnare her suitors as necessary, but never would she have stooped to using an unintended pregnancy to get her way. Actually, she'd never really thought about having children, had never experienced any driving desire to have a family.

Now, however, as she looked up into Landon Beck's kind, handsome face, she thought she might need to revisit her ideas on the subject.

First things first, though. She sat up and pushed her hair back from her shoulders. "Do you think our main course is still warm? Because I just worked up a hell of an appetite."

He smiled at her an extended a hand. "We'll just have to find out, won't we?"

———

She slept next to him, long dark hair—finally dry—spread out against the pillow. After they'd finished the rest of their dinner and the bottle of wine, they'd come back and made love once again before falling asleep in each other's arms.

Landon woke in the dark watches of the night, and got up to use the bathroom and belatedly clean his teeth. Afterward, he climbed back into bed next to Dhani, moving as carefully as he could. She didn't stir, and he was grateful for that. While they both needed their sleep, he thought she most likely needed it even more than he did, since at least he had gotten regular rest up until the time this entire adventure had begun, while she'd been trapped for days in a cell in the bowels of Zeta Tau station, trying to sleep on a hard cot with an even harder mattress.

The mention of her sojourn in the prison cell had troubled her, he could tell. Possibly it had been unwise to bring it up at all, but he truly was sorry for what she'd suffered there. Although he understood the need to get away to a small, obscure world where no one could find them, at some deep, atavistic level, he almost wished they could have a final confrontation with Colonel Owens, just so Landon could kill him and rid the galaxy of such a villain.

But endangering Dhani and himself just to enact such a personal revenge was foolish. Their best revenge would be to get safely away and live happy lives together. Owens might never know what had happened to them, but Landon hoped that somehow, deep down, the colonel would realize all his efforts had been in vain, and that somewhere far from his reach, the two of them were away, prospering together.

In order to do so, however, they would have to have some sort of destination in mind. His handheld had been rescued from the pocket of his discarded uniform jacket and now sat on a table next to the bed. He reached for it, triple-checked the settings to make sure that all the tracking on it that he'd disabled had remained disabled. Yes, it was still untraceable, and he let out a small sigh of relief.

The hotel had a fast network available to guests; Landon accessed it, wondering how many who weren't staying at the Flower of the Desert lingered nearby in order to use that same network. Well, that was the hotel's affair. As long as everything remained safely encrypted and shielded, he should be fine doing a bit of research.

Dhani shifted, and Landon went silent for a moment, worried that the faint light from the handheld's screen had been enough to wake her up. But no, it seemed she had only been looking for a more comfortable position, because once she was settled on her side, she went still and quiet again. He watched her, even though he wasn't able to make out much more than the fall of dark hair against the pillow, the faint outline of her bare shoulder above the sheets she'd pulled up to cover her breasts.

God, he loved her.

It almost hurt, this intensity of emotion that seemed to sweep over him when he looked at her. Once in his youth, before he'd even left for the GDF academy, he'd thought he was in love, but he now realized that had been a boyish infatuation, nothing more. It hadn't been the realization that he would do anything to protect this woman and make sure she was safe...that he would die for her.

Somehow that wasn't the most comforting of notions. However, Landon accepted it, just as he accepted the color of his eyes or the shapes of the constellations in the skies above the hotel that sheltered them now. Some things simply couldn't change, and, deep down, he knew that he would gladly give up his life if it meant that Dhani, precious, beautiful Dhani, would continue to live.

Enough of that for now, though. He navigated to the Consortium's database of planets, glad that the hotel's network would shield his identity and keep anyone from discovering exactly who was accessing that information. Oh, it was harmless enough, because the database was made freely available to all Consortium citizens, but Landon still wanted to make sure that he didn't attract any undue attention.

The database was slow to load, however, and he wondered whether the hotel's network was the culprit, or whether the disruptions occurring across the galaxy had made it all the way to the heart of Gaia. After all, a good deal of the government's data-processing centers were located on Gaia's moon, and he and Dhani had already heard about the insurgency's attacks there. Redundant centers had been scattered around the galaxy, but if his requests were getting bounced from world to world, looking for a functioning server, he could understand the reason for the delay.

Eventually, though, he had full database access. Finger tapping against the screen, he narrowed down the parameters—a colony world on the outskirts of settled Gaian space, atmosphere and gravity Gaia-normal, light on industry and heavy on agriculture.

In less time than he'd expected, a list of likely candidates appeared—five in all. Two of them he rejected immediately, because it seemed the database's concept of what was remote seemed to vary widely from Landon's. The third he decided against after a more in-depth examination of its agricultural development, since it seemed that most of it was concentrated in greenhouses and high-rise arcologies, and he had no interest in any of that. If he was going to go back to his roots, so to speak, then he wanted someplace where he could get his hands dirty.

The fourth planet shouldn't have been included at all, as far as Landon was concerned, because the terraforming process there was not yet complete, and so again, all food production took place within enormous domed greenhouses. After spending far too much of his life in Zeta Tau station's artificial environment, the last thing he wanted was to be confined to yet another one just as he had managed to break free.

But the final planet…it looked promising. Its natural atmosphere had been so close to Gaia-normal that it had required only minimal terraforming, and the colonies in place on its surface had been there for almost twenty-five years now, indicating a fairly stable environment. The crops grown there were specially modified versions of staples most Gaians would recognize—wheat and rice and quinoa, spinach and lettuce and kale and many, many more.

Even its name was a promise.

*Aurora.*

Dhani stirred, then rolled over and blinked at him with droopy dark eyes. "What on earth are you doing up, Landon?"

He turned his handheld's screen toward her, although he wasn't sure how much she could see with her vision probably still a bit blurred from sleep. "Research. I think I've found our new home."

"Oh," she said, and yawned. "I suppose that means you're sticking around, doesn't it?"

"Yes," he replied, before bending down to kiss her on the cheek. "I'm afraid you are stuck with me."

"Good." She blinked again, her vision a little clearer this time. Her gaze shifted to the handheld he still had in one hand. "Why don't you put that thing down? You've woken me up, so we might as well do something productive with our time."

That sounded like an excellent idea. He put the handheld down on the table next to the bed, then turned and gathered her into his arms. As she nestled against him, her mouth seeking his, he thought he could get used to this.

Yes, a whole lifetime of it.

## CHAPTER THIRTEEN

————————

IT FELT SO GOOD TO WAKE UP HERE NEXT TO Landon, to have him roll over almost as soon as she stirred so he could pull her into his arms. They'd made love again late last night, and she was feeling satisfied enough—for the moment—and yet she still thought there was nothing better than to have him hold her, his embrace warm and strong and utterly reassuring. The sensation was alien to her, because Dhani would be the first to admit that most, if not all, of her former lovers hadn't exactly been the reassuring type. But Landon was different. Once upon a time, she would have thought "reliable" was an utterly damning description for someone. Now she realized that it was exactly what she'd been looking for all her life.

"I was half-asleep," she told him. "Did you really say last night that you'd found a place for us to go?"

"I did," he replied as he idly played with a lock of her loose hair. "Aurora. It looks quite beautiful, and it's quiet and out of the way."

"Populated?"

"Yes, but the colonies—there are three main ones, from what I've been able to tell—are not terribly large, no more than four or five thousand residents in each of them." Once he'd finished speaking, he gave an abstracted frown, as though he'd realized that possibly Dhani, who'd spent most of her life in big cities of one sort or another, wouldn't find that type of scenario precisely appealing.

However, she realized that she needed to look beyond what she'd done in her past and hope for a different kind of future. To tell the truth, after being shot at over the past few days—and cooling her heels in Zeta Tau's brig for several weeks before that—she was ready to settle down and go someplace quiet. Landon had already proved to her that quiet didn't necessarily have to mean boring.

"It sounds like a good place," she said. "You think they'll accept outsiders like us?"

"We'll say we're refugees," he replied. "It's not that far from the truth, after all. And Eustis Penn's credit vouchers will go a long way in helping us to procure some land. Money's usually fairly tight in far-flung colonies like Aurora."

His explanation made sense. However, Dhani

couldn't help feeling unease stir within her. Sure, they had money piled up on those vouchers, probably more than they could spend in a lifetime, especially in a backwater like Aurora. But how long would the credit on those vouchers even be good? If things were as bad as they sounded, wasn't it just a matter of time before the central banks began to collapse as everyone withdrew their electronic funds in order to have some hard cash on hand?

Apparently, Landon noticed her hesitation, because he said, "If you don't think Aurora is a good fit, I can keep looking."

"No, that's not it," Dhani replied at once. "I suppose I'm worried about how long those credit vouchers will actually be any good."

He gave a thoughtful nod. "That is a cause for concern, but I think we have some time. The Consortium is too big and too unwieldy to collapse overnight. And honestly, I'm not sure whether the core of it will collapse at all. What I visualize is more of a contraction—possibly pulling all the way back to Gaia's system and letting the other worlds that were once part of its government free to go their own way. If that's the case, then while some value will be lost, I don't think it will be the free-for-all you're worried about."

Those words did help to reassure her a bit, or maybe it was just Landon's low, soothing tones, the warmth of his body as she hugged him. Either way, she told herself that of course he was right, and that they should be fine as long as they didn't linger here on Iradia for too long.

Which had never been the plan, anyway. They would need to pick up a few odds and ends—if nothing else, they'd need to get some food and water to take with them, since Aurora sounded as though it was far enough away that the journey would last at least twenty-four standard hours. The ship that had brought them here was very fast, but even so, Landon hadn't been talking about a short jump from Gaia to Eridani, for example.

"All right," she said. "I suppose I should have thought of that. This is my first civilization collapse, after all."

He smiled down at her. "Let's not think of it as a collapse. More like...a restructuring."

Fair enough. She could work with that. "Restructuring, then." Really, hadn't she had to do the same thing in her own life, over and over again whenever something didn't work out?

Hopefully, those days were now behind her.

"In the meantime, we should resupply here as best we can. I trust you have enough clothing to last you for a while"—he paused and gave her a somewhat arch look, to which she raised an eyebrow in reply but didn't say anything—"but we'll need consumables for the ship and various odds and ends."

"What are you going to do about the guns?" Dhani asked, recalling the contraband currently taking up valuable space in the hold. "Are you still going to try to unload them?"

Landon didn't quite wince at her question, but she could tell he hadn't much liked the tone of it, either, as if it edged them a little too close to illegal dealings for his comfort. He straightened against the pillows, sitting up all the way, and so Dhani was forced to do the same. She hung on to the sheet, though, guessing this wasn't the time for bare breasts.

"As much as I'd like to get out of here quickly, we probably should do something about them," he told her. "What I wish we could do is shoot those damn guns out the airlock, but if anyone manages to salvage them—and I have to guess that this system is crowded with space junk collectors—the guns could still have some kind of identification that could lead them back to Eustis Penn. Since we're still connected to him because of the ship we're using—"

"Someone might be able to trace them back to us." Dhani held back a sigh. It would have been so much easier to dump the guns that way, but the risks weren't worth it. For all she knew, the guns might have already been scrubbed, but she had no idea how to check something like that, and she had a feeling Landon, didn't either.

He nodded. "Also, I don't like the idea of taking them with us to Aurora. Most colonies have strict policies about the sorts of firearms that can be brought in, and the last thing we want is to fall afoul of the local authorities before we even get started. It wouldn't to do start out with everyone believing we're arms dealers or something even less savory."

Dhani hadn't realized that restricting weaponry was a policy for the Consortium's colony worlds. Then again, she hadn't spent much time in agro-colonies, since there wasn't a lot of opportunity to use her particular set of talents in that kind of a setting. She could see why it was necessary, though. Out in the hinterlands, the last thing you wanted was a bunch of colonists shooting each other up with overpowered artillery.

"Well, after we're up and showered, we can venture out to get something to eat, and then we can start poking around," she said. "You'll have to prepare yourself for some slumming, though."

A wry smile pulled at Landon's mouth. "After the past few days, slumming sounds like a relatively harmless pastime."

All she could do was chuckle then, and shift her position slightly so she could plant a kiss on his cheek. "Then slumming it is. Do you mind if I shower first?"

"Not at all."

Maybe that was just so he could look at her naked body as she slipped out from under the covers and made her way to the bathroom. Dhani found she didn't mind so much, though. She liked the idea of him looking at her, admiring her. A little flush passed over her as she closed the bathroom door, and she wondered for a moment whether she should invite Landon in to share the shower with her. There was certainly enough room.

But no, they had a mission to accomplish, and sometimes it was better to tease at the things you wanted than to lay it all out there. Even if they managed to get rid of the guns today, they'd probably spend another night here at the hotel, and there would be plenty of opportunity for more fun before they set out for Aurora.

Smiling to herself, she turned on the controls for the hot water, then stepped into the stone and glass shower enclosure.

***

As soon as Dhani was inside the bathroom with the water running, Landon got out of bed, retrieved his underwear and his trousers, and drew them on. Handheld with him, he went out to the living area and got himself a pouch of water from the refrigeration unit, then checked the tracker app on the device to make sure that all was well with their ship. Despite all its safeguards, all its biometric locks, he knew the expensive arrow-shaped vessel presented a tempting target to would-be thieves, and he wanted to reassure himself that no one had absconded with it in the night.

But the ship was still there, and didn't appear to have been tampered with at all. In fact, the faint coating of yellow dust that now marred its shiny surface seemed to prove no one had even attempted to touch it.

Good.

He drank some more water, then set the pouch down on the table in the dining area and went over to the window. After activating the controls to lighten the room-darkening filter embedded in the glass, Landon gazed out at the streets far below, which, if possible, were even more crowded than they'd been the evening before. In a way, he supposed that made sense. Most likely, the citizens of Aldis Nova would prefer to get as much business as possible taken care of before the full heat of one of Iradia's afternoons descended on them.

The frightening thing was that, according to the data stream provided as they'd descended to the local spaceport, it was already late autumn here. He didn't want to think what it must be like in the middle of Iradia's summer. Not for the first time, he wondered why anyone would voluntarily settle on a planet with such a hostile environment.

But that wasn't his problem, or Dhani's. They'd be long gone before summer arrived here on Iradia.

Another day to divest themselves of the illegal arma-ments they carried, and then they'd be off to Aurora. He could only be reassured that, so far, there hadn't been any sign of pursuit. Surely if Colonel Owens had any idea of where they were headed, he'd be here already with his commandos.

Or perhaps not. It was one thing to descend on a privately held world like Nelos, a place where he knew he wouldn't encounter much resistance. Iradia, on the other hand, had already declared its independence from the Consortium. Landon had no idea what sort of local defense force they had—if any—but he had to believe that the local Iradians wouldn't be very pleased to see a group of hated GDF troops descend on their city.

Imagining that scenario, Landon was very glad that he'd been wearing some of Eustis Penn's clothes when he and Dhani arrived here.

"I'm out!" she called from the other room. "Show-er's yours."

"Thank you," he called back. After turning away from the window, he headed back into the bedroom. Dhani, clad in one of the robes the hotel had supplied, stood in front of the open closet, frowning slightly. "What's the matter?" he asked.

"Oh," she said with a smile. "I suppose I'm trying to decide which of my new outfits would be most appropriate for meeting with arms dealers."

That remark made Landon want to wince, but he

tried to sound casual as he replied, "Anything that doesn't attract too much attention, I suppose. Once you're dressed, why don't you order something for breakfast? I'm sure I'll be out of the shower by the time the food gets here."

"Of course." She reached into the closet and pulled out a sleeveless shirt in a sort of blush color, along with a pair of dark brown pants. "Is there anything you want me to avoid?"

"No," he replied at once. "After eating mess food at GDF bases for the past ten years, I can manage just about anything."

That comment made her grin. "Yes, I suppose room service here at the Flower of the Desert is a bit better than that. I'll see what sounds interesting."

Landon thanked her and went into the bathroom. As he shut the door, he couldn't help marveling how relaxed and easy matters were between them, even after the intimacies they'd shared the night before. No awkwardness, no embarrassment. Already they were interacting as if they'd known each other for much longer than a few days, and he could only be gratified by that. Their current ease seemed to bode well for their future together.

Now all they had to do was get rid of those damned guns and get the hell out of here so they could move on to enjoy that future.

Most of the breakfast food on the menu was Gaian-style, with not much that seemed local. Just as well, since Dhani didn't really want to expend the energy to figure out what was edible. Much better to order a few vegetable omelettes and toast and coffee, and be done with it.

That task taken care of, she combed through her hair another time before slipping it back into a silvery metal clasp, then applied some light cosmetics, just enough to look "done" without expending too much effort…or putting in the effort to create a look designed to attract attention. That was actually the last thing she wanted, and part of the reason why she'd opted for such a simple outfit in the first place. Finding someone to buy their guns was going to be difficult enough without those same buyers wondering whether she was for sale, too. The Consortium had tried to sweep the whole business under the rug, but it was pretty much an open secret around the galaxy that slavery still prospered in Iradia's underworld, as well as on other planets located in the hinterlands.

The water in the bathroom shut off, and Dhani went over to the bed and straightened it up as best she could. She supposed she could have left that task to the housekeeping staff, except she guessed that Landon would lock down their room while they were gone. He was far too wary to leave the place open during their absence, even for the hotel's house-keeping staff.

Besides, they would only be here one more night at the most, so it wasn't as though the bedding really needed to be freshened during such a short stay. As she plumped the pillows and smoothed out the silky coverlet on the bed, she wondered what sort of accommodations they could expect to find on Aurora. After all, it wasn't as though agro-colonies were known for their first-class hotels. Did they even have hotels?

Dhani paused to ponder that question for a moment. Yet another topic she'd never researched, simply because she'd never thought she would ever travel to such a world. She knew that in most colonies, settlers were provided with the materials to build their own homesteads, and everyone was accommodated that way. Still, surely those worlds must have visitors from time to time—representatives from the Gaian Exploration Commission, or resupply ships, or vendors seeking to sell the latest agro equipment.

Having reassured herself that there must be some-place suitable to stay on Aurora until she and Landon bought their own homestead, Dhani finished making the bed, then paused to check her reflection in the mirror to make sure all her hair was still in place.

"You're beautiful," Landon said from behind her. "You don't need to check to make sure."

She turned around and saw him standing a few paces away, a faint smile on his lips. The sleeves of his new shirt were rolled up, showing off his muscled forearms. Once again, Dhani was surprised by what he'd been hiding under that GDF uniform. It wasn't until she'd seen him in civilian clothes—well, all right, and without any clothes on at all—that she'd realized how well built he truly was. He must have spent a decent amount of time in the gym at Zeta Tau station.

"You're not so bad yourself," she returned, and he only shook his head.

"If you say so."

Clearly, he wasn't comfortable with her noticing his looks. She wondered why. Maybe someday she'd ask him. For now, it probably wasn't important.

"I ordered breakfast," she said. "It should be here soon enough. And after that we'll head out."

"Any idea where?"

Dhani shrugged. "I don't think we'll have to go too far. Pretty much every city I've been in, the questionable types tend to hang out around the spaceport."

"For a fast getaway?"

She grinned. Like it or not, Landon seemed to be picking up on some of this stuff. "More or less."

The door chime sounded then, and he headed out to answer it. Dhani followed, mostly because she knew they were going to have to go into the dining area to eat anyway. Standing directly behind him, she could see the way he tensed before he touched the controls to answer the door, as if he was expecting someone other than the room service mechanoid to be waiting out there.

But the mech was the only thing in the hallway. No Colonel Owens, no boogeyman. Relaxing slightly, Landon took the tray from the mechanoid, thanked it, and then closed the door behind him.

The silver pot of coffee perched at one end of that tray looked a little precarious, so Dhani snagged it before Landon could take a step. "Don't want anything to happen to the caffeine, after all," she said.

He offered her a small smile. "No, of course not."

They went into the dining area, and Landon set down the tray and gave Dhani her plate of food before taking his own and sitting down. She noted that he was still tense, although his expression was calm enough. Maybe ordering the coffee hadn't been such a good idea.

Well, there wasn't anything she could do about it now. She poured some for each of them, doctored hers with a little sugar and cream—she wondered where on Iradia they raised the cows for cream, or whether it was synthetic—and said, "It's going to be fine, you know. All you have to do is stand there and look tough, and let me do the talking."

He gave her a tight little smile. "I'm afraid I'm not very good at looking tough."

Probably not. He was handsome and strong and obviously competent, but he'd been working a desk job at Zeta Tau station. It wasn't as though he'd been one of the guards there, or one of Colonel Owens' commandos. But at least he was tall and had impressive shoulders. Things could have been worse.

"It's all about attitude," she said. "Anyway, we're not going to be doing any tough negotiating. As long as we're offered a price anywhere close to what those guns are worth, we're going to take it. We don't need the money, after all."

"True," he agreed, taking a sip of his own coffee. He put down the cup so he could cut off a piece from his omelette. "Of course, I suppose it would help if either of us knew anything about what those arms are really worth."

"Don't you?" she asked, surprised. He'd been in the military, after all. He must know something.

One eyebrow lifted. "Why would I? Those guns are prototypes, something that hasn't been released yet —and probably never will, with the way matters are headed now. Besides, even if I'd known of their existence, had fired one, it would have been supplied by the GDF. It's not as though I would have gone out and bought it for myself."

Right. Dhani supposed she should have thought of that. Well, time for a little mental arithmetic.

Several years ago, she'd bought a new pulse pistol for self-defense. It had cost her nine hundred units. Those contraband guns in their ship's hold were an order of magnitude larger and more powerful than her little pistol—and certainly were not readily available—and so she thought they must be many times more expensive.

"Five thousand units each?" she suggested, and Landon frowned slightly.

"Possibly. We can start there, at least, and then when they want to lower the price, we won't argue very much."

"No, but we need to haggle just a little, or they'll wonder why we're so eager to get rid of them."

"And this is why you'll be in charge of the negotiations." He smiled at her before returning to his omelette.

His confidence in her ability to handle the sale of the guns made a small flush of pride wash over Dhani. So often her lovers had been dismissive of her, or convinced that they knew the best way to handle a particular matter. But Landon wasn't like that at all. He knew he was out of his depth here, and so he was willing to defer to her. She was his equal in this venture, and not just a piece of arm candy.

It was a new feeling for her, one she'd need to get used to. But she thought she could get used to it… and would like it.

"I'll do my best," she said casually. "I assume we're going to stay another night?"

"If all goes well."

"And if it doesn't?"

He offered her a taut smile. "Then I suppose we should be glad that we have one of the fastest ships on Iradia."

## CHAPTER FOURTEEN

LANDON HAD TO ADMIT THAT IT WAS SOMEWHAT surreal to head out of the Flower of the Desert and walk deliberately toward one of Aldis Nova's seedier sections, an area that bordered the eastern edge of the spaceport. The buildings grew shabbier, with patched duracrete that gave the lie to the material's name, and most of the people they passed didn't want to look directly at them, but hurried past with their eyes averted. The few who did meet their gaze were obviously giving them the once-over, making note of their new, expensive clothing.

Perhaps it hadn't been all that wise to order new clothes, but he and Dhani hadn't had much of a choice. If there was a type of shop that specialized in used clothing, he guessed Iradia might be the place to find it. However, he doubted Dhani would have been too happy to put on something worn and shabby after spending weeks in prison garb, and so they would simply have to make the best of their not terribly inconspicuous appearance.

Doing his best to look tough—whatever that meant—Landon strode alongside her, jaw set, eyes narrowed slightly. Of course, that was due more to the merciless light of Iradia's sun beating down on them, because even their borrowed eyewear was straining to keep up with the fierce solar radiation. Next to him, Dhani didn't seem terribly fazed by the glare, but perhaps her dark eyes were better suited to manage the fierce sunlight than his blue ones.

To his relief, they didn't have to walk for very long. Turning off the main street, Dhani brought him to a low, unobtrusive-looking building with an equally unobtrusive electronic sign that declared it to be the Sun Dog Tavern. It seemed an early hour to be drinking, when it was not yet noon local time, but Landon supposed that the people who frequented this sort of an establishment weren't necessarily concerned with such niceties.

At least it was blessedly cool inside, refrigerated air gushing out of the vents in the walls. He had to blink to adjust his eyes to the dimness of the room, such a sharp contrast to the brilliant, white-hot sunlight outside. And, once he'd regained his focus, he wasn't sure he was glad that he had.

The place was half empty, and most of those

who were there had clustered at the long bar of polished metal that stood against the far wall. Humans, for the most part, although Landon was surprised to spot a couple of tall Stacians standing at one end of the bar, heads bent toward one another as they spoke quietly, the low light above the bar glinting off the metal ornaments in their long, dreadlocked hair.

Technically, the Gaian Consortium was at war with the Stacians. But Iradia had already pulled itself out of the Consortium, and so Landon supposed it wasn't that strange to see some of those fierce aliens here on this outpost world.

Next to him, Dhani had paused, her gaze moving quickly over those present in the bar, assessing, evaluating. That gaze lingered on the Stacians for a moment, but then she gave a small shake of her head, as if telling herself that they weren't the right choice for this particular transaction. Instead, she leaned toward Landon and murmured, "Over there."

He did his best to look where she had indicated without being too obvious about it. Unfortunately, he didn't know how successful he was, since the place was so poorly lit that he had to strain to see who she was talking about.

The object of her interest was a human male probably ten or fifteen years older than Landon himself. He had fair, thinning hair and a sharp beak of a nose, and was so completely unremarkable that Landon wondered what it was about him that had drawn Dhani's attention.

He didn't have time to comment, though, because she'd already begun to move in the stranger's direction...and once again, she'd altered her posture slightly, just as she had back on Ordon. This time, though, she didn't look like an exiled queen, but rather a businesswoman, brisk and controlled. She approached the stranger's table, then paused and said, "Tira O'Malley."

The man looked up from his drink. For a second, his expression sharpened with interest... until he saw Landon stop and stand behind Dhani, arms crossed, face impassive. Or at least, Landon hoped his features weren't betraying any sort of emotion. Ridiculous as it was, he almost felt inclined to laugh. Playing a role didn't suit him at all, and he wondered how Dhani managed it so effortlessly.

"Never heard of you," the man said, reaching for the tall glass in front of him.

"You don't need to have heard of me," she replied without missing a beat. "But I think you'll want to listen to me, once I tell you what I have to offer."

"Not interested," the man said. His gaze shifted toward Landon, and he frowned slightly. "Not very smart of you to bring a cop in here."

Landon opened his mouth to protest that label— he might have been in the Gaian Defense Fleet, but he most certainly was not local law enforcement—but Dhani was too fast for him.

"Ex-cop," she said mildly. "He makes a very good bodyguard."

"And I can see why you would need one," the stranger returned, his gaze moving over her body in an insolent way. Landon stiffened, wishing he could say something that would let the man know such attention wasn't acceptable, and knowing he needed to keep his mouth shut and allow Dhani to do her work.

"Thanks," she said, her tone casual. "Well, if you're not interested, maybe you can point a girl toward someone who would be? I've got some... special...cargo that needs to find a home."

The man's pale gaze sharpened a bit. "Special? In what way?"

"I thought you said you weren't interested."

"Maybe you've piqued my interest."

For a second, she didn't reply, only stood there as she gazed across the table at the stranger. Then she said, "Mind if I sit down?"

He shrugged and took another swallow of his drink, which Landon guessed was some kind of ale. "Suit yourself."

Dhani didn't appear put off by this grudging invitation. She pulled out a stool from the table and sat, while Landon maintained his position behind her. The pistol tucked into the waistband of his pants suddenly felt far too bulky. Would he really be able to pull it out and deploy it in any sort of useful way if negotiations suddenly turned sour? Yes, he'd gotten the impression that he was more window dressing than anything else, but….

Neither one of them made any movement that Landon was able to see, but suddenly an ancient mech trundled over with a drink that looked identical to the one the stranger was drinking. The mechanoid server set it down next to Dhani, spilling a little of the ale—or whatever it was—onto the dull metal surface of the table where she sat.

"Thank you," she said, addressing her words not to the mech, but to the man who sat across from her.

He shrugged. "It's a hot day. Now tell me what you're offering."

"Guns," she said briefly.

The stranger didn't quite roll his eyes, but he did appear singularly unimpressed. "Lady, I've got guns coming out of my ass. I don't need more."

"Even experimental GDF prototypes?"

He went quite still at that question, pale eyes narrowing. "How do you know that's what they are?"

"I know guns, that's how," Dhani replied before taking a sip from her drink. "I used to date Garrett Chase. I assume you've heard of him."

Of course, Landon had never heard of such a person, but the same couldn't be said for the unassuming man who sat across the table from Dhani. The lighting in here was dim, true, but it was still bright enough to reveal the recognition that flared in the stranger's eyes, the way his lips pressed together for a second before he assumed a neutral expression once more. And Landon knew if he'd been able to detect these tells, then of course Dhani had, too.

"Sure," the man said, his tone grudging. "So he educated you on guns. Where'd you get 'em? If you lifted them from Garrett Chase, then I don't want any part of 'em."

"No, they're safe," she said quickly. "The—the man who was transporting them is dead."

"You killed him?" the stranger asked with a curl of his lip.

Dhani's dark eyes flared with anger, mingled with sorrow. Her true reaction, or one she was putting on for her audience? Sometimes it was hard to know for sure. "Of course not." A pause before she added, "Gun smugglers generally don't have long lifespans, but I had nothing to do with the death of the man who was transporting these guns. They're clean."

"Well, as clean as stolen GDF prototypes can be," the man remarked. Landon noted how he'd never offered his name, and how Dhani hadn't asked for it. He doubted that was an oversight on either of their parts.

A faint lift of her shoulders. "You really think the GDF is worried about a few missing prototypes right now?"

"Probably not." The stranger drank some more of his beer and set the glass down. It was now nearly empty. Settling against the back of his chair, he said, "I'll need to see one before we can talk price. Don't suppose you brought one with you."

Of course they hadn't, because there would have been no way to conceal even a compact pulse rifle in the clothing they wore. Dhani didn't look terribly worried by this omission, however. "They're too valuable to carry around on the street here. You can come by our ship and take a look, though."

Mild alarm flashed through Landon. Was it really wise to invite this gun runner—or whoever he was—to visit their ship? Then again, the final transaction probably would have had to take place there anyway, since it wasn't likely that they'd want to cart a dozen contraband pulse rifles halfway across Aldis Nova.

The man gave her an unpleasant smile. "You're a trusting one, aren't you?"

"No," Dhani replied immediately. "Stealing spaceships isn't your thing."

"You might have misjudged me."

One delicate dark eyebrow lifted. "Have I?"

A long pause. Then the stranger actually chuckled. "No, you're right. Jacking ships is a game for the kids. More trouble than it's worth. Guns are much neater." He drained the remaining beer in his glass and said, "Where are you docked?"

"Bay 872."

The man nodded, obviously committing the number to memory. "Okay. I'll be there at twenty hundred hours."

Dhani didn't look particularly pleased by this suggestion. "That's a long time from now."

"You want to do this in broad daylight?"

"No, probably not." She got up from the table and extended a hand. "You trust me not to sell them out from under you between now and then?"

Another one of those supremely uninterested shrugs. "Doesn't matter one way or another. Eventually, those guns will make it to me anyway." He shook Dhani's hand briefly and then let go.

So this man was the head of all the gun smuggling operations here on Iradia? He certainly didn't look all that prepossessing, but then, Landon supposed it was in the stranger's best interests to keep a low profile. Whether there were any local security forces operating right now was a good question, but discretion generally paid off, no matter who you were trying to avoid.

"We'll see you at twenty hundred, then," she said.

The stranger's pale eyes glinted. "I look forward to it."

She offered him a confident smile and then turned away, going to Landon and giving him a brief nod. He took that as her indication that it was time to leave, and went ahead of her to the door, whose lock he touched briefly with his palm. At once the glaring light and heat of Iradia at midday surrounded them, and he blinked.

Dhani's hand stole into his. "Thank God that worked," she said in a murmur. "Now let's get the hell away from here."

Landon thought that sounded like an excellent idea. Fingers twined around hers, he headed back toward their hotel, since he wasn't quite sure where else they should go. He certainly had no desire to roam around this rough city, dripping sweat the entire time. Better to be in their comfortable hotel room, where at least they could relax. He could think of several enjoyable activities they might indulge in to pass the time.

As he and Dhani entered the lobby of the Flower of the Desert, cool air immediately washed over them, and he couldn't help pulling in a small, relieved breath. And he was doubly relieved when the clerk at the front desk smiled at them when they headed over to the bank of elevators. Although he'd reassured Dhani the night before that their credit vouchers were fine and that they shouldn't encounter any difficulty using them, he still couldn't be completely certain that the bank funding them might have decided to cancel them and keep those assets for itself. With institutions collapsing and planets pulling out of the Consortium, who would even be left to pursue a lawsuit?

However, his fears appeared to be for naught. No one stopped them from taking the elevator to the top floor, and no one stepped out to tell them that they couldn't enter the luxurious penthouse suite where they were staying.

Almost as soon as he closed the door to their suite behind them, Dhani turned and threw her arms around him. "I can't believe it was so easy!"

Her negotiations with the arms dealer had seemed to go quite smoothly, and he wondered what she had feared might go wrong. "Does that mean we have to worry about a trap?"

At once her expression sobered. "No, I don't think so. You might find it hard to believe, but most of the people involved in gun running—or any kind of smuggling, really—have a code. Mostly because it's bad for business if you get a reputation for being a cheat, but still, when someone like our friend says he'll be there at twenty hundred, he will be, and he'll only be there to conduct business."

"And not steal our ship."

"No, definitely not that." Dhani went over to the small refrigerator discreetly hidden in the wall and pulled out two pouches of cold water. After handing one to Landon, she went on, "Our gun-running friend doesn't want our ship. It's fast, but it's also new and shiny and way too distinctive for the kind of work he does. I'm not saying there aren't people here on Iradia who'd be all too happy to boost the thing and sell it on the black market, but he's not one of them."

Landon cracked the seal on the pouch of water and took a sip. That was better. Now he didn't feel so much as if he had sand caught somewhere in the back of his throat. Some of his misgivings began to retreat, although he had to wonder whether part of his newfound serenity had to do with being back here in this suite. It wasn't a true sanctuary—any determined adversary could probably knock down the door in less than a minute—and yet he couldn't help feeling safe here.

He said as much, and Dhani smiled, although there was something a little strained about her expression.

"I'm glad you feel that way," she said. "It doesn't mean our friend didn't have us followed here, though."

"'Followed'?" Landon repeated blankly. "What on earth for?"

"Information. That's all." She shrugged and drank from her pouch of water. "I mean, he knows where our ship is docked because we told him—and you'd better believe he sent some of his people to go and check it out, make sure it isn't some kind of a setup—but I know he also wanted to find out what we did after we left him."

"In case we actually did go talk to a rival gun dealer?"

"Probably." Another sip of water, and then she came over and laid a reassuring hand on Landon's arm. "It's nothing you need to worry about, though. They'll have seen we're staying here, and they'll see that we're flying an expensive ship, and they'll let him know, and he'll guess that we're either a couple of silly rich folks who stumbled into something they didn't quite understand, or he'll think we stole the ship and are off-loading the guns because they're too hot a property for us to handle."

Which wasn't all that far from the truth. Yes, no one knew what he and Dhani were carrying around in the hold of their ship, but that blessed anonymity wouldn't last forever. As soon as they landed on Aurora, someone would be along to inventory the contents of their ship's hold, and then the guns would be discovered.

Of course, that wouldn't be a problem, because the contraband would be long gone by then. Assuming this deal actually happened the way Dhani seemed to think it would.

"But the gun dealer won't care either way."

Dhani chuckled. "No. Our friend has much more important things to do with his time. With the Consortium falling apart, gun dealers and smugglers are going to be busy, busy people. He's not going to give a damn about our story, because he'll have too much on his plate to care about who we really are or where we came from. Speaking of time"—she paused and eyed the open door to the bedroom—"we have a lot of time to kill. Good thing we didn't let the housekeeping staff in, isn't it?"

As she took him by the hand and led him toward the bed, Landon reflected that Dhani just kept giving him new reasons to love her.

## CHAPTER FIFTEEN

———————

WHEN WAS THE LAST TIME SHE'D BEEN ABLE TO BE so blissfully hedonistic? Dhani wasn't sure if she ever had, not really, because even when she was staying in five-star hotels and wearing expensive clothing and eating exotic food, she'd always been somewhat on edge. She'd known she was playing a role and running the risk of getting caught, and so she'd never allowed herself to relax all the way.

Maybe she wasn't completely relaxed now, either, but she knew this was about as close to it as she would ever get. The meeting with their gun-running friend was coming closer and closer as the hours passed, true, and yet she had no real reason to think that the trans-action wouldn't go smoothly. He wanted the guns, and they wanted to get rid of them…and didn't care too much about the price they got for them. It seemed like a match made in heaven, really.

In the meantime, she was able to stay in this luxu-rious suite with Landon, to have him make slow, impassioned love to her, to snuggle up against him when they were done, to order the most outrageous things they could think of from the room service menu. Somewhere in the back of her mind, she knew they were enjoying all this largesse thanks to Eustis Penn's credit vouchers, but she refused to feel guilty about that. Poor Eustis wasn't around to enjoy the money, so someone might as well use it.

Late in the afternoon, though, after they'd shared another bottle of fizzy wine—their last one, since Landon insisted they allow themselves enough time to sober up before their meeting with the gun dealer—he sat up in bed and gave her quite a serious look.

"What is it?" Dhani asked, not entirely sure she liked the way he was staring down at her. She pushed herself up to a sitting position, one hand holding the bed sheet against her bare breasts.

"I was just thinking."

"About?"

"You."

She lifted an eyebrow at him. "What's there to think about?"

Now he smiled at her, even as he gave a slight shake of his head. "A lot of things. But I was wondering about your childhood, where you came from. You haven't spoken of it very much."

The glow from all the delicious food and the sex

and the wine immediately evaporated as if it had never been. Still hugging the sheet to her naked body, she said, "You know I'm from Chicago. There isn't much else to tell."

Landon's head tilted to one side, and he gave her a considering look before he said gently, "You don't need to hide anything from me, Dhani."

Oh, damn it. Maybe she didn't, but she couldn't help thinking that once he knew about her origins, he wouldn't want anything to do with her. Yes, she'd had her files altered because London seemed like a much more glamorous place to be from. That hadn't been the whole reason, though. Far from it.

As she remained silent, he said, "All right, I'll tell you a little about me first. Possibly that will make you feel more at ease." He shifted slightly, as if to find a more comfortable position, and then went on, "I'm from New Madrid, a small farming colony not too far from New Chicago. A brother and a sister— my brother stayed at home to help with the farm, while my sister Lissa went to school on New Chicago and ended up marrying and settling down there."

"It all sounds very respectable," Dhani commented, still not quite looking at him.

"On the surface, I suppose. But my father wasn't happy that I decided to go into the Gaian Defense Fleet, thought I was betraying the family."

This revelation made her shoot him a surprised

glance. "I thought it was supposed to be a big honor to serve in the GDF."

"To most people, maybe," Landon said. His expression was abstracted, his gaze very far away. "But my father tended to agree with most of the residents of New Chicago and Nova Angeles that the Consortium had no right to annex their colonies the way they did—never mind that all that happened more than a hundred years ago. My father thought I was throwing my lot in with the enemy, so to speak. There wasn't any real reason I was needed on the farm, not with him and my brother working it, and all the automation they had in place, but that was another reason he used to browbeat me about my betrayal. Needless to say, over the years I've come up with a variety of excuses for why I haven't had time to go back for a visit."

"I'm sorry," Dhani murmured, and she truly was. It didn't seem right for Landon to be estranged from his family for such a small reason, but then, she supposed that neither he nor his father looked on their differences of opinion as small.

A shrug. "It's the way things have been for quite a while. I've gotten used to it. And really, I wasn't given enough leave that it would have been all that easy to go back and see my family very often anyway." Under the bedclothes, his hand sought hers, covered her fingers, warm and strong. "I only wanted you to know that you're not the only one who has a difficult family history."

Oh, how she wished that was true. But there was difficult, and then there was impossible. Still, she knew he would be hurt if she continued to remain silent, even if her story was so very much worse than his.

Without looking at him, she said, "My father took off when I was two. I don't remember much about him. I think he was tall, and he had dark hair and eyes like I do."

Landon's fingers tightened on hers, gave them a reassuring squeeze. Tone quiet, he asked, "Do you know why he left?"

"Not really." Dhani let a brief sigh escape her lips and amended, "That is, my mother claimed it was because he was a loser asshole, but I think it was because he couldn't take her addictions anymore."

"Addictions?"

She'd deliberately used the plural because there had been so many. Drinking at first, but then her mother had moved on to bigger and better things. "She'd go to rehab, get therapy, get 'cured'—there was a joke—and then move on to something else. After they got her off the booze, it was some kind of painkillers. I'm not sure what exactly, because I was still too young to really know what she was taking. But then her doctors got wise to her recreational use of artificial opiates, and back she went to rehab. That one took for almost a year"—a year during which Dhani had hoped the nightmare was behind them, even as she waited for the inevitable shoe to drop—"but she relapsed, this time with street drugs because she couldn't get anything else. It was frightening for me because she'd hook up with men to get her drugs, bring them back to our apartment."

"I'm so sorry," Landon said. His fingers tightened on hers. "Why didn't your father take you away from that situation?"

"By that point, he was off-world. I think he got a position on Ganymede, but I don't know for sure. He was good about sending child support, I'll give him that." Dhani touched Landon's hand briefly, then moved so she could tuck her knees up against her chest and hug them against her. Despite having him so close by, she couldn't quite dispel the unsettled feeling that had descended on her as soon as she started talking about her dysfunctional childhood. "I don't think he knew what was going on, not really. My mother held it together enough to send him a new picture of me every year, made sure I was cleaned up and looking presentable. But then...then she got into TIEs."

Total immersion experiences. They'd been billed as the next generation in virtual reality, but what the games' developers had neglected to mention was that, for a small portion of the population, they were a hundred times more addictive than the most powerful opiates. Money changed hands, reports from watchdog groups got swept under the rug, and everyone did their best to pretend that the games didn't turn a small number of their users into glassy-eyed addicts hooked up to their computers twenty-four hours a day, seven days a week.

"Dear God," Landon said.

"I'm not sure He was involved, but yes." Dhani gave him a weak smile, about the most she could manage right then. "My mother had already pretty much fried her brain, but that was the last straw. She basically turned into a zombie. At least by that point I was fourteen, could manage on my own, could even get her to eat sometimes. It wasn't enough, though."

"What happened?"

"She died right after I turned fifteen." Was that her own voice, so hard, so tight? Presumably, although Dhani couldn't hear anything of the laughing careless-ness that had such an effect on the men she needed to beguile. "And I've been on my own ever since."

"You didn't have any relatives to take you in? Your father—"

"By the time he was notified, I was long gone. As for other relatives?" Dhani shrugged and wished they hadn't drunk all of that bottle of fizzy wine. "My mother was an only child. She never talked about my grandparents, so I don't know if they were dead, disin-terested, or off-world. Not that it matters now."

Landon's face was a study in pity, and Dhani

hated that. She didn't want him to feel sorry for her, or suddenly view her as a responsibility because she'd been let down by everyone else in her life. She wanted him to love her for who she was, not for what her family had done to her. And the last thing she wanted was for him to stay with her out of obligation rather than affection.

"It's fine," she said. "She taught me one thing, and that was how to manage on my own. I did okay."

"How?" he asked, but there was a world of worry in that one syllable.

"How do you think?" she returned, now forcing herself to look at him directly. If he truly loved her, wanted her in his life, then he needed to know the worst. "There are always men, Landon, men willing to take you in if you make things pleasant for them."

"You were only fifteen, for God's sake—"

"Well, I didn't *tell* them I was fifteen," she said reasonably. "People hear what they want to hear, believe what they want to believe. I said I was eighteen, and no one asked too many questions. Anyway, I got along. I watched and listened and absorbed as much as I could. I learned how to get along in their world. It wasn't so bad. Some of them were even… nice, I guess. And once I knew what I was doing, had some money of my own, I got off Gaia and never looked back." She paused then, watching Landon's face, trying to gauge even a little of what he might be thinking or feeling. Now he only looked as though he was concentrating on something, although on what, she wasn't sure. Knowing she needed to say it—and hating that she had to—she went on slowly, "If any of this changes your mind about me, it's okay. I understand."

"'Changes my mind'?" he repeated, as if he had never heard the phrase before. "Why on earth would anything you've said change my mind?"

"Because I'm damaged goods, Landon." His question had awakened some small hope in her, but she needed to be absolutely sure. This was not a time to mince words. "I have a past. You—you come from a nice family, have a normal background. I've been sleeping with people to survive since I was fifteen years old. A lot of guys can't handle that sort of thing. I wouldn't hold it against you if you walked away."

For a moment, he was silent. Then he reached over and took her hand, pulled her against him. Still without saying anything, he held her tightly, his arms strong and reassuring. Was this his answer? Dhani wanted to believe it was, but....

"You think I care about any of that?" he asked, his voice rough with emotion. "Well, yes, I care, but only because of everything you've had to suffer, all the hardships in your life. Those men—what you did was your business. I would certainly never judge you for what you had to do to survive. I only need to know one thing."

"What's that?" she asked, finally daring to look up

into his face. All she saw in his eyes was concern, and possibly anger at everything she'd had to endure. That anger wasn't directed at her personally, though, but rather at a cruel universe that had made her suffer such tragedies.

"I only need to know you meant it when you said you loved me."

"I did, Landon," she replied at once. "I do. I love you, and I want to go to Aurora with you, and live the most boring existence ever, raising kale or whatever it is you have planned for us. Because I know it won't really be boring. Not if I can be with you."

His hands touched her face then, gentle and strong. Then he kissed her, firmly and quite thoroughly, before he pressed her down onto the mattress, his desire for her all too evident. This would make the fourth time this afternoon, but she didn't care. She wanted him more than she'd wanted anything in her life, and as their bodies joined, she cried out, knowing this was also his answer to her, that he cared only about her, Dhani Warlow, and not what she had done or who she had once been. Because now she was the woman who loved him, and that was all that mattered.

---

This time they shared a shower, hands moving over one another, smoothing body wash against skin, fingers helping to knead shampoo into scalps. Landon already possessed an astonishingly intimate knowledge of Dhani's body, and yet he learned new things even now, such as that ticklish spot along one hip bone, or the tiny mole at the nape of her neck, usually hidden by the fall of her thick dark hair.

Perhaps she was also learning new things about him.

Curiously, neither one of them tried to initiate any sexual contact beyond the mere sensuousness of soaping the other person's body, but he supposed that was probably because they had already spent so much of the afternoon in intimate contact. Now they both seemed to realize that they needed to focus on the meeting ahead and not expend any energy in further sexual play.

Dhani stepped out of the shower first, reaching for one of the towels hanging on the hooks next to the luxurious marble-tiled enclosure. After she'd wrapped the towel around her body, she handed the other one to Landon. He took it from her gratefully, glad of its warmth. Odd to think of how welcome something warm was in this moment, when it was all blazing heat outside their hotel suite's window. However, the hotel's air conditioning units were obviously extremely efficient, because the air here was downright cold on his bare skin.

He dried himself off, then asked, "What's the time?"

His handheld was sitting on the marble countertop of the built-in vanity. Still with the towel wrapped around her, she went over and retrieved the device, then looked down at the screen. "Nineteen oh eight. We have time, but we need to start getting ready."

"Not a problem." He replaced the towel on the hook—and got an admiring look from Dhani in return—before he went out into the bedroom and gathered up some clean underwear. It had crossed his mind to put on a new outfit, rather than the one he'd worn to their previous meeting with the gun dealer at the pub, but Landon decided against it. Wearing fresh clothing would either signal that he was more concerned about this meeting than he appeared to be, or it might reveal the kind of activities he and Dhani had been up to this afternoon. That was private, and certainly none of the gun dealer's business.

On the other hand, she didn't appear to be concerned by such constraints, for she selected a new outfit to wear, an embroidered tunic in a deep purple hue, and slim black trousers. Such an ensemble would have looked far too warm for Aldis Nova in the daytime, but Iradia's fierce white sun had already dropped behind the horizon, and all beyond their windows was now dark and dim. Not entirely pitch black, since the city provided some illumination for its streets, but it was certainly nothing like what he'd seen in New Chicago's population centers, or on Gaia itself, for that matter.

Landon doubted he and Dhani had much reason for concern, however. The arms dealer wanted to buy their guns, and he would most certainly do whatever was required to make sure they remained safe until after the transaction was completed. Once it was done, they would be on their own, but Landon doubted they would be lingering here on Iradia anyway. Speaking of which....

"Perhaps it would be wiser if we packed our things now," he said, while Dhani fussed with her hair. She'd put it up in a clip during their shower, and so it was mostly dry, with just a few damp ends. "I know we'd discussed staying here for another night, but it seems wiser for us to head out for Aurora as soon as our business is complete."

She turned away from the mirror, brush in one hand. "Intuition?"

"Possibly." That was as good an explanation for the feeling of doubt that had suddenly come over him. No, it wasn't that he doubted Dhani. He knew unequivocally that she loved him, just as he loved her. Their feelings for one another seemed to be the only constant in this ever-shifting universe. What he was experiencing now could merely be butterflies over the transaction they'd be handling in less than half a standard hour, but he didn't think so. "This suite is wonderful, but that's mostly because of having you

CHRISTINE POPE

here with me. And I can enjoy your company just as easily on board our ship."

"Or on Aurora," she added. "You're probably right. If we leave right away, then our gun-dealing friend will know that we only had the one transaction to handle, and that we don't have any plans to stick around and create any kind of competition for him."

"God, no," Landon said emphatically. That particular angle hadn't even occurred to him.

Dhani smiled but didn't say anything, probably because she didn't want to point out his naïveté. Well, he would be the first to admit that he didn't know much about these sorts of worlds, and he really had no desire to. He only wanted to get rid of these guns so the two of them could go on with the next stage of their lives. "Go ahead and get started," she said. "I'm almost done getting ready. Then I'll pack up my things, and we'll get out of here."

"Good idea."

He went and packed the items she'd bought for him, folding them carefully into a lightweight black case. This didn't take very long, so once he was finished with that task, he went ahead and logged into their account with the hotel, setting a departure time of 21:00. That was well after their meeting with the gun dealer, but Landon figured it would allow some extra time in case they needed to come back here for any reason.

Hair done and flawlessly minimal makeup

complete, Dhani packed her own things with the ease of someone who'd had to do the same thing many times before, on many different worlds. How many, Landon wasn't sure he wanted to know. He'd told her earlier that he didn't care about the men in her past—and that had only been the truth—but he also had a feeling it would be better if he never discovered just how many partners Dhani had collected along the way.

When she was done, she zipped her case shut and asked, "Are we checked out?"

"We will be, as of 21:00."

"Good."

Landon pulled out his handheld. Twenty minutes until their meeting. "We might as well head over to the ship. That way, we can get our things stowed, and I can get the course to Aurora set up and ready to go."

The approving smile she sent him was enough to make little ripples of warmth move through his body. God, he loved her. He'd never realized it could be like this, that her smiles would be enough to make him want to do whatever it required to be worthy of her. "I like a man who thinks ahead," she said. "As fun as this suite has been, I'm ready to move on. Let's go."

She picked up her case and he got his, and the two of them headed for the front door of the suite. When Landon let the door shut behind them, he experienced a small pang of regret. As Dhani had said, their room here at the Flower of the Desert had been the setting for some extremely memorable moments. He rather doubted they would find anything quite so luxurious on Aurora.

*But it will be away from here, and safe,* he thought. *And soon we'll be able to purchase a home-stead, and we can focus on our future together.*

That sounded like a wonderful idea.

The clerk wasn't at the front desk when Landon and Dhani crossed the lobby. Well, there was a small office immediately behind the desk, and perhaps she had gone in there to fetch something. Since Landon had already checked out, there was no need of the young woman's assistance, and yet he experienced another pang, this one much smaller. Saying goodbye to her would have made their leave-taking seem more official.

A warm night wind blew past them as they exited the hotel and began to make their way toward the spaceport. It was almost friendly compared to the super-heated blasts Landon had suffered while traversing these streets in the daylight hours, and he wondered why more of Iradia's business wasn't conducted at night. Tradition, or some other reason?

Unfortunately, they wouldn't be staying here long enough to discover why.

Even though he knew the ship was fine, thanks to the app on his handheld that gave him updates on its status, Landon still let out a relieved little breath when he and Dhani came to the landing bay and saw the vessel still sitting there, its sleek outlines now a bit blurred by Iradia's ever-present chalky yellow dust. The bay was actually better lit than the streets they'd just covered to get here, with a circle of orangey-yellow lights recessed into the duracrete that ringed the area.

"Everything looks okay," Dhani ventured, pausing next to him as he gazed at the ship.

"Yes, it seems to be fine," he replied. "Let's get everything inside."

He went over to the hatch and let the biometric scanner set in the wall next to it analyze his retinal patterns. The door opened, revealing the interior of the ship, now coming to life as lights flared on and the oxygen generators began to do their work. At the same time, the automatic gangway descended, touching down on the dusty duracrete with a small thud.

Smiling over her shoulder at Landon, Dhani had just begun to walk up the gangplank when a familiar —and hated—voice emerged from somewhere in the darkness beyond the landing bay's circle of lights.

"Going somewhere, Captain Beck?" asked Colonel Owens.

# CHAPTER SIXTEEN

HER VEINS FELT AS IF THEY HAD SUDDENLY BEEN filled with liquid nitrogen. Oh, God…she'd thought she would never have to hear that voice again. Dhani couldn't say that it haunted her dreams, but she'd done her very best to push it away, lock it down in the same mental compartments that held some of the more abusive men in her past.

She turned and saw Owens step forward into the landing bay. Flanking him were six of his commandos. Not the entire complement that had attacked her and Landon on Nelos, but still enough to be effective. Where were the rest of them, though? Guarding their ship? Or possibly the colonel had lost a few of his henchmen on the world Eustis Penn had bought as his plaything. The firefight there at the end had been furious enough that she hadn't kept track of all the combatants.

Landon stood frozen next to the gangplank. No, not exactly frozen. From her vantage point, she noted the way he had one hand tucked behind his back, fingers resting on the grip of his pulse pistol. While she admired his courage, she didn't see how he thought he could possibly prevail against seven armed men. Well, six at least. Owens' hands rested easily at his sides, although he wore a pistol in a holster at his hip. It looked as though he expected his commandos to handle his defense.

"What, no words of greeting?" the colonel asked, taking another step forward. Now he was only a foot away from the base of the gangplank. The commandos moved with him, closing their ranks slightly. "I thought at the very least that you'd be impressed by the way I tracked you here."

Landon spoke then, his tone just faintly sarcastic. "It doesn't take Sherlock Holmes to figure out that Iradia would be a likely destination for people on the run from the Consortium."

"So you admit that much at least, deserter."

A shrug. Looking at him, cornered like this, Dhani could only be impressed by his apparent nonchalance. He didn't appear terribly worried about being confronted by his former commander, although she also noted how he hadn't glanced up at her even once, as if doing his best to make sure that Owens would pay as little attention as possible to her. "As far as I'm able to tell, colonel, there isn't that much of a

Consortium left. It seems to me that the people still running the government have better things to do with their time than chase after one lowly captain."

A little barb there, the insinuation that Colonel Owens had his priorities skewed if he was wasting resources and manpower to come all the way to Iradia in search of a couple of low-level fugitives. The comment wasn't lost on the colonel, whose thin lips pressed together so tightly that they practically disappeared.

"I wasn't about to let one of my officers go AWOL and not suffer the consequences. Sad, actually." He paused, steely gray eyes turning a strange, almost tawny color in the reflection from the lights that circled the landing bay. "You had so much promise, Landon, and yet you were willing to throw it away for a piece of tail."

Dhani didn't even flinch. She'd heard much worse, after all, and Owens wasn't even speaking to her directly. However, judging by the way his gaze flickered up at her, she could tell he'd registered her presence, had probably inventoried every detail of her appearance. Thank God there wasn't much for him to see—the tunic and slim pants she wore fit well, but they certainly couldn't be called revealing.

"'Promise'?" Landon echoed, still in that faintly ironic tone. "Is that why I haven't had a promotion in five years...sir?"

Owens chuckled. "Surely you're not bitter over

that. I made my recommendations—it was up to Command to decide whether or not those recommendations were followed."

Another lift of his shoulders. However, Dhani could see the way Landon's fingers tightened on the grip of his pistol, and she went very still. While she understood his desire to take that gun and blow the colonel away, she feared he wouldn't be able to get off more than one shot...if even that much. The commandos who flanked Owens held their rifles at the ready, and she knew they'd unleash holy hell if Landon made even the slightest suspicious movement.

Things were dangerously close to getting out of hand. Time to step in.

"Colonel Owens," she said, and immediately the colonel's gaze was fixed on her. Landon startled a bit, but his grip on his pistol remained steady.

"Hello, Ms. Warlow," he returned. She didn't miss the greedy flicker in his eyes as he looked at her, or the way his tongue briefly passed over his thin lips. "You are looking very well."

"Captain Landon knows how to take care of a woman."

Meaning, of course, that Owens did not. Once again, his gaze grew narrow, although he didn't immediately snap out a retort.

Taking this as a good sign, she went on, "Really, colonel, although your dedication is admirable, what's the point in tracking us down now? I doubt that the MaxSec on Titan is in any position to be receiving new prisoners right now. Or is it? When we heard what happened on the Moon, we naturally assumed—"

"MaxSec is still functioning normally," Colonel Owens gritted, clearly annoyed by her insinuation that the entire Gaian system was in a state of collapse. "And since the orders to take you there were never rescinded, it's my responsibility to make sure you're delivered to the proper authorities."

*You'd enjoy that, wouldn't you?* Dhani thought, doing her best to hold back a shudder. *Trapped in a transport ship with you for the several days it would take to get all the way back to Titan, with your commandos trained to look the other way no matter what....*

Because she'd had to do the very same thing more times in her life than she could count, she was able to hold back a shudder of disgust. Barely.

"Well, if everything is functioning normally the way you say it is, then I'll also be able to file a complaint, won't I?" she inquired, and Owens frowned, even as Landon shifted his weight slightly, the only way he was able to express his concern over the way the conversation was going.

"A complaint for what?"

"For my treatment at Zeta Tau station, of course," Dhani replied, doing her best to look as guileless as

possible. "Someone needs to know about your unprofessional behavior."

"There was no unprofessional behavior," he
gritted.

She cocked her head at him. "Really? That's not
how I recall the situation."

"Your 'recollections' are faulty, Ms. Warlow,"
Colonel Owens said. "Do you really think anyone is
going to believe your word over mine?"

"Well, not under normal circumstances, no," she
admitted.

Owens gave her a thin smile. "Then I am not
quite sure what you think to accomplish by making
empty threats."

Dhani allowed her eyes to widen. Probably the
colonel would see right through her innocent act, but
she didn't much care. Right now, she was having fun
toying with him, getting her own little bit of payback
for the emotional torture he'd put her through while
she was being held at Zeta Tau.

"Oh, they're not empty," she told him. "I can see
why you might think that, but you see, a while back, I
had a micro-recorder implant placed here." She
pointed at her right eye. Such implants did exist—
she'd heard Eustis talking about them once—but of
course she'd never actually had the surgery to get one.
They were very expensive little toys, valuable in their
own way, but she had never been in a position to

require one. Of course, Colonel Owens didn't know that. "Mr. Penn paid for it, actually. He knew I had a way of getting access to people that he didn't, and since the implants are basically undetectable unless you know to look for them, I can see why no one picked up on it when I was scanned in at Zeta Tau. Still, it was on the whole time…recording everything."

The muscles in Owens' neck stood out as he gritted his teeth. "No one's going to care," he said. "Make whatever report you like…submit whatever evidence you want. It won't change the fact that you're just a common little grifter, and not good for much except a few nights of pleasure."

A few days ago, those words might have stung. Not too much, because over the years, Dhani had done her best to grow as thick a hide as possible, or she wouldn't have been able to survive for as long as she had. Still, she might have felt some shame at the colonel's insinuation. Now, though, knowing that Landon loved her, wanted to spend the rest of his life with her, Owen's words had no bite to them, none at all.

"So you're admitting that you assaulted me?" she asked.

The commandos, who'd been standing silent and unmoving during this entire discussion, suddenly seemed to grow uneasy. Several of them shifted their weight from one foot to the other, while the others suddenly seemed very interested in looking at anything except their commanding officer.

And Landon's finger still hovered over the fire button of his pulse pistol, although he hadn't moved, hadn't reacted.

"It was hardly assault," the colonel retorted.

"Semantics," she replied, allowing a faint smile to touch her lips. "I suppose we'll have to let the GDF's internal affairs people sort that out, won't we?"

"I have nothing to hide."

All Dhani did was lift her shoulders. She had a feeling Colonel Owens had a great deal to hide; her own experience had taught her that once an abuser, always an abuser. If she'd been a betting woman—and she wasn't, despite using a gambler's tricks against her marks more than once—she'd have guessed that she was only the last in a long line of the colonel's victims.

"Stalemate?" Landon said, speaking at last. His voice was hard, precise, carrying clearly to the watching commandos and the colonel himself. "Do you really want to take the risk, colonel? It would be a shame to see a long and distinguished career such as yours tarnished by these sorts of accusations, even if they came to nothing in the end. You may have us outgunned now, but you might just end up losing in the long run."

For one long, drawn-out moment, the colonel hesitated. Impotent anger glared from his cold gray eyes, and he finally snapped, "Your threats mean nothing." He glanced to one side, at the now-hesitant commando who stood next to him. "Take them."

Was that hesitation? Yes, there did seem to be a pause, just for a second or two, but then the commandos began to move forward, rifles pointed directly at Landon and Dhani. She cast about frantically for something else she could say, something she could do to stop them. Unfortunately, it seemed as if the eye-implant gambit had been the last weapon in her arsenal. She really didn't know how she could hold off the inevitable, not when she was unarmed and Landon only had that one fairly underpowered pulse pistol.

However, just as the first of the commandos began to step onto the gangplank, the night became alive with pulse fire, bolts in bright blue and green flashing out of the darkness. Two of the commandos fell right away, collapsing before they even had a chance to turn and face their attackers. Since there wasn't much else she could do, Dhani dropped to the gangplank, doing her best to present as small a target as possible. Out of the corner of her eye, she saw that Landon had dropped to the ground as well—and her heart was suddenly in her throat. Had one of the shooters hit him?

But then he pulled himself into a crouch, pistol no longer tucked into the waistband of his trousers, but out and pointed at one of the commandos. A single shot to the chest, and the man fell, just as another of his comrades was taken out by the invisible shooters in the darkness beyond the perimeter of the lights that surrounded the landing bay.

Colonel Owens had his sidearm out as well, but he seemed oblivious to the attackers who'd already felled several of his bodyguards. Instead, he was moving forward, eyes narrowed with hate, gun trained on Landon where he crouched next to the gangplank.

No....

"Clever of you," the colonel said, wincing just a bit as a pulse bolt whizzed past his ear and impacted harmlessly on the hardened durasteel of the ship's hull. "I should have realized you would hire mercenaries to protect you while you were here on Iradia."

Of course, Dhani knew that she and Landon had done no such thing, but there was no point in protesting now. Best guess, the unseen shooters were their gun dealer friend and his own hired muscle. She had to admit that their timing was pretty impeccable —if they'd gotten here even a minute or so later, the situation might not have been salvageable.

Not that it seemed terribly salvageable now. Both Landon and Colonel Owens had their guns trained on one another, and she had no idea who would be able to get off the first shot. She'd seen standoffs like this in vids before, but she'd never expected to witness anything like it in real life, even with all her exposure to the admittedly seedy underbelly of galactic society.

"You know how careful I am," Landon said. He

held himself so still, he might have been a statue, except for the way Dhani could see the rise and fall of his chest as he fought to maintain control.

"Yes, you were always the cautious sort, Captain Beck. That's why it surprises me so much that you'd be taken in by the likes of my captive over there."

Landon didn't blink. "She's not your captive. And she never will be."

Another flurry of pulse bolts, and a cry from one of the commandos as he fell to the landing bay's duracrete floor. Dhani risked a quick glance toward the firefight and saw that only one of Colonel Owens' bodyguards remained standing. He was firing gamely away into the darkness, but his expression was that of a man who knew he wasn't getting paid enough for this shit.

And for a brief second, distracted by his need to know how his commandos fared, Owens looked in that direction as well. Dhani took advantage of his momentary loss of focus to launch herself from the gangplank, catching the colonel by the knees so he stumbled and lost his balance.

That was all the opening Landon needed. He fired, gun pointed directly at Colonel Owens' head. The bolt seared into his temple, and his eyes opened wide with shock before his body went slack and he fell to the ground.

At once, the single commando who still remained

standing dropped his rifle and held up his hands. "I surrender!" he called out.

"Smart move," said the gun dealer from the pub as he stepped forward out of the darkness. Around him was a motley group of muscle—a hard-faced woman probably not that much older than Dhani, several Gaian men in the pale, loose clothing favored here on Iradia…the two tall Stacians she'd seen at the bar earlier that day. The dealer looked over at the woman. "Get him out of the way, will you?"

She nodded and went over the commando, and unclipped a pair of military-issue handcuffs from her belt and put them on the soldier. "Come on, kid," she said, not unkindly. "Let's see about sending you home to your mother." Taking him by the arm, she led him away from his fallen comrades.

The arms dealer stepped forward and glanced down at Colonel Owens' body for a second or two before returning his attention to Dhani and Landon. "Looks like we showed up at the right time."

"Yes, you did," Landon said. He seemed some-what shaken by the outcome of the firefight, but then he straightened and took in a breath. "Thanks for that."

"No problem," the man replied. "Especially if it gets me a discount."

Landon smiled, even as Dhani nodded at him. "I believe we can arrange that," he said.

# CHAPTER SEVENTEEN

THE ARMS DEALER INSPECTED ALL OF THE GUNS carefully, taking his time with each one, making sure that they were all functional, that none of them possessed any flaws which might prevent him from getting top dollar for them. He set the last one down and gave Landon an appraising look. "Six thousand."

Beside him, Dhani raised an eyebrow, but she didn't say anything. Landon cleared his throat. "Look, I was agreeable to a discount, but six thousand units for twelve prototype weapons simply isn't acceptable."

The man offered him a grin, watery hazel eyes almost disappearing into the heavy lines cut into his skin, probably the result of decades spent in Iradia's harsh climate. "Six thousand *each,* my friend." He paused and added in almost friendly tones, "You don't have much experience at this, do you?"

"Six thousand each is fine," Dhani said hastily. "Cash."

"Is there anything else?" The arms dealer turned toward one of the Stacians and made a brusque gesture with one hand. Landon wasn't sure what it was supposed to mean, but clearly the burly alien didn't have any problem interpreting the command. He left the ship's passenger compartment, where the negotiations had been taking place, and disappeared briefly outside. When he came back, he was carrying a brown synth-leather satchel, which he handed over to Landon before exiting the ship once more.

He looked inside, saw a sizable amount of the gleaming gold-colored coins used for currency in the outer worlds. Without saying anything, he gave Dhani the satchel. He figured she would do much better at counting the coins, since presumably she had handled these things before, whereas Landon had only read about their use and had never actually seen them in person.

"It's all here," she said after a moment.

"So we have a deal?" the arms dealer asked.

"We do," Landon replied, glad that he sounded firm and in command of the situation. Inwardly, he was still trying to come to terms with the way he'd coolly shot that pulse bolt into Malachi Owens' temple. One could argue that it had to be done, but—

"Nice doing business with you," said the dealer. A

pause, and he added, "However, I think it's probably a good idea for you not to ever come back here."

"Not a problem," Landon responded. He could safely say that avoiding Iradia for the rest of his life wouldn't be much of a hardship. Still, there was one loose end that needed to be tied up. "And the colonel…?"

"We'll handle it. And the other men we took out. It's probably best if you don't know anything other than that."

Dhani spoke up. "What about the one who survived? If he makes it back to Gaia and lets his commanders know what happened here—"

The gun dealer cut in, "He won't. Thalia—she's the one who led him away—is making sure that his memory is nice and scrubbed. We'll put him on a ship to Gaia, put some civilian clothes on him. He won't remember anything. Of course, the authorities will be able to I.D. him once they do a retinal scan, but they sure as hell won't be able to figure out exactly what happened to him…and neither will he."

"Thank you," Landon said. Really, their gun-running friend was being downright expansive. The only reason he could think of for the other man's largesse was that even six thousand a piece was a ridiculously low price for the guns, and he'd decided to celebrate the profit he was about to make by being magnanimous.

"Yes, thank you for that," Dhani chimed in.

"All part of the service." The gun dealer got up from the chair where he'd been sitting and headed for the open door. Once there, he paused for a moment before saying, "If I were you, I'd be on my way immediately."

"We will. Our luggage is stowed and our course laid in."

"Well, then." He nodded at the both of them and went out through the open door, his footsteps clanging on the gangplank as he made his way back to solid ground.

Landon looked over at Dhani. "Ready?"

"I've never been readier." She got up from her own chair and headed to the door, then activated the controls to shut it and seal it. Once that was done, she said, "Let's get the hell out of here."

A sentiment he could definitely agree with. He nodded and went forward into the cockpit, taking the pilot's chair. Dhani sat down in the co-pilot's seat and watched as he went through the usual preflight checks, although on this sleek, lovely ship, doing so was more a formality than anything else. Their reactor wouldn't need a recharge for years, and they had enough oxygen and water to make it across the galaxy and back again.

But they wouldn't be going nearly that far. Only to Aurora, which, according to the nav-computer, was less than twelve hours away.

As the ship lifted from the landing bay, though,

Landon couldn't quite prevent himself from tensing. Despite the gun runner's assurances, he was worried that more GDF forces were on their way, ready to shoot the ship out of the sky, and its passengers along with it. However, as the night side of Iradia dropped away and the planet became a warm, sandy-hued disk once more, Landon realized that no one was coming after them. A few ships moved in the darkness of the Iradian system, but none of them seemed to show any particular interest in the sleek vessel he was piloting. And a minute or so later, they were far enough away from the planet's gravity well that it was safe to activate the subspace drive, and watch the universe blur into tangled ribbons of strange, shifting colors.

Landon looked away from the view-screen and over at Dhani. She, too, was watching the tortured heavens outside the ship, but he didn't see any particular worry in her expression. Instead, she appeared thoughtful, as if her mind was very far away. Then she said, "We did it, didn't we?"

He had to smile. "I believe we did."

Her fingers worked the buckles of her safety harness, and a second or two later, she stood and went over to him, laid a kiss on the top of his head. "You were amazing. The way you took out Owens…." She paused there and watched him carefully, dark eyes full of concern. "Are you all right?"

Landon knew she really meant, *Are you all right with killing him?* And the strange thing was—even though he'd never lifted a hand against another person in his life—he thought he was at peace with what he'd done. It was a terrible thing to kill, true, and yet, if anyone deserved killing, it was Colonel Malachi Owens. The man was bad to the core. If he'd been allowed to live, to return to Gaia, then he most certainly would have found a way to add to his roster of victims.

But now—now he couldn't ruin any more lives. And, thanks to the gun dealer who'd taken those problematic weapons off their hands, it seemed very unlikely that anyone in GDF command would be able to discover the truth behind Owens' death.

"I'm fine," Landon said, then unhooked his own safety harness so he could stand up and face Dhani. With their entry into Aurora's system a good eleven hours off and the ship on autopilot now that the subspace drive had been activated, he no longer needed to remain in the pilot's seat. "Thanks to you. If you hadn't knocked Owens off balance—"

A pleased little flush touched her cheeks. "It was the only thing I could think of to do. When I saw that look in his eyes, I knew he was about to shoot. If he hadn't stumbled…." She shook her head. "I don't want to think about it."

"Then don't." Landon brushed a stray strand of hair away from her face, then glanced downward and realized the knees of her trousers were smudged, prob-ably from hitting the surface of the landing bay as she tackled the colonel. "We're safe now—and more than seventy thousand units richer. All in all, I'd say it was a successful endeavor."

Dhani grinned at him, a happy twinkle returning to her eyes, one that he was all too happy to see. "Yes, I suppose when you look at it that way, you can say it was. And now…."

"And now we fly to Aurora, and we start over." He took both her hands, held them tightly. "Assuming you still want to."

"'Want to'?" she echoed, as if puzzled by his comment. "Of course I do. I've never wanted anything so much in all my life."

Landon had seen her put on an act more than once, but he could tell she wasn't acting now. No, sincerity rang in her tone, was echoed in the earnestness of her big dark eyes as she gazed up at him. She truly wanted to go to Aurora with him, be his wife, learn how to enjoy the simple pleasures of a life lived on the land.

There was nothing he could do then except bend down and kiss her, taste her glorious sweetness, feel the lithe promise of her body pressed up against his.

When she pulled back a few inches, however, her eyes were dancing. "Well, actually, there may be *one* thing I want more."

Puzzled, Landon asked, "What's that?"

Her gaze slid away from his, toward the rear of the ship where the cabins were located. "It's going to be a long flight. We might as well make the most of it."

With that she was off, running to the luxurious stateroom that was now theirs. Landon gave chase, knowing she wanted him to catch her, to push her down onto the bed so their bodies might be joined once more, so they could spend these hours until they arrived at their new home in joyous lovemaking.

And that is exactly what they did.

*The End*

Strange Magic

The Arrangement

Defender

Bad Blood

Deep Magic

Darktide

Books 1-3 and Books 4-6 of this series are also available in two separate omnibus editions at special boxed set prices. Chronicles of Cleopatra Hill includes the series' two "back in time" novellas, *Bad Blood* and *The Arrangement*.

---

THE DJINN WARS*

(Paranormal Romance)

Chosen

Taken

Fallen

Broken

Forsaken

Forbidden

Awoken

Illuminated

Books 1-3 and Books 4-6 of this series are also available in two separate omnibus editions at special boxed set prices!

Enemy Mine

Get the first three books of this series in an omnibus edition, or read the complete six-book series in one super-low-priced boxed set!

---

## TALES OF THE LATTER KINGDOMS

(Fantasy Romance)

All Fall Down

Dragon Rose

Binding Spell

Ashes of Roses

One Thousand Nights

Threads of Gold

The Wolf of Harrow Hall

Moon Dance

The Song of the Thrush

Snow Fall (first half of 2019)

Books 1-3 and Books 4-6 of this series are also available in two separate omnibus editions at special boxed set prices.

---

## THE GAIAN CONSORTIUM SERIES

(Science Fiction Romance)

Beast (free prequel novella)

Blood Will Tell

Breath of Life

The Gaia Gambit

The Mandala Maneuver

The Titan Trap

The Zhore Deception

The Refugee Ruse

Books 1-3 of this series are also available in an omnibus
edition at a special boxed set price!

* Indicates a completed series

---

STANDALONE TITLES

Hearts on Fire

Sympathy for the Devil

Taking Dictation

Night Music

Golden Heart

# ABOUT THE AUTHOR

*USA Today* bestselling author Christine Pope has been writing stories ever since she commandeered her family's Smith-Corona typewriter back in grade school. Her work includes paranormal romance, fantasy romance, and science fiction/space opera romance. She makes her home in Sedona, Arizona.

*Christine Pope on the Web:*
www.christinepope.com

[f] facebook.com/ChristinePopeAuthor

[t] twitter.com/ChristineJPope

[p] pinterest.com/ChristineJPope